Three Small Coinkydinks

I0657992

Aaron Rosenberg

CRAZY 8 PRESS

Ned's already got another of his gadgets out—this one looks like a cross between a thumb drive and a possessed rag doll, all big eyes and feverish grin and USB ports. "Hold on!" he shouts after a minute, just as a bright light sears its way onto my eyeballs and a fierce wind appears out of nowhere. Hold on? To what? To Ned? I reach for his arm but he bats me away—maybe he's seen *The Fly* too many times and is afraid we'd merge together, which gives me these horrible notions of a DuckBob with a vegetable garden growing from his/my bill and overalls on top of his/my dragon shirt. Huh. Just then the light turns blindingly white, and I feel a weird lurch like the whole universe took two quick steps to the left.

And I'm not standing in the Matrix chamber anymore.

I'm in Brooklyn.

Wait, no.

I look around again, blinking after-images from my mind. No wonder MiBs have really good sunglasses. If they didn't, they'd all be blind by now. I have this sudden mental picture of a bunch of blind MiBs trying to grapple your typical killer-lizard alien and flailing about all over the place, unable to do anything but tap at him with those white canes as he just waltzes right by them, only the canes shoot lasers. Yowza.

Regardless, just now at first glance I thought I was in Brooklyn. Now that my eyes are mostly recovered, though, I see that I'm not.

Not by a long shot.

Crazy 8 Press is an imprint of Clockworks.

Copyright © 2014 by Aaron Rosenberg
Design by Aaron Rosenberg
ISBN 978-1-892544-12-4

First edition

For Jenifer, Adara, and Arthur, as always—and that's no coincidence

With thanks to Phil, David, and Bob for helpful comments

Chapter One
Freebird translated is Lame Duck

"Hold still!" Ned half growls, half whispers, which is fine since he's practically climbing on my head at the time. "I don't want to put your eye out or anything!"

"And if that isn't a ringing endorsement for using tranquilizers, I don't know what is," I snap back. But without opening my bill. Which makes me sound like I'm whistling down a long tunnel or something. I guess it's like being my own reed instrument? Huh, who knew: "New DuckBob action figure, with built-in bamboo flute action!"

I'd rather have the Kung-fu Grip.

Ned's filling the right side of my vision, so I focus on the left. Which isn't really all that much better, since it means I'm staring at the pair of Grays standing there watching this whole rodeo. Great, I love an audience.

Actually, I usually do. Ma always said I was born without shame—actually, I remember her telling cousin Phyllis once that most babies are hauled into this world kicking and screaming but I leaped in, did a somersault, and shouted "Ta-da!" I'm pretty sure she was exaggerating, though. It was probably just a barrel roll. Anyway, yeah, I don't usually have any problem doing whatever whenever and not worrying about what other people think. But these aren't other people, exactly. They're Grays. Which means, first off, they're aliens. I know, after all this time you'd think that wouldn't faze me anymore—I've seen all kinds by now, from ones that look just like you and me (or at least, just like you) to ones that are nothing more than colored lights to ones that're weird combinations of animals and minerals to ones that look like cartoon scribbles and so on. Maybe I haven't seen it all, but I've sure gotten a good sampling.

But these are Grays. The original "Ahhh, it's little men from outer space coming to suction out my brain and graft the head of a monkey onto my butt!" boogeymen. The same little, gray, big-headed, big-eyed, no-noses, no-hair creepy dudes depicted in everything from ancient Mayan tablets to Internet memes to cute bumper stickers.

Also, not coincidentally, they're the ones who abducted me and gave me the head of a duck. Not on my butt, just where my old head was. And human-sized, because I guess having a full-grown guy with the regular-size head of a duck on his shoulders would've looked weird?

And, oh yeah, they're also my bosses. I'm the Guardian of the Matrix, after all, the official living component to, and watchdog of, the device designed specifically to protect the borders of our reality from incursion by outsiders trying to invade, conquer, and get us to switch to a new cable provider.

The same Matrix designed and built by the Grays who sent me here to take over after the last operator died during an attempted incursion. I got here—eventually—got the Matrix up and running again with myself plugged into it, and stopped the invasion. Ta-da!

In return, the Grays hired me on to stay here full-time. Which, actually, I kinda had to anyway, since being part of the Matrix means I'm literally plugged into it twenty-four-seven. At least Ned figured out how to splice in a headpiece with a really long extension cord, so I could sit and sleep and basically laze about the Matrix headquarters rather than having to constantly jog around the Matrix chamber—which looks an awful lot like a football field—to keep up with the device's slow but constant rotation.

Though at least if I had, I'd be really fit by now.

Aw, who am I kidding? I'd have bullied Ned into outfitting me with a cross between a Segway and a lounge chair and I'd be the size of a small whale, being carried around in circles like some kind of avian Caesar.

All I need to complete that picture is my lovely lady friend Mary walking along beside me in a toga, feeding me grapes.

Mmmm.

And maybe Tall following along behind to shade me with a giant palm leaf.

Heh.

Back to reality—sadly—that's why the Grays can still creep me out: a combination of old trauma, ancestral fear, and issues with authority. Freud would've given me up as a lost cause long ago. Or he'd have had me stuffed and put in a big glass display case beside his desk.

This is also the first time the Grays have bothered checking up on me in person since I started this gig. Normally they just trust Mary to report back to them. Hopefully she isn't reporting everything, since that could be awkward.

I'm pretty sure I'd still get a good performance review, though.

So yeah, I was a little surprised when the Grays turned up an hour ago. And equally surprised, if a lot happier, to see Ned with them.

"Is it check-up time already?" I'd asked when I answered the door and saw him there. Ned's not only my buddy he's also the official Matrix handyman and my personal IT guy, so he stops in at least once a month to make sure the Matrix is running smoothly and that my headgear is functioning correctly. Of course, the fact that he also comes by to shoot pool, play foosball, watch TV, drink beer, order pizza, and generally just hang around means I don't mind in the least. Like I said, we're buds. Have been ever since we saved the universe together—him, me, Mary, and Tall. The old gang. The core unit. The A team. The top dogs. The saw horses.

Okay, I'm gonna stop now.

But Ned was here just last week, catching up on the latest episodes of competitive fish-basting with me—the trick is to coat them while they're mid-leap, then fillet them in the air and have them land directly on top of the grill so that there's no wasted motion and no loss of flavor or freshness—which is why I was surprised to see him again so soon.

And he's never shown up with the bosses in tow before, either.

"Not exactly," was his answer as I stepped aside to let him in. Hey, the front door's wide and all but Ned's almost as broad as he is tall, and with my bill I take up a ton of room already. There was no way we were both going to fit. And I was already inside, so I figured I'd be nice and let him in. I debated stopping the Grays, but like I said, they're the bosses, and as I know from bitter experience it never goes well when you slam the door in your landlord's face. Especially since they have their own keys.

"Uh, hi, guys," I'd said after they were all inside and I'd shut the door behind them. "What brings you here?" The way the Grays stare at you—with those cold, unblinking eyes, their little mouths pursed in what could just be their natural expression but always feels like a tiny moue of disapproval, like they can't believe you're really taking up valuable space like this—it always leaves me feeling tiny and worthless and weak.

In other words, they're just like HR.

So when two of them show up at your workplace, that's never a good sign.

Damn, and I really like this job, too. Other than the whole "you can't ever leave the building because you can only go as far as your tether, lest the whole universe collapse" thing. Which is, I'll admit, a bit of a drag sometimes. Sure, I have every cable channel in the universe and could watch movies until Earth's sun went supernova and never see the same thing twice, but it'd still be nice to get out and take in a show occasionally. Especially since right now my dates with Mary consist of her coming back to my place. Which I am definitely not complaining about, but I'd love to be able to take her out somewhere nice and show her a good time. And not have to worry about the dishes afterward.

Still, that's like the only downside. Otherwise this is a basi-cally a dream job—I get paid really well to sit on my butt all day and do whatever the hell I want. I only wish I'd known this job existed back when I was in college, so I could enjoy the fact that some day all my studying really would come in handy.

Of course when the Grays show up I immediately start run-ning through all the ways I've screwed up at this job. Like you do. Stuff like "Okay, I probably shouldn't have used that one spot in the Matrix to cook my PopTarts, but I was hungry and it was right there and it barely stained at all!" and "Yeah, maybe, but how was I to know it would start smoking? I only offered it the one out of courtesy!" and of course "you never said I couldn't use it to make personal calls! I'm sorry that it got routed to an entire spiral galaxy at the same time! Especially that call. On the plus side, Mary and I got a lot of compliments, a whole heap of congratulations, and four offers for our own late-night cable show." I don't think any of those are firing offenses, though maybe all together. Could they just be here to issue an official reprimand? I've certainly had plenty of those—at one job the HR lady told me she'd never seen anybody with as many rep-rimands on file as I had, and for so many different but equally minor offenses. I probably shouldn't have pointed out what a waste of time and money it was to keep dinging me with those things, and how if the company would spend less time worry-ing about its employees daring to speak to each other and more thinking about the official products and sales and such, we'd all be doing a whole helluva lot better and they wouldn't be forced to justify their very existence by dragging good employees away from their actual work in order to answer questions about ridiculous things that shouldn't matter anyway.

But hey, at least my file gained another reprimand from it.

The Grays don't say anything, which is actually pretty common for them. They're not exactly the chatty type. Ned, on the other hand, definitely is.

"Not really a check-up," he tells me cheerfully, which totally confuses me for a second—not that he's cheerful, Ned's a pretty happy-go-lucky guy, but the reply, which forces me to cycle back through my thoughts until I hit the one that had sparked his reply. Yes, I often have to go back and figure out what I was talking about or hearing about or smelling about or whatever, unraveling the chain of events that led to a particular conversation.

And yes, that often winds up requiring diagrams and flow charts and pie graphs.

Mmm, pie.

But Ned's still talking. "This is more of an upgrade," he assures me, pulling something from his tool belt and snapping it open with the flick of his wrist and a loud, ominous-sounding click. It looks like . . . like one of those cheapie plastic tiaras kids wear when playing dress up. If those were made out of wood, stone, proper metal, and glowing, blinking lights.

Whoa, did I win Miss(ter) Congeniality of the Universe and nobody bothered to tell me ahead of time? I'd better write up a quick acceptance speech, stat!

"Uh . . ." is all I can manage on such short notice, though. Hey, I've never been any good as a speech writer—back in college whenever I was the one tasked with making our frat's opening announcement at the start of a party I usually just went with some variant of "hi, welcome, go ahead and get trashed but don't puke in any of our rooms." Which covers almost every occasion, when you stop and think about it.

Fortunately, Ned's used to me by now. "It's your new head-gear," he tells me, holding it up so I can admire it more. Yep, still looks like "Techno Elf-king Barbie." Ned's grinning like he's just invented sliced bread, though, or reinvented it, or gone back and stolen it from whatever guy did come up with it originally, or whatever, so I try to be nice.

"Oh. Cool. Yeah, looks real snazzy," is the best I can do. "Uh, way more glittery than the current model." I tap my headband, which looks a lot like if Richard Simmons had been assimilated by the Borg: "That's it, alien races, give me twenty more and then let's do one lap around the Andromeda galaxy!"

Ned laughs, though. "So, yeah, it's a bit bulkier than that one," he admits. "But that's 'cause it needed room to house the transmitters." He waits for it, and that grin gets bigger when he sees my eyes widen. "Yeah, exactly." He waves my new party accessory again, turning it so I can see every angle. "Notice there's no place to plug in the cord? That's because it doesn't need one."

"Wait, you mean—" He nods. "Completely?" Another nod. "What's the range?"

Now he looks really pleased with himself, his little broccoli-stalk earbud thingies practically vibrating. "If I built it right? Anywhere and everywhere."

I look over at the Grays, who haven't said a word or moved except to follow us into the main Matrix chamber. "So you guys are here to watch because I'm about to go wireless?" They don't respond, don't even blink. Man, they're a tough room to read! Ned's nodding, though, and it does make sense. Something this big, the top brass'd want to be present for it, like at a ribbon-cutting.

If they pull a pair of oversized scissors, though, I'm defending myself. Once was enough, that's all I'm saying.

Anyway, Ned tells me I need to sit back and relax while he calibrates the new gear and switches over to it.

Which is where we came in.

"Are you done yet?" I ask him, still with my bill clamped shut.

"Almost." He tugs at the headgear again, settling it further into place on my noggin, and I swear I hear a faint click. "Ah, there we go!"

"Tell me you didn't just drill holes in my head and bolt that thing in place," I beg. Look, I know this head of mine isn't exactly the original hardware but I'd like to think I've kept pretty good care of it so far, and I'd hate to perforate it now.

Besides, that might create a draft.

"Naw, I went one better," Ned answers, stepping back a pace to admire his handiwork. "There're organic magnets all along the inner edge, and I just synched them with your DNA. It's locked in place now, anchored right to your skull but no cutting or bolting required."

"Oh. Okay. Cool." Hey, I got "you don't have to worry about

losing it or having it slip off when you tilt your head back," so
I'm good. "So, is it all set?"

"Just about." He pulls out one of his little tech gadgets—
most of which look like a cross between lockpicks, digital wands,
finger puppets, and small vegetables—and fiddles with it for a
second. There's a beep just above my cranium, and then a faint
hum. Which stops, fortunately, because if I had that monoto-
nous buzzing vibrating through me every second of every day
I'd go nuts. "There!"

I look around, then over at the Matrix doing its usual
merry little crawl around the room, then back at him. "Yeah?"
Everything looks fine. I know better than to just trust that,
though.

But Ned nods. "Yep, all good. Nice, strong signal, and it's a
unique frequency and pattern so it'll stay connected anywhere
in the universe, full strength." He claps me on the back. "Looks
like you're free!"

"Really? Sweet!" I jump to my feet—okay, I stand with
marked enthusiasm—and head straight for the front door.
Throwing it open, I step outside, which is the first time I've
done that for a few weeks. The Grays don't know that occasionally Mary or Tall or even Ned will spell me on the Matrix long
enough for me to essentially jog around the block, just so I don't
go completely stir crazy. That's all they can do, though, since
you've gotta be attuned to the Matrix to maintain the connection—it'll tolerate an unattuned mind for maybe twenty minutes before it gets cranky and starts to shut down.

Not this time, though. I'm still plugged in but I can go

outside, go down the block, go get drunk at the nearest bar. I can do whatever I want!

Wa-hoo!

"We'll test it slowly, expand the range little by little," Ned tells me when I burst back in. "The hell with that," I reply. "I've got my wings back and I'm ready to fly!" I look over at the two Grays, who've been watching all this without even moving. "Yo, send me home!" I tell them.

The next instant there's a bright flash.

And everything—Ned, the Grays, the Matrix and its whole glittertastic stadium—are gone.

Chapter Two
Do fish and game get half-fare?

"**YES!!!**"

I spin around again, just to take it all in—and nearly brain some lady who's trying to shove past me. "Oops, sorry." She just glares at me, shakes her fist in my general direction, and keeps right on moving.

Which only proves I really am back home.

Manhattan. The Big Apple. New York City. The City That Never Sleeps. The King of the Hill, Top of the Heap, and so on. The best city in the world, if you ask me.

And I'm not just seeing it through some kind of wacky projector, or dreaming about it, or hallucinating it—at least, I don't think so, since there aren't any supermodels on hand to offer me drinks or any albino alligators rising up from out of the sewer grates offering to shine my shoes. I know, I don't really get that one either, probably something to do with irony and watching *Romancing the Stone* too many times in my teens. But this—this is real. I can smell it. There's a particular odor to Manhattan, a mix of people and cars and the ocean and hot dog stands and everything else that all comes together like no place else, and that's filling my head right now. And, yeah, making me slightly dizzy, but it's a good dizzy.

I'm back.

"I'm back!" I shout. Most of the people walking past ignore me, of course. A few turn to stare. Some shrug. One yells, "Hey, welcome back, my man!" He looks like he probably hasn't bathed since the Roman Era, and his clothes might actually be made of duct tape, but it's still a nice gesture. The follow-up one, after he holds out his cup and I stuff a bill into it, only to realize belatedly that it's Arcturan slime-centavos left over from my last pizza run, is a lot less friendly.

But still just as familiar.

Okay, so I'm really here. I rub my hands together. This is great! What'm I gonna do first?

Huh.

My first thought is Mary, of course. But that's a no-go—she's away on the job right now, doing whatever it is she actually does for the Grays (I try not to pry, especially since it would suck if she accidentally told me something I wasn't supposed to know and our creepy little bosses decided to wipe my mind or just scramble all my memories to keep me from revealing it. Yeah, workplace conduct training's got nothing on these guys!), and that means she's completely incommunicado until she gets back.

Well, if your best gal isn't available, try your best pal instead, right?

"What'd you break now?" Tall growls into the phone when he answers. There's a weird sound in the background, a soft hissing, like he's in a really big snakepit or maybe touring Yosemite or something.

"Nothing, I swear," I tell him, which is mostly true. At least, I'm pretty sure I can put it back together again and nobody'll ever be the wiser. That's what he gets for asking if he can store some of his stuff at my place, anyway. And collectibles don't have to be in their original packaging, really, right? "That's not why I'm calling," I continue, as much to distract myself as him. "Guess where I am?"

"Why, what'd you do?" It's amazing how fast he gets suspicious of me. That's what made him a good MiB, of course, but does he have to do it to me every time? Even if he is usually right?

Not this time, though! This time I'm totally innocent. "I'm in Manhattan," I practically sing into the phone. "Ned came up with a wireless headset for me, which means I'm free to roam, baby! No extra charge!"

"Huh. Well, good for you." Ah, Tall. As demonstrative as ever—which puts him right on par with a block of marble or a hunk of Styrofoam, though at least that makes obnoxious squeaking sounds. Speaking of which, there are those weird noises again. Or still.

"I know, right? Wanna meet me for lunch? We can go to that kebab place you like."

"Ah, can't right now, sorry." And he does sound sorry about it, too. Which only shows how much he's loosened up—when I first met him Tall might sound angry, frustrated, bored, violent, suspicious, or just plain dangerous, but sorry? Not really in his wheelhouse. "Heidi and I're transporting a flock of Vengalisian steam-sheep out to a colony by Polaris IX." Heidi's his partner, they do interstellar trucking together. Good guy, for something that looks like a shy electric eel skulking inside a floating bowling ball.

"Vengalisian steam-sheep? Never even heard of 'em. What're they, steamed from the inside out?" That sounds handy—and tasty—but dangerous too, like the way you can singe off your own eyebrows if you're a little too hasty in opening a bag of microwave popcorn. Hey, I was hungry! And they grew back eventually.

Tall laughs at me, which is a common occurrence. "Always thinking with your stomach," he chides. My stomach's had some darn good ideas over the years, thank you very much! "Naw, they're actually made of steam, like little superheated clouds. The colony's on a permafrost moon, so these things'll help thaw it out, raise the ambient temp a dozen degrees or so. And they feed off the sublimated water, which'll keep the humidity from going through the roof." More hissing and rumbling behind him, which I now realize must be the sheep. "Listen, I gotta go. But we'll definitely grab lunch once I'm done, yeah? And congrats, man. That's awesome news."

"Thanks," I tell him, but he's already hung up. Tall's never been big on long good-byes. Or idle chitchat. Or utili-kilts, which is a shame because he could really work one.

None of which changes the fact that he can't come hang with me right now.

Okay, so including Ned who might be angry I took off in such a hurry those're my three closest post-Matrix friends. What about everybody I knew before, though? I could call—no, he's not speaking to me anymore, after that thing with the cab fare. Like I knew the guy was gonna want to take the FDR and then the Hudson River Parkway to get from Clinton to the Village? Both ways? Why was I the one assigned to watch that stupid little "you are here" map on the screen in the back seat? Anyway, forget about him, whatever, his loss. And his credit rating, I guess, but screw him if he couldn't take a joke. And a second mortgage.

What about—oh, right, he moved upstate. Why was that again? Oh yeah, some lame-ass excuse about "my great-aunt passed away and left me this mammoth house on this huge estate just outside this little town and now I need to go live there and throw massive parties every weekend for anyone who wants to schlep all the way up here." Well, no thank you—I don't care if you do have twelve bedrooms and a wine cellar and a private grotto, you're still no Hugh Hefner and you can keep all your wannabe bunnies. Gee, I wonder why he never came back down to visit?

Well, maybe—no, that's right, he's always working, can barely manage our monthly poker games. Poker! That's it—I can go to poker again, in the flesh this time, none of Ned's wacky tech hocus-pocus to make it look like I'm there!

Oh, but we just played last weekend. No game for at least three weeks, depending on schedules.

Damn.

Hm, well, I can visit the old homestead, I suppose. Though I did leave in a bit of a hurry, and Nate and Greg weren't exactly happy I was cutting out like that. Hey, I gave them two months' rent just to make up for it! I guess it was more the fact that Greg realized he wouldn't have an ally against Nate's slobbiness anymore, and Nate figured out he wouldn't have anybody to make fun of Greg's anal tendencies with anymore, either. Huh. Yeah, maybe I shouldn't go see them. Besides, that place was a dump. The entire thing could've fit in my bedroom and still left room for my bed, a circular sofa, a Ping-Pong table, and a small racquetball court. But only a small one.

Hey, wait a second. I stop in the middle of the street, which causes a whole cacophony of horns and beeps and curses all around me. Ah, music to my ears! But I'm a little distracted by the thought I just had. They tend to do that to me, just completely blindside me, the little devils—it's not like there's ever any warning a thought might be rolling down the pike. I'm ambushed by my own thought processes. And right now I just got hit with a doozy—

—what if the Grays kick me out?

I mean, with this new headgear I don't have to live at the Matrix anymore. What if they decide they'd rather have me work off-site? It'd save on cleaning bills, and food delivery, and Internet connection, and charges for violating various galactic shipping laws and local noise ordinances and possibly a few public indecency charges. Hey, what can I say, I'm a *Risky Business* fan! But with me working from anywhere they could, I dunno, rent out my room? Rent out the entire rest of the Matrix building? Even not counting the main Matrix chamber you could still fit an whole mid-sized company in there, half a dozen if they're dot-coms. Hell, you could probably fit a small school in the building if you really wanted, there're enough rooms and halls and alcoves. There's even a locker room! And it's prime real estate, smack dab at the center of the universe, easy access to everywhere at once, great connectivity, lots of food delivery options. If the Grays are smart they'll realize they could turn a healthy profit by using that space for something other than just little ol' me.

But that would leave me out on the streets. I could move back here to Manhattan, sure, but even with the fat salary they're paying me I'd only be able to afford a place the size of a postage stamp here. That's the way New York real estate works, the closer you get to Central Park or the UN or Saks Fifth Avenue the smaller the apartment and the higher the rent—go anywhere near Times Square or Bryant Park and you're looking at a closet for as much as a large house would cost in most of the rest of the country. We are on an island, after all—there's only so much space to go around.

I could move out to Queens again, or Brooklyn, or even the Bronx. Not Staten Island—I'm not that desperate! Rents are a lot lower in the other boroughs, and apartments are bigger, but after the Matrix I'm a bit spoiled. If I don't have enough room to fit my bowling alley I'm not sure I'll be able to cope.

And that's assuming I still have a job at all. Because if this headgear really works—and since the universe doesn't appear to be collapsing around me or hanging up "under new management" signs I'm guessing it does, not that I really doubted Ned for more than a few minutes there—and the Guardian can be connected from anywhere, it doesn't have to be me anymore. I was handy because I was already attuned to the Matrix, thanks to the Grays' screwing with me in the first place, and because I was the one they sent so I was on-site and willing to serve once I got the Matrix back online, but now they could literally hire anybody qualified—meaning anybody else who's been altered by them at some point, or even somebody who hasn't but who's willing to be—and have him or her work from home. What if they decide they want somebody more reliable? Somebody less obnoxious? Somebody who won't repeatedly set parts of the kitchen on fire? What, is it my fault the dials to light the burners on the stove look exactly like the one for the protective firecage? And yes, I know that one isn't actually on the stove. It doesn't matter, it's still too close.

So maybe the Grays are about to hand me my walking papers. Maybe they're going to pick a new Guardian, one who's calmer and quieter and doesn't get plastered and walk around with flippers on his head shouting "Hey, look at me, I'm Flapman!" Though I only did that the one time. Lately.

Oh, crap. What if the reason the Grays were willing to send me back home was because this was basically the easiest way to get me out of the office? Like the old "Hey, DuckBob, why don't you go grab some donuts for everybody from that place down the block? Oh, what's that, your key card no longer works to get back in? And a box with all the crap from your desk is sitting out on the curb? Why yes, I'm trying to tell you something—but give me my damn donuts first. And my change."

I hate it when they do that.

I look around frantically, half-expecting to see a big cardboard box filled with all my stuff, like my mug that sings when you drink from it and my sub-zero computer and my semi-animate couch thing. Of course, that last one could be the box, which would certainly make packing easier, assuming it didn't decide to turn itself into a funnel or an archway or a late-night pawnshop all of a sudden.

I don't see my stuff anywhere.

Whew.

Though they might've just shipped it to me. Admittedly, I don't know what that would entail, if they're kicking me out of my current home and it's not like I've even had a chance to fully process that idea yet, much less find someplace new. Those boxes're gonna be circling around in outer space, watching me like some weird storage-container vulture, ready to swoop the moment I settle somewhere, landing on me like homing beacons with moving trucks attached. Now I'm picturing myself running through the city, all my worldly possessions spiraling about over my head, news copters getting caught up in the maelstrom that is my shirt collection and my array of fancy party hats and my antique Crab nebula cookware set. It'd be like *Hoarders* meets *Twister* meets *The Amazing Race* with a bit of *House Hunters* thrown in.

And the really sad thing is, I'd totally watch that, too.

So what'm I gonna do now? I'm back in New York, sure, but I'm homeless and jobless, or as good as. Does this mean I'm gonna have to get my old job back?

I look up and suddenly realize I'm actually standing outside my old office building. It's like Fate brought me here. Or, more likely, I was so used to doing this walk every morning for all those years that my feet just knew the way and figured I wasn't bothering to give them directions so they'd take control and go the easiest place they knew.

I hate it when my feet get uppity like that. Just because they've never been the ones responsible for any of our really impressive screw-ups, they act like they're so superior. Well, you guys've made me trip and fall on my face plenty of times! Sometimes even when I'm standing completely still! So there!

Meanwhile, I'm outside my old office. Should I go in? Should I tell my old boss, Phil, that I want my old job back? Should I grovel? Should I just stroll in like I own the place, say, "Yo, Phil, how's it hanging? I was busy saving the universe and all but that gig got old so I figured I'd swing on back, you don't mind, do you? And hey, can you grab me an espresso? I'll be at my desk," and see how long it takes anyone to wonder what I'm doing back or to point out that I don't actually work there anymore? I'm pretty sure I saw this movie years ago and it worked pretty well, especially for Teen Wolf and Supergirl.

Thing is—thing is, now that I stop and think about it, I hated my old job. Really hated it. All I did all day was scroll through screens on my computer, click a bunch of boxes on and other ones off, submit the form, and then repeat the process. It really didn't seem to make much difference which boxes I checked, either. I know because I got bored after a while and started doing patterns, just like I used to do on the old standardized tests back in school. Which might explain why I almost got held back a grade twice but the NSA wanted to recruit me right out of middle school. So I used to check boxes in squares and rectangles, triangles and rhombuses, fleur-de-lis and stars, spirals and ankhs and infinities and subway maps. Nobody ever complained, at least to me, but I'm pretty sure we destabilized a small third-world company and brought a busload of tourist gamblers back to life. That's bound to balance out whatever else happened, right?

Even if it does, though, can I really stand to go back to that? I mean, I saved the universe, man! I fought off an alien invasion! I stopped a galactic menace with nothing but taffeta and taffy! I fried a killer shrimp! After all that, how'm I gonna be able to survive working in that tiny little cube again, hunched over that tiny little screen, clicking buttons?

Wow, I had no idea just how much my old life sucked. Good thing I haven't bumped into anybody I know yet—that's the thing about being this distinctive, it's not like my old friends and former co-workers could walk past and think, "Huh, weird, another guy who was modified by aliens and given the head of a duck just like DuckBob, and is leaving a trail of broken things behind him, what're the odds?"

Which is, of course, right when a hand lands on my shoulder. A big, meaty hand, caught up in the cuff of a dark suit. And there's the rest of the suit behind it, along with a white shirt, a dark tie, a dark hat—

—and a pair of dark sunglasses.

"Mr. Spinowitz?" It's a surprisingly high voice for such a big guy, and it quavers a bit at the end.

But I don't care. Right now I'm actually happy to see a MiB. That's how weird my life has become. "That's me, agent," I tell the poor guy, resisting the urge to throw my arms around him because that would be awkward and because I'd likely brain him with my bill. Trust me, my days of spontaneously hugging people are over unless I decide to become the world's cuddliest serial killer. Plus I really don't want to hurt him. Right now, he's my only link back to the wild and wacky life that was mine right up until a few minutes ago.

Which is why, when he says, "I need you to come with me," I practically skip after him to the dark sedan idling by the curb.

It's amazing what can look good to you—familiar, comforting—when everything you've been taking for granted suddenly gets yanked away like that meal you're only half-finished eating.

Which should teach me not to take the "Dare to attempt our five-pound hamburger!" challenge anymore, at least.

I still think they cheated. The lettuce and tomato filled me up before I could finish. As did the onion rings, cheese fries, jalapeño poppers, mozzarella sticks, and chocolate malted.

Great, now I'm hungry again. I wonder if Mr. Agent Man would be willing to hit a diner along the way?

Chapter Three
I swear I have no idea
what I'm talking about

The drive to MiB headquarters takes all of twenty minutes. Not surprising, considering I was standing in Midtown and they're based maybe twenty, thirty blocks south. A block a minute is about right for New York City traffic. It's also how long it takes to walk the same distance, which explains why we're such a walking city. If you can get there just as fast on foot and not have to pay for gas or worry about being rear-ended, well, it seems like an obvious choice even to a certified couch potato like me. Of course, if I had my way I'd be carried everywhere by a large armchair with animatronic spider legs so I could get fresh air and be ridiculously lazy at the same time, but what can I say? I'm an overachiever.

Riding in the MiB-mobile is funny. You know how lots of cars and houses and sunglasses and privacy shields on desks are tinted so you can't see into them from the outside? Well, this car's windows are like that—but from both directions. I couldn't see into it when we were outside, and now we're inside it I can't see out, either. There's a pane separating the front from the back, just like in a cab or a limo, and it's just as dark. I'm guessing the front windshield is clear from the inside, otherwise the driver's doing a darn good job navigating by touch and sense memory. Then again, a lot of people in New York seem to drive by sonar, honking and shouting and cursing and then using the returning sound waves to map out their route, so I suppose I shouldn't be all that surprised.

Finally we pull up onto a curb and then into an underground garage—I can tell by the way the sound changes. A minute later the car shuts off. Then my door opens.

"This way," Mr. Agent Man tells me. He's holding the door like a chauffeur but his tone is more irritated soccer mom, not "would you care to exit, sir?" but "get out of that car this instant, and how many times do I have to tell you to stop pouring your juice into the video player and all over your siblings?" I get out nice and quick, and he leads me across what looks just like any other parking garage except that it's completely filled with MiB-mobiles, over to an elevator. He pushes the button, we wait a minute, the door opens, and we get in. This whole time I didn't see who was driving the car. I wonder if it was this guy and he was sent to get me all on his own or if the driver's still sitting in there, waiting for us to go so he can leave. Maybe he's bashful? Maybe he's got a bad case of acne? Or maybe he just doesn't want to ride in the elevator with us. It is a tight squeeze, on account of my bill. I can't remember the last time I managed to fit into a photo booth, but unless they make double-wide versions I have a feeling I won't be trying one again any time soon.

The ride is completely silent, just like the car. Mr. Agent Man doesn't speak, and for a change neither do I. Hey, try something different every now and again. Besides, I can't imagine what I'd say to him. Well, okay, yes I can:

Me: So. Been a MiB long?

Him: [silence]

Me: How're you liking it? They treating you okay? They offer decent dental?

Him: [silence]

Me: Do you ever get tired of always wearing black suits? You guys don't have Casual Friday, do you? You should. Imagine, you could come in wearing a navy pinstripe and really shock people!

Him: [silence]

Me: So, how about those Mets?

Him: [silence, but with a distinctly disappointed look on his face]

Yeah, glad I didn't try that. Whew.

The elevator dings and opens, and we step out into the lobby of the main floor. I've seen this place before, of course, but I can't admit to that—after all, I only saw it while I was using a spy-cam to keep an eye on Tall, back when Tall still worked here. So I try to act all shocked and surprised by what I see, which is hard seeing as how it looks like any other boring corporate office.

Any other boring corporate office manned entirely by MiBs. Who aren't exactly the life of the party at the best of times.

Mr. Agent Man grabs my arm and tugs me down a short hallway running off to one side of the main room. There are doors all along it, and he yanks open the nearest one. "In here." Looking over his shoulder, I see a bare concrete room with one table and a pair of chairs on either side. At least it doesn't look like a torture chamber.

"Does it have to be this one?" I ask as he slides to one side of the door and waits expectantly. "What about the next one over? I might like the lighting better. Or the feng shui, it might have better lines." I honestly can't tell you why I'm putting up such a fight over which room I'll be held in. Maybe I have a deep-seated psychic sense that being in this room will damage me in some way. Maybe I'm worried about being close to the bathroom and the vending machines. Or maybe, like my kindergarten teacher said to my mother several times, I just can't do anything the easy way. Regardless, Mr. Agent Man doesn't even respond—he simply shoves me the rest of the way in and closes the door on me.

Yeah, it's nice to be made to feel welcome.

I sit down on one of the chairs—I don't think it matters which one, they look exactly the same. And then I wait.

When I get bored of waiting, I get up and start pacing out the room. Then I lean back in my chair, prop my feet up on the table, and take a short power nap. Then I bounce back to my feet and pace some more.

That takes care of the first ten minutes.

I'm mentally numbering, naming, and repainting the blocks of the wall—and by "mentally" I mean "out loud, in a deep operatic voice, complete with fake German accent"—when the door opens and two more MiBs step inside.

Well, technically one MiB, one WiB. And I know them both. Oh, goody.

"Mr. Spinowitz." Agent Smith nods at me, the kind of nod you might give something you found stuck to the bottom of your shoe after you've decided it isn't poop or bubblegum and isn't actually eating through the sole but you still don't know quite what it is or how to clear it off properly, especially without letting it touch your bare flash, and steps over to the table. "You're in my seat."

"Really?" I glare at him. "You drag me in here off the street, toss me in this little cell like I'm some sort of criminal, and then tell me I'm in your seat? What's next, stealing my pudding and giving me your tattoo?" I look past him at the other agent. "Hello, Agent Jones."

She just nods at me. And here I thought we had something—not friendship, exactly, but we did work together nicely to save Tall from the former WiB who'd captured him and, oh yeah, tried to take over not only the MiBs in general but the whole world. Shouldn't that have given us a nice, warm, fuzzy bond of some sort? Or at least matching scars and a nifty secret handshake? Instead she gives me the same cool "I register you as a semi-intelligent life-form but all that really means is I've marked all of your vital spots so I know where to shoot you if necessary" stare I've always gotten from her. She doesn't bother going for a chair, at least—she just stops right inside the door, which closed behind her, and stands there with her back against it, arms crossed. She still looks like a bulldog in an ill-fitting black suit. At least Agent Smith wears his well.

And I guess he's tired of messing with me, or has realized it isn't worth the hassle, or just noticed the chairs were identical, because he pulls out the second chair and sits in it without further protest. Whew, I really didn't want to have to reenact the inevitable prison-fight-in-the-cafeteria scene, especially without one of those metal trays handy. And a few dozen other inmates who inexplicably take my side and start bashing on the guards and anyone else who tries to interfere.

"So," I start out, drumming my fingers on the table. "Nice place you've got here. Real homey. Shame about the wallpaper. And the decorations. And the windows. And the rest of the furniture."

"It serves its purpose." Agent Smith smiles at me, that same smile he's always had where it feels like any second lasers will shoot from his eyes and start stripping the flesh from my bones, one layer at a time. "I was surprised to hear you were back in town, Mr. Spinowitz. I thought you were permanently stationed at the Matrix now, to better maintain and protect it."

"Yeah, well, change of plans." I stretch and crack my knuckles. It isn't as impressive a display as Tall can do—the man can perform whole symphonies—but I have been practicing. "I'm mobile now."

"I see." Smith frowns slightly, which means the corners of his mouth are no longer perfectly crease-straight. "We had not been informed."

"Just happened, no time to send out a memo yet," I tell him. "You'll get one any second now, though." I smile at him. "So I figured I'd stretch my legs a little, see the old homestead, look up a few pals. And here I am! Didya miss me?"

"How do we know you're telling the truth?" This is from

Agent Jones. She hasn't moved except for her mouth. "You're a known liar, after all."

"Well, sure," I concede, "but that's usually only when I'm really bored, and never about anything important." Not what I'd consider important, anyway. I'm still not sure where I'd classify "confidential information about my grade-school teachers and the little love nest/pot farm they had on the side"—I know *they* thought it was important, but to the rest of the world? Meh. I give Smith my best serious look, which I know is kinda ruined by the whole duck-head thing, but still. "Look, you know I take my job as Guardian of the Matrix seriously." Assuming I still have the job, that is. "I would never leave it unmanned." Though maybe I just did. Ned did say this thing should work at any range, though. I just took him at his word. Quickly. "Everything back at the Matrix is fine"—I hope—"and will continue to stay that way." I rise from my chair. "Now if you'll excuse me, I've got a date with a kimchi taco truck." Mmm, kimchi tacos.

Agent Jones doesn't even twitch. And Agent Smith only tilts his head back slightly so he can still look me in the eye. Don't ask me how, but even though I'm standing and he's still sitting I somehow feel like he's looking down on me. Must just be an attitude thing. "I am glad to hear you will continue to maintain the Matrix," he tells me, though he doesn't exactly sound happy about it, more like resigned. "But if you are indeed mobile, that changes certain . . . parameters in our working relationship. We had agreed to leave the Matrix headquarters untouched, given the delicate balance of the device itself and also the extreme distance from here to there, provided we were given regular status reports by a trusted agent." That's Tall, even though he isn't a MiB himself anymore—he's still a consultant for them, and their official intermediary. I don't miss the look that flickers across Agent Jones's face, either—it's the same look a bulldog gets when he sees a particularly juicy steak bone. Clearly she still has a thing for him. Ew.

Smith is still talking, though. "If you are now once again taking up residence here, however, we will need to adjust our arrangement." He smiles at me again, and I do a quick check to make sure I still have all my fingers and toes and vital organs. "You will report in here once a week to confirm the Matrix remains operational. You will also inform us any time you intend to leave Manhattan, and will check in with us each day as to your location and status. Furthermore—" I'm pretty sure he's about to tell me that Jones will be babysitting me twenty-four-seven and that I'll be fitted with a dog collar and a leash and probably a homing beacon or at least a wildlife tag when the door bursts open. That in and of itself might not have stopped his little dictatorial tirade except that Jones is still standing in front of it, and so when it flies inward the door nails her right in the small of the back and sends her flying forward—right toward us. Ever have a two hundred pound MiB come sailing at your head, arms flailing, mouth wide, jowls shaking? It's not a pretty sight. I'm still on my feet so I backpedal fast, putting the table between me and her. Smith doesn't move. He barely twitches.

And then he's buried beneath Jones, and the two of them go down in a heap.

I wish I had popcorn.

"There you are!" Ned rushes into the room—I guess he was the one behind the door-catapult. "I've been looking all over for you!" He glances down at the duo tangled on the floor. "Oh, hey, Agent Smith. How's it going?"

"What're you doing here?" I ask Ned. "And how'd you find me?" Not that I'm ungrateful, of course. I just wasn't expecting him. I figured he was still back at the headquarters with the Grays.

"I wanted to make sure everything was working fine on your end," he answers, pulling out one of his doohickeys and waving it toward my new headgear. "All looks good, though, and the Matrix is reading strong and smooth, so that's fine." He glances down at Smith, who is still disengaging from Jones, and sidles closer, lowering his voice. "As to how I found you—" and he glances up at my headgear again.

Ah. Yeah, that makes sense—I'd put a GPS in it too, if I were the one building it. And I'm glad he didn't tell Smith that. Though I guess it would save them the trouble of putting one in me directly. Probably "by accident."

"Thanks," I tell him. I look down at Smith, who's just now getting to his knees. "Well, this has been oodles of fun, Agent Smith, but I really must be going. Lots to do, you know, keeping the universe safe from invaders. Not to worry, though, I'll shoot you that memo about me being mobile now. And we definitely have to do this again sometime, maybe over tea and crumpets or just beer and pizza. Okay? Cool. Take care!" I hit him with my biggest, cheesiest smile and lead Ned out of the room. There are more MiBs out in the hall, of course, including Mr. Agent Man, but I just smile and wave at them. "Hey, how's it going, Guardian of the Matrix here, have to get back now or the whole thing explodes, take care." I keep moving, dragging Ned along behind me, and I guess the MiBs don't know if I'm kidding or not so they all back away and let us pass. Whew.

"What was that all about?" Ned asks as we step out of the elevator, cut through the lobby, and pass out through the glass doors and back out onto the street. Man, least fun "take your altered-by-aliens semi-employee to work day" ever!

"Smith thinks now that I don't have to be at the Matrix full-time I should be his little lap dog and report in every time I wanna scratch my balls," I answer. "Which, y'know, not happening."

Ned laughs. "Naw, not so much. Don't worry about it, the Grays won't let him take control like that." That's a relief, at least. Of course, it assumes the Grays still want me to be Guardian, but Ned doesn't say they don't or try to wrestle the headpiece back off my noggin, so I decide not to mention it. No reason to push my luck.

I am about to ask him what the Grays said when I left, if anything, but just then something somewhere nearby starts playing the Imperial Death March from *Star Wars*. Oh, wait, that something is me. More specifically, my right thigh. I reach down into my pocket and pull out my cell phone. I don't need to check the Caller ID—I know who it is. I only assigned one person that ringtone, after all. This ought to be fun.

"Hey, Ma," I say after hitting Answer. "What's up?"

"I hear you're back in town, Robert," she says. "What, you weren't going to come visit?"

I actually spin in a circle, looking for surveillance drones. Ned is eyeing me like I might burst into flame, or into song, or both, any second. I mouth "my mom" at him before answering her. "Uh, Ma, I've literally been back less than an hour. How did you even know I was here?" It's not like I filed a flight plan! Though I'm sure I'll hear about that one later—Wildlife Services likes to keep a close eye on my movements. Sheesh, maybe they can team up with Smith and all get together to watch me eat or something.

"A mother knows," is all she says, which is typical. And true. I have no idea how she does it, but growing up she always knew exactly where each of us was, even when we were trying to keep it a secret. Fortunately she didn't usually care too much what we were doing, or with whom, as long as she could get her hands on us if she needed or if the property damage started getting too much. But apparently her powers are increasing or something.

"Well, I was gonna call," I tell her, which is true, more or less. I would have called eventually—I always do. I'm just not sure it would've been in the first few days. Or months.

"Never mind," she replies. "You're here now. Dinner's at seven. Don't be late. Oh, and bring your friend—I'd like to know what kind of people my baby is associating with these days." Then she hangs up.

"What's going on?" Ned asks. I'm sure I look like somebody just ran over my dog. With a Sherman tank. That was on fire.

"We're having dinner with my mom," I tell him. "I hope

you've got some kind of forcefield or something." He gulps a little.

Hey, maybe I can disconnect this headgear, just for a few minutes. Just long enough to make the Matrix wobble a bit, so I've absolutely got to head back straightaway and check on it.

Of course, that would leave the universe open to attack again, at least until I got everything up and running again.

But between that and the prospect of having dinner with my mom? Especially with Ned in tow?

I'm seriously debating which would be worse.

Chapter Four
Time to Clam Up

"Are you sure this is a good idea?" Ned asks for like the twelfth time as we get off the LIRR. My mom and stepdad and whichever of my siblings is currently getting divorced/being evicted/between jobs still live in the house I grew up in, right here in Little Neck, and it's a short walk from the train station. Of course, almost everything here is a short walk to the train station. But hey, at least that makes commuting into the city easy.

"No, I'm not sure," I tell him yet again. "Actually, it's probably a very bad idea. But I don't really have a choice. Which means you don't either. Come on, it's this way." The town hasn't changed any that I can see—it still looks more like a sleepy little fishing village than a suburb of New York City. But that's the way people around here like it. I still remember back when I was a kid and there was a huge fight over the motion to install street signs. Not replace the old ones, mind you—install them on streets that didn't have any and never had. Those who opposed the motion said, "We've always been able to find our way around without those darn things, why change now?" It was a close vote, as I recall, and I'm not sure they weren't right, in the long run. Certainly we got a whole lot more junk mail after strangers could find our house. That, and court summons.

"Do I look okay?" is Ned's next question as we trudge down the steps from the station, cross the street, and start up the hill. The house is near the top, which is great during sledding season, other than the fact that you always wind up sledding right across the street at the bottom. And, if you're not careful, you can even slam into the side of the station platform. That never stopped us, of course—hell, the idea that you might get run over by a car always added a certain spice to the whole thing. My mother still mutters occasionally about how the odds totally suggested at least one of us would get hit. She never sounds entirely happy that we didn't, but I think that's because she probably had money on it. Our old neighbor, Mrs. Brooks, on the other hand, always looked insufferably smug about our surprising good luck. I guess I know who took the longshot there.

"You look fine," I tell Ned. He does, too. Mostly. When I told him we were coming to dinner he panicked a little, going on about how he couldn't be seen by locals and it could violate all sorts of directives and get him in hot water with the MiBs and then with the Grays and so on. None of which made any sense to me.

"You're standing here in plain sight in the middle of Manhattan," I told him. "How is this any different?"

But he shook his head. "I got a monotony overlay up," he said. "So I don't have to worry about it."

"A what now?"

"It's like an image overlaid on top a' me," he explained. "You know how, if you have to read a contract or tax form or some other legal document, after a minute your eyes start to glaze over? This broadcasts the generic equivalent to that, but as a subvisual so you see it and your brain registers it as a part of my whole visual identity. It makes your brain glaze over so you can't notice details about me, like my skin tone." He grinned. "Pretty clever, right?"

"Yeah, actually." And it really is. "So, wait, if I had one of those nobody would notice I had a duck head?"

"Exactly. They'd see you, they'd know you were there, but their brain would decide to sort of skip over the details."

Wow. If bank robbers had this thing, they could be the greatest ever. Nobody would ever be able to agree on what they looked like, so they'd never get caught. Y'know, unless they gave their name or used the back of their own deposit slip for the "Give us all your money" note or something like that. Spies would love it, too—they wouldn't need disguises because they could walk right by in broad daylight and nobody would recognize them. "So if you have that," I ask, "why're you worried about dinner?"

"'Cause it only works on the casual observer," Ned answered. "If somebody really takes the time to look at me properly, they'll see me." He shuddered. "And I get the feeling your ma wants to get a real good look at me."

He's probably right, too. Ma can be a bit overprotective, even with me, and she's not crazy about strangers, plus she does like to know what's going on. Ned'll be lucky if he doesn't come away with stripes all up and down from the grilling he's about to receive.

"Oh, wait, I just remembered—okay, hang on," Ned said, patting down his toolbelt and dipping his thick fingers in a few spots before finally coming up with something that looks like a small stethoscope attached to one of those little handheld fans that sprays water at you. If he even started to say "proctology" I was ready to toss him overboard. But he turned the thing toward himself instead, and then twisted a spot here, tapped a spot there, and flicked one end. It started vibrating and humming and glowing a little, and a soft blue light wafted from it like thick steam, right toward Ned's face. The light sort of settled on his skin, clinging to him like glow-in-the-dark face paint, and then it slowly sank in and faded. Only now his skin looked dark tan, like one of those guys who worked outside a lot. And his face was still flat but not pane-of-glass flat, just a little smushed. And the weird broccoli-like tufts above his ears were now curly brown hair, almost an Afro, while his ears themselves weren't as batlike anymore, though they were still pointed at the tips. Whoa.

"Whoa," I told him. Yeah, I still don't have much of a verbal filter. "That's awesome. You look like a normal Earth dude now."

He beamed at me, enough that I could actually see the little ladybug that's carved into one of his teeth. I'd forgotten about that, or tried to. I can still remember it winking at me. "Really? Sweet! I thought it'd work, but I wasn't one hundred percent sure." He patted the doohickey just behind the spray part, and I swear it seemed to push up against his fingers like an attention-starved cat. I'd always assumed Ned's devices were, well, devices, but what if they're actually alive? Although, given some devices like my computer, there may not really be that much of a difference.

Regardless, it did the trick. Which is how the two of us are currently trudging up the hill, heading to Ma's house for dinner. Whee.

"Anything I need to know before we get there?" Ned asks from behind me. I'm not exactly an Olympic athlete but I did live in Manhattan for years and you pretty much have to develop strong leg muscles there unless you're one of those types who has the limo take you from your own front door to the front door of the shop so you can wait there, looking bored, while your chauffeur runs around collecting the items you want and then stands in line so you only have to walk up to the cashier at the last possible second and pay for it all. In which case I'm guessing you don't worry about the state of your legs. Though of course some of those uber-rich ladies have personal trainers and are actually in scary good shape even if they never so much as open their own mail.

Anyway, even after all these years I find I can still manage the hill home without a problem. Ned's exhausted, though, and wheezing, and with the new coloring it's much easier to see that he's gone beet-red in the face. We definitely need to stop and take a break, maybe just spend the night here. I'm sure Ma won't mind.

Who'm I kidding? She'd send out a search party. It's what she always did to us when we were growing up. I was ten before I realized most families didn't have Saint Bernards—and hadn't trained the dogs to retrieve small children, carrying us home by the back of our collar or the scruff of our neck. And I'm pretty sure Ma still has Bernie VII. Ick, I really don't want to run into him out here. He might decide I'm some sort of new chew toy— or the first person in the world to combine two of his favorite things, ducks and a leg to hump. If I had a red nose like a Superball I'd be irresistible.

But, oh yeah, Ned had a question. What does he absolutely need to know?

"I don't know who all's going to be there," I tell him. "Definitely Ma and my stepdad, Harold. Probably Eddie, my oldest brother, and his wife Caitlyn and their two girls. Could be some of my other brothers and sisters and cousins, too. Everybody's mostly friendly, though if my sister Lila's there don't make eye contact, tell short person jokes, or ask her to pass anything." That evokes a momentary shudder, remembering the last time anyone did. Who knew you could use a gravy boat like a throwing knife? At least the poor kid, one of Eddie's friends, wasn't allergic to gravy. That could have been bad. As it was, the sudden subcutaneous infusion had done wonders for his acne, and the scar became a good conversation starter for him. The worst part was, Ma stopped serving gravy after that, just to be safe.

"How many brothers and sisters have you got?" Ned asks.

I have to stop and think about that one for a minute. I know, I know, but trust me, it's necessary. "Eleven, I think. No, wait, twelve."

"Twelve?" Ned stops and stares at me. "And what do you mean, you think?"

"It's complicated." I sigh and turn back to wait until he can catch up again. "My mom and dad had a bunch. Then they got divorced. Ma remarried and had a few more. My dad had a few more too, though he never married again—he said he'd been through Hell once and survived, trying it again would just be tempting fate. But a few of the women he was with over the years had kids of their own, so they were almost like half-siblings. Same with Harold, Ma's second husband—he already had two kids, and they gave the rest of us enough hell, and got enough of it back, that they're pretty much kin, too." I shrug. "I'm pretty sure there's thirteen of us in all—I vaguely remember jokes about us being our own witches' coven—but I could be missing somebody somewhere."

Ned shakes his head. "That's . . . odd." He studies me. "Isn't it? I don't know Earth customs real well. Is it not odd here? It sounds odd."

Ned can get a little motormouthy when he's nervous, I've noticed. So can I, of course—when we're both worried it's like a verbal deluge, torrents of words just spilling out all over the place. Good thing I can swim like, well, you know.

"Yeah, it's probably a little weird," I admit. "Growing up, most of my friends came from good-sized families but not as big as ours. They'd have four or five or even six or seven, and we had twice that many. Not all under the same roof at the same time, except for family gatherings, which got a bit crazy, but even so." I grin. "Still, there were a few advantages. Any group of kids in the area was bound to know at least one of my brothers or sisters, so that was like an immediate in. And you could always find somebody to go along with any crazy idea you had or any errand you had to run or anything like that."

Ned nods. "That musta been nice," he says. He's finally starting to breathe normally again instead of like a stegosaurus with a head cold. "I've got only the one sister, and she's a bit older than me, so I had to go outside the house to find other kids." This is the first time I've ever heard Ned say anything about his childhood, or about his life in general, really. For a guy who can talk your ear off, he's really private about his personal life. I've often wondered if he's actually some sort of pod person. It would explain the ears.

We finally arrive, and I stop in front of the house and do the whole Vanna White thing. "And there she is, the old homestead! Glorious, ain't she?"

I can tell that Ned's trying to figure out if I'm being sarcastic or serious. Which is fair—half the time I wonder that myself. And in this case it's at least half and half. I know the house isn't the grandest around—no columns, no stained glass, no turret. Still, it's in decent shape even now, looks like it was repainted within the past year or two and the shutters are a crisp green against the white stucco and the faded red brick, and it's big, and the wraparound porch has always been one of the place's best features.

And, hey, it's home.

We head up the walk, which isn't half-blocked by go-carts and bikes and baseball bats and miscellaneous other toys and tools like it used to be when I was a kid, and step up onto the porch. Somewhere inside, Bernie VII howls, but there isn't a thunderous crashing noise approaching so I'm guessing Ma has him corralled in the pantry or the basement. I give Ned a sec to make sure he's caught his breath before hitting the doorbell. A second later, the door gets yanked open and somebody small and blonde almost puts her own eye out by flinging herself at me.

"Uncle Bob! You're here!"

"Hey, Lizzy. Yep, I'm here. Wow, you got big! This is my friend Ned." I gently disengage from her and turn, keeping one arm around her shoulder. Lizzy's always been my favorite and she knows it—don't ask me why but we bonded when she was just a baby, and we've been close ever since. Of all my family members, she's the one I missed the most when I went away. "Ned, this is my niece, Lizzy."

Lizzy eyes him dubiously, then thrusts out her hand. "I'm his favorite." She grins at me, then swivels to include Ned in that blinding light. I swear, if the lighthouse ever goes out all they'll need is to get her to stand there and beam out over the water. I think that's part of why I like her so much. You can't be around Lizzy when she smiles and not feel a whole lot better about life in general.

"You're not supposed to say that," I remind her. "Remember? Tricia gets mad."

Lizzy doesn't care, though, which is another reason why I've always liked her. She just humphs and tosses her head back. "She should've tried harder, then," she declares. She thrusts one arm through mine and the other through Ned's and drags us inside. "Come on, everybody's waiting." I only just manage to kick the door shut on my way past. Good to know these pontoon-feet of mine are good for something! Bernie VII howls again, but it's clear he's not getting loose tonight, which is definitely safest. We're all a little big for him to be lugging around, even Lizzy.

She wasn't kidding about people waiting—they're all seated around the table already, and the hungry stares we get when we enter make me wonder if we're the last diners or the first entrée. Which would be awkward in so many ways. Ma's the only other one not seated yet, since she won't sit down until all the food's on the table, and she comes bustling out of the kitchen, apron still on over her blouse and skirt, and gives me a one-armed hug. The other's waving a spoon from the mashed potatoes.

"You're late," she tells me. "Train trouble?"

"The usual." Which it was—there were delays due to track work, and then when we did get on the train it crawled its way through Queens, stopping several times between stations. Which is pretty normal, but I'm a little out of practice so I didn't build in enough time for it. "Sorry." I gesture with my free arm—Lizzy's still attached to the other. "Ma, this is my friend Ned. Ned, this is my mom."

"Pleased ta meetcha," Ned tells her, offering his hand and letting out a surprised "Umph!" when she hugs him instead. I probably should have mentioned that my family tends to be very hands-on. Hopefully there won't be any of the traditional "wrestle for the last piece of pie" tonight. "I brought this." He holds up the six-pack of beer he's been carrying—and the bottle of Scotch. I know my mom well.

"Well, aren't you the thoughtful one?" she gushes, patting

him on the cheek. I'm half-afraid that stuff he used will rub off on her hands—and wouldn't that be a sight, Ned with one green cheek and Ma with a tan hand!—but it doesn't. "Thank you! I'll just set them on the counter. Grab a chair, make yourself at home, and I hope you brought your appetite." Ha, she has no idea. I've seen Ned put away more food than a whole construction crew, and that was between meals. Then again, Ma usually cooks like she's feeding the entire U.S. Army, so this could get mighty interesting.

There's two places open, one on either side of Ma's chair. Of course. I take the one next to Lizzy and motion Ned to the other, which puts him next to Lizzy's older sister Tricia. "Hey, Tricia," I say as I sit. "Eddie. Caitlyn. Frank. Dolores. Jimmy. Harold. This is my friend Ned." There's a whole chorus of hellos, and Ned sort of half-waves back. Yeah, my family's a bit overwhelming at first. And second. And third. At least nobody's throwing anything. Yet.

"Nice to see you, little brother," Eddie booms in that bank-president voice of his. "You're looking good." He's looking the same as always, which means it's like he's about to pose for a portrait to be hung in the great hall, him in his pinstripe suit and silk tie with matching pocket square, the diamond tie stud gleaming almost as much as his teeth—Lizzy gets her smile from him except hers is a lot less predatory—and a little more than the distinguished white wings at his temples. Wings I happen to know he brushes in every morning to make himself look more dignified. But that's always been Eddie to a T, more concerned with looking and sounding the part than actually doing the work. Of course, growing up I was mostly just jealous because no matter what sort of shenanigans we pulled—and sure, I was often the one who came up with the plan, especially if it was completely half-baked and more than a little dangerous, but he was almost always willing to take part—Eddie somehow always came out smelling like a rose. I can't even count the number of times he used the "I was just going along to make sure they didn't get in too much trouble, or hurt themselves or anybody else" excuse, and it worked for him every time. Every. Single. Time.

And now here he is, president of the local bank branch, a member of the city council, and vice-president of the Moose Lodge. All his dreams come true. And he knows it, you can see that in the smirk hiding just beneath the surface. The smirk that says, "and what've you done with *your* life, hm?"

If he knew even half the things I'd done the past year, his head'd explode, fake wings and all.

"You too, Eddie," is all I say, though. There's no point in anything else, really. He probably wouldn't hear it anyways.

"I thought your new job was overseas somewhere?" Harold asks me. Poor Harold. I don't hate the man, I really don't, in part because there just isn't enough there to hate. If you looked up the definition of "milquetoast" in the dictionary, you'd see a picture of Harold but from right before he met my mom. Now take that guy, who had barely enough spine to keep himself upright, and thrust him into the middle of my family, which makes the Bad News Bears look like the Brady Bunch. We were like Tom Sawyer's gang and Fagin's crew but all related and living under one roof. It was enough to crush the spirit of any normal person, and Harold had been beaten down by life plenty before he ever met us, so you can imagine what we did to him just by general proximity. Still, he's stuck with my mom all these years, and he's done his best to do right by all of us, so yeah, no hate here. No love either, but I try my best to be nice to him because, gosh darn it, somebody sure as hell ought to.

"Yeah, it was," I tell him, cutting a quick glance at Ned, but he's keeping his head down and his expression blank, "but they're looking to open a new branch in Manhattan so I may be moving back soon." *Or they may be cutting me loose completely, in which case can I have my old room back?* I think but don't say out loud. No sense letting that worry out into the world just yet.

Ma re-emerges, carrying a brisket the size of the Hindenburg. But hopefully with less gas. She sets it on the table, and I see Ned's eyes go wide and bright. Literally. Guess that stuff he sprayed on himself couldn't exactly stop the whole searchlight-gaze thing. Hopefully it's bright enough in here that nobody'll notice. "Dig in," she declares proudly, and then there's a few minutes of frenzy as everybody just stabs in with their forks, trying to scoop up as much meat as they can before it disappears. Which is better than it used to be, with only a handful of us here and all but the girls getting a little older and a little slower. When I was a kid it was like those fistfights you'd see on cartoons, where it was nothing but a big swirl of dust and motion with the occasional head or fist popping back into view—there'd be a complete whirlwind and when it settled the food would be gone like it'd never existed, all the plates picked clean. The trick, we all figured out early on, was to concentrate on a single dish. As long as everyone didn't go for the same one, you were likely to get something to eat that way. My own method was to go for the vegetables but then to catch anything that fell off my brothers' forks between the serving dishes, their plates, and their mouths. And, yeah, sometimes I might've jabbed them somewhere to make them drop a little more, too. Hey, a kid's gotta eat.

Like I said, this is a little slower and more civilized than those days, so even though it takes Ned a second to catch on he still manages to get a healthy slab of meat. Ma had gone back into the kitchen, and now she returns with a big pot of mashed potatoes, which she proceeds to circle the table with, dumping a portion onto each plate as she goes. Good thing her eyesight's still sharp or Eddie'd be needing some dry-cleaning on that fancy suit of his! Then she's gone again, only to swing back around a minute later with green beans and corn and roasted peppers. There's fresh-baked bread already on the table, and butter, and cheese and crackers in case people're still hungry. One thing I have to say is that we always ate well in our house. Of course, if we'd had a little less fuel we might've gotten into less trouble, but at least we were fast enough to outrun irate adults most of the time.

There's not a lot of talking for a bit while we all chew and swallow, but eventually everyone's finished with the first round and settles back into their seats. Which is, of course, when the barrage of questions starts.

"So, Ned, what do you do?" That's Frank asking. My cousin Frank has had at least a dozen different jobs over the years, everything from lifeguard to schoolteacher to carpenter to the guy who stands out on the construction crew holding up the sign that says "Caution—Workers Ahead." That's a good job, too—I did it for a few summers back in college. You get paid a surprisingly good wage, thanks to the union, and all you have to do is stand there holding a sign and working on your tan. The problem was, when Frank did it, he kept falling asleep and dropping the sign.

"Tech support," Ned answers after swallowing his last bite of brisket. "This is amazing, ma'am," he tells Ma, who beams at him like he's the Second Coming—or the first, since she nominally converted to Judaism before Eddie was born and never officially left even after she and Dad split up. "I don't think I've ever had such good brisket before." Which could just be because he hasn't spent a lot of time here on Earth, but Ma does make a mean brisket.

"And you work with Robert?" Jimmy asks. Nobody in the family calls me DuckBob, even though it is legally my name now. It's all still "Robert" and "Bobby" and "Bob." But what can I do, disown them? Turns out that's only an option if you have money. I checked once.

Ned nods. He's got a piece of bread in one hand now and is buttering it with the other, using all the care and concentration of a surgeon about to thread the left ventricle. "Yeah, though I'm not full-time like him. I'm an outside contractor, really. I just come in a few times a month to make sure the hardware's all running okay."

"What's with the tiara?" Tricia asks. I hate to say that she's my least favorite niece but, well, there it is. She takes after both her parents but in all the wrong ways—she inherited Eddie's self-importance and Caitlyn's cattiness, whereas Lizzy got her dad's fearlessness and her mom's poise. Not that Tricia's a terrible person but she thinks she knows everything, hates to be proven wrong, and can get nasty when that happens. Huh, I guess we are related after all.

"It's actually a Bluetooth setup," I tell her, glancing at Ned, who shrugs and nods at the same time. Impressive. "Like one of those ear-and-throat things you see a lot." I tap my bill. "I couldn't really do the regular configuration, so Ned set this up for me instead."

Tricia nods like the answer is satisfactory, if only barely, and I pretend not to notice the angry red blotches that just bloomed on both cheeks. The rest of the table's gone silent. Even though it's been years, my . . . altered appearance is clearly still a taboo topic here, particularly during dinner. After it happened I came home, not sure how to deal with my new look or all the stares, and my mom sat me down and told me "those horrible little things may have done something to you on the outside, but on the inside you're still my same darling boy, and that's never going to change." Then she basically stopped noticing my new look. She refused to talk about it and wouldn't let anyone else, either. And maybe that wasn't the healthiest way to handle the situation, but it did get me through my own coping problems. Even now, though, when I'm completely comfortable in my own skin, feathers and all, it still bothers Ma, so we try not to talk about such things around her. Here I'm just your normal, average, ordinary guy.

I just have to steer clear of Harold's den—he's an avid hunter, or was back in the day (which is why all of us got lessons on gun safety at a young age and learned at least the basics of hunting as we got older, a fact that probably didn't help curtail our evil plotting any and may have actually made matters worse since we'd learned basic strategy and the art of the ambush)—and the walls in there feature mounted proofs of his success. Including several ducks. After it happened I had a recurring nightmare that I'd come home and Harold would mistake me for an actual duck, shoot me, and mount my stuffed head in there with all the rest.

Hey, at least that way I'd never miss another family gathering.

Chapter Five
My dinner isn't settling, it's plummeting to its doom

"Who's ready for dessert?" Ma calls out, which prompts the thunderous clatter of chairs being pushed back and plates being stacked. One thing we had drilled into us from an early age was that you cleared your own place when you were done. If you didn't, well, you certainly didn't get any of whatever might be coming next, usually meaning dessert but sometimes meaning the next meal instead. Nobody forgot or tried to skate more than a few times. It was a smart move on Ma's part—after all, there were an awful lot of us, and though she's a lot stronger than she looks, especially her left arm from carrying so many of us over the years, that would still be a massive pile of dishes to cart off by herself. Plus, although we all hated having table manners shoved down our throats as kids and avoided them like the plague in our own home, whenever we went to friends' houses the parents were always wildly impressed. It's funny the amount of crap you can get away with when somebody's parents thinks you're "the nice kid"—"You're going where? Oh, Robert's going with you? That's fine, then." Most of them caught on after the first few calls from the cops, admittedly, but even then a lot of them were willing to believe I had been dragged into whatever scheme it was against my will. Ha!

There's a nice little procession into the kitchen, each of us lugging our own plate plus at least one serving dish, and Lizzy manages to wind up next to me by the simple expedient of hip-checking Jimmy out of the way. Did I mention that I love my niece? "When did you get back into town?" she asks as she slides into the kitchen just ahead of me.

"This afternoon, actually." I shake my head. "I don't know how Ma knew." We just leave that there—Lizzy's had plenty of experience with her grandma's seemingly psychic ability to know where her kids and grandkids are at any given time. Made her one hell of a babysitter when the girls were little, though.

"How long're you staying?" is her next question as we add our plates to the stack in the sink and put the serving dishes on the counter to the side. Those'll get scraped, any leftovers packaged and put in the fridge, before being soaked and then washed. Ma doesn't fool around when it comes to dishes, probably because with the amount of food that gets prepared here on a daily basis, and all the dirt and who knows what else we used to track in all the time, she'd wind up with a full-scale mold factory otherwise. Or maybe a penicillin farm, which could've been a great second income.

"I'm heading back tonight, actually," I tell her, and feel bad when her face droops. "I should be back in a few days, though, and I'm hoping this time it'll be for good."

That brightens her back up again. "Great! Maybe you can come to my show? We're doing *My Fair Lady* at school and I'm playing Eliza!" Of course she is—Lizzy's not only one of the smartest of the bunch, she's also darn cute, and she can sing. And act. And do almost anything else she puts her mind to. Not that I'm biased or anything. Then she leans in a little closer and her voice drops to a whisper that might only be audible with spy gear. "You could meet my girlfriend."

Ah. Yeah, I'm the only one in the family Lizzy told, a few years back. She knew her parents would be mortified—more from how this would prevent them from making an advantageous match for her someday than anything else—and her sister even more contemptuous than usual, and that Ma and some of the others probably wouldn't understand. I'm not sure anybody in my family would've actually condemned her or anything— we're all a bit too messed up ourselves, and too aware of that fact, to go pointing a lot of fingers—but there might have been a lot of confusion and a lot of well-meaning attempts to "help her straighten out." Pun intended.

I don't know that I'm the most open-minded person in the world, myself, but I can say that one benefit of being modded by the Grays is that "to each his own" means a whole lot more to me now. So of course I was supportive, told her it was cool, we were cool, nothing had changed, etc.

It kills me that I can't tell her all the things I've done and seen. She'd love it—when she was little I introduced her to *Doctor Who*, comic books, the whole shmear, and she took to them right off. We'd sit and watch cheesy sci-fi movies together whenever I babysat—Tricia would either sulk or sit off to the side making snarky comments or just hole up in her room with a book. But of course both the Grays and the MiBs warned me not to tell anybody, "for security reasons." I really want to make an exception with Lizzy, though. Especially because she's always stood up for me whenever any of the others have started in on the whole "yeah, you've got a duck head, but what else have you done with your life?" crap, and this would finally vindicate her faith in me.

Unless I just got fired and have to go back to some crappy little office job, in which case maybe it's better I don't tell her.

"That'd be great," I say instead. "And if I'm back in town, I'm there." She beams at me again, and I'm in a good mood as we make our way back to the dining room—until I see Ned.

Who's been cornered by Eddie, Frank, and Jimmy.

Uh-oh.

". . . really good opportunity," Eddie is saying as I approach them—fortunately there's enough clatter still that they don't hear me. "You'd be getting in on the ground floor, and from there the possibilities are endless." Frank and Jimmy are matching Bobbleheads, trying to convey sincerity by the force of their nods.

"Hey, what's going on?" I ask loudly, breaking into the little circle. I'm pretty sure the words "Help me!" just flashed across Ned's forehead. I don't know if that's a side effect of that stuff he sprayed on or just a trick he never revealed before, but either way it'd be darn useful at rock concerts and other loud, crowded venues.

All three of my kin start and get that look, the one where you know you're caught but still think you can get out of it if you talk fast enough. "Oh, nothing," Eddie tells me, doing his usual "what, me?" grin. "I was just chatting with your friend here about this new business opportunity I found. I thought maybe he'd be interested, a bright guy like him."

"You should get in on it too, Bobby," Jimmy tells me, earning him a glare from Frank and Eddie, but Jimmy's never been the brightest bulb. "Lots of money to be made."

"I think I'm good, thanks." And I am, at least for now. The Grays pay me well, and I really only spend money on food and sometimes clothes and whatever random stuff catches my eye from any of the thousand-plus home shopping channels I get. Plus I still have all those extra credit cards lying about. I grab Ned's arm and steer him back toward the table. "Time for dessert, Ned, and you don't want to miss it. Ma makes a killer cheesecake." Which isn't her fault—she had no idea that one kid had a dairy allergy. He was fine afterward, anyway—turns out that having the entire clan leaning over you screaming is enough to get the adrenaline pumping, and once he was able to drag out his epi-pen he was okay. And yet again it proved to be a good thing that the local ambulance knew the way to our house—when Ma got through to them all they said was "Yeah, we're on our way." I honestly think they were just surprised it wasn't one of the family for a change.

"Sorry about that," I tell Ned. I don't bother to keep my voice down, either. "They're always hitting on these get-rich-quick schemes and trying to rope the rest of us in." Most of us learned to steer clear of Eddie's "opportunities" after the first time or two. Hell, I still own an acre on the Moon and another on the bottom of the sea somewhere, if I can find the paperwork. The minute we set up colonies in either location, I'm good as gold.

It's always Eddie, Frank, and Jimmy, too. Frank and Jimmy are the ones who find these ridiculous things, and Eddie's the one who sells other people on it. He's always been good at conning people into stuff, and of course now he's the bank president so he's got that aura of respectability about him. Frank and Jimmy are too squirrelly for most people to trust, but they know a lot of equally unsavory types, which is how they keep hearing about these things. This is also one of the reasons Frank's had so many jobs—he'll work at one for a bit, set aside some money, then fall for one of these schemes and lose it all. At least Eddie's not dumb enough to put any of his own money into them. He just gambles with others' savings. I shudder to think what'll happen if the feds ever decide to audit his bank.

Ned just shrugs. "No worries. I wasn't going to give them money anyway, and it was a kick listening to the sales pitch." He grins at me. "I'm having fun."

That, of course, was exactly the wrong thing to say—it's basically another way of saying "This isn't so bad," which is always the kiss of death.

Because just as we're sitting down to dessert—the aforementioned cheesecake, plus brownies, apple pie, and ice cream—the front door slams.

And in walks Lila.

Oh, crap.

"Lila, honey!" Ma is out of her chair like a shot and has her arms wrapped around Lila before my little sister is halfway across the room. "I didn't know you were coming! You missed dinner but I can fix you a plate." She's trying to drag Lila into the kitchen but though she's petite Lila's made of wrought iron and isn't budging. In fact, she's still trying to make headway despite Ma's bear hug.

And she's gunning straight for me.

"I heard you were back," she says, her voice sharp enough to cut and laced with enough poison to kill a dozen rat warrens. "Just couldn't stay away, huh?"

"Hi, Lila." I give her my best smile, the one that says "don't mind me, I'm not doing anything, I'm just here for the pie." Of course, it doesn't work any better now than it did growing up. Apparently I don't do "innocent" well. "Clueless," yes, but that's different. "How are you?"

"How am I? How dare you!" She manages to drag Ma a step or two closer, and now Eddie's up from the table and coming around to lend a hand. "Get the hell away from me," she snaps at him, and he stops dead. Then she shakes Ma off and suddenly she's in my face, which would give most people pause but not Lila. She's never been afraid of anything, least of all me. "I should kill you for what you did." Her voice is so low it's almost subsonic, vibrating through my bill from inches away, but from the shocked expression on Ned's face I'm pretty sure everyone heard her.

"Give it a rest, Lila," I tell her, too annoyed to be as scared as I probably should be. "It's been over a decade."

"There's no statute of limitations on something like this," she snarls at me. "And yet here you are, sitting down to family dinner like you never did anything wrong. How cozy." She flicks a finger against my bill, which stings a bit though I notice her eyes tightening afterward too. Good. It's nice to know that hurt her a little, too.

"That's enough, Lila Josephine!" Uh-oh. When Ma breaks out the first middle name you know you're in trouble. The more she adds, the higher the Defcon rating—we each have at least three, and if you get all your names called you're better off just finding a bunker somewhere and hoping it's stocked with enough rations to last you the year or two before the fallout dies down enough for you to resurface. Lila actually flinches and pulls back a foot or two, giving me enough room to scoot my chair away from her. "You're welcome to sit down and join us for dessert," Ma continues, "and I can make you a plate if you'd like dinner, but I will not tolerate squabbling at the table!" Which has always been true, actually. We all learned at a young age that we could mix it up in the backyard, in the basement, in our rooms, even in the living room, but not out front (too many potential witnesses), not in the kitchen (too many sharp objects), and definitely not at the table. Fortunately most meals we were too busy trying to grab food to fight anyway.

"Fine." Lila steps back, both hands up, but I know her too well—I'm watching for a knife to appear in one of them. She's always had dangerously good aim. "Some other time, big brother." She manages to hurl the title at me like the words are bullets, hard enough to pierce flesh. Amazing how a simple declaration of kinship can become such a vile insult when said just the right way. While the words are still ringing in my head, she turns on her heel and storms out.

Lila was always good at storming.

There's silence after that, the kind of silence that everybody's afraid to break because they know there's a chance of delayed explosion, like when you've just shattered a family heirloom right in front of your parents and have the crazy notion that if you stay frozen they won't really register what they just saw and you'll escape with your skin intact. That never actually works, by the way. Trust me on that.

Ned, fortunately, steps up. "Could somebody pass the pie?" he asks, doing the whole "why no, I didn't just witness an awkward family drama" bit. Which is exactly what's needed here, as Dolores deftly serves up a slice for him and everybody falls back into the rhythm of eating and carrying on small talk.

But there's still that pall over it all, and even Lizzy's smile isn't as bright anymore.

Lila was always real good at that, too.

Two hours later, Ned and I get up and make our good-byes. Which takes time in and of itself, because following long-standing Jewish tradition the good-byes last almost as long as the meal did. I don't know why that is but I once heard the phrase "says good bye but doesn't leave" and it really fits. Everybody wants to chat just a little bit more before we go, even after the "okay, take care, we're leaving now," and it's like running a well-meaning gauntlet to reach the front door, moving a few feet at a time with long pauses in between. Never try to leave my family's house when you've got to catch the last train, not unless you've allowed a whole heap of extra time—like an entire day—just to be safe. Finally we're at the door, and only Ma and Lizzy are left. Lizzy's got her arms wrapped around me like she can either keep me from leaving or at least get carried along with me, and much as I'd love that second one to be true I know she's got school in the morning so I pull free as gently as I can.

"It was great seeing you, kid," I tell her softly, brushing her hair out of her face. I give her a peck on the forehead—no, not a real peck, that'd leave a permanent mark and probably a concussion—and one last squeeze. "I promise I'll be back soon. And email me the date of your play—I'll be there."

"Okay." She wipes away a few tears—unlike my generation, Lizzy's not afraid to show emotion. Then again, she doesn't have as many siblings waiting to pounce, and she's been able to take Tricia since she was five. "I love you, Uncle Bob."

"I love you too, kid." Now *I'm* getting all teary. I turn to my mom. "Ma. Thanks for dinner, it was excellent as always."

She shrugs that off. "Eh, after all these years feeding you, I'm gonna stop now?" Yes, she absorbed a lot of Jew over the years. She gives me a quick hug, then studies me. "You look good, like you lost some weight." Which is all thanks to Tall and his ruthless attempts to whip me into shape. Even though they've been only partially successful, I'm not quite as much of a marshmallow as I was. "Next time you'll bring this girl of yours, yes?"

"As soon as she can, yeah." And won't that be fun. Then again, Mary can hold her own against Tall, the Grays, the invaders. At the very least Ma would know she'd been in a fight. "Love you."

That gets a smile out of Ma, at least, and she ruffles the

feathers atop my head. "I love you too, Robert." Next she turns to Ned. "You I like," she tells him. "You're welcome any time."

"Thanks," Ned says back. "I really appreciate you having me, and dinner was excellent." He says good-bye to Lizzy too, and then we're outside. Finally.

"Wow," is all he says on the way to the train station, and that's when we've already gone a good block and a half. "So that's your family."

"Yep."

"Huh." He gives a little laugh. "That explains a lot, y'know." I give him the hairy eyeball, but it doesn't faze him much. "You've always been tougher than you look," he goes on, sounding completely serious for a change, "and I can see where you'd need that, growing up there. Nothing against them, they just made you work for it."

I scratch at my bill. "Yeah, that's certainly true. Speaking of which, keep your eyes open. I wouldn't entirely put it past Lila to be laying in wait somewhere."

"Uh, yeah, what was the deal with that?" he asks, though he does pick up the pace a little, and glances nervously at the shadows lining the sidewalk. "She seemed pretty pissed at you."

"She is. Has been for years now." The train station is in sight, and I make a beeline for it.

"What happened?"

I sigh. "It's a long story, but basically I called her on her birthday and her answering machine ate the message, so she thought I'd forgot. And the post office lost the present I sent her, which convinced her she was right."

Ned actually stops on the stairs to stare at me. "That's it? You forgot her birthday and she's hated you ever since?"

"I didn't forget it—I actually did call, and I *did* send a present. In time to get to her, for once. But between the answering machine and the post office, yeah, she thought I forgot. And then I wouldn't apologize, because I hadn't actually done anything wrong." I shrug. "Lila's always been the kind to hold a grudge."

"Yowza." We step out onto the platform, which is nice and well-lit and has excellent sightlines. "That must make family events fun."

"You have no idea." I sink down onto one of the benches. "The worst part is, before that? We were really close. She was my favorite sibling, growing up."

"Oh." Ned sits next to me, leaving the requisite "macho space" between us so nobody'll think we're together, which can get particularly funny—and annoying—on a crowded subway car. "Sorry."

"Eh, I'm used to it by now." Though I can't say it doesn't still hurt. I slap him on the back. "But hey, look at you, you survived dinner with my family!"

That makes him grin. Then the grin widens, and his eyes light up again. "Not only did I survive," he proclaims happily, producing a tinfoil-wrapped object almost the size of my head, "I took prisoners!"

I guess Ma gave him the rest of the cheesecake.

That figures.

Chapter Six
Somebody set that hallucination on Repeat

I'm still a little down the next day when Ned stops by to check the headgear again. "Just playing it safe," he tells me as he fiddles with it and with one of his little gadgets. I can't see what he's doing, of course, but it feels like when you get your teeth cleaned with that little whirry thing that makes them vibrate, only on the top of my head. If I still had ears they'd be ringing for sure. "Everything looks good, though. Nice steady signal, strong output, battery's got a full charge. You're all set."

"Cool. Thanks."

He puts his tools away and studies me. "Still messed up over dinner, huh?" I half shrug and half nod, which I guess makes it a snod. At least it's not a snood, 'cause I'd look terrible in one of those. "Sorry, man." He brightens. "I know, I'll take ya to lunch! We'll go to my homeworld. You'll love it!"

"Yeah?" Okay, my interest is officially piqued. First off, this whole wireless-headgear-mode is still brand spanking new, so the thought that I really can go out to lunch somewhere is pretty darn exciting. Second, I'm dead curious to see what Ned's homeworld looks like. All I know about it so far is that it's a small planet in the vicinity of Betelgeuse and all I can picture is a cross between a plumber's convention and *Veggie Tales*. I'd love to see if I'm right.

Besides, I bet Tall twenty bucks that everyone there has what looks like veggies growing out of their heads. Y'know, like farms with faces.

"This'll be great!" Ned assures me, dragging me to my feet. Boy's got decent arms, I'll give him that. I know from experience that I'm hardly a lightweight. Though I guess you could legitimately call me a "featherweight." Ha! "We'll go to Gus's All-You-Can-Eat Melva Buffet. Remember I told you about it? Trust me, you're gonna love this place!"

"A buffet?" I do vaguely recall him saying something about that, back when he and Tall and I were at Red's Diner that time. "Okay, sure, count me in." Hey, I love places that let you eat all you can stuff in your face for a set price. They don't always love me back, mind you. Especially since I realized I could shove food in my bill and carry it out that way. What? Most buffets don't actually think to say "all food must be fully consumed on premises." I am actually putting it in my mouth, so really I've already started eating it—it's just that sometimes that process can take a while.

Like two hours and a subway ride, followed by a few days in a carton in the fridge.

The thought of never-ending food—and free at that—is definitely working. I can practically feel myself perking up. That might just be pins-and-needles, though—I think my arms fell asleep again. I grimace a little as I try taking a step, but I'm still optimistic when I say, "Right, let's go!"

Ned's already got another of his gadgets out—this one looks like a cross between a thumb drive and a possessed rag doll, all big eyes and feverish grin and USB ports. "Hold on!" he shouts after a minute, just as a bright light sears its way onto my eyeballs and a fierce wind appears out of nowhere. Hold on? To what? To Ned? I reach for his arm but he bats me away—maybe he's seen *The Fly* too many times and is afraid we'd merge together, which gives me these horrible notions of a DuckBob with a vegetable garden growing from his/my bill and overalls on top of his/my dragon shirt. Huh. Just then the light turns blindingly white, and I feel a weird lurch like the whole universe took two quick steps to the left.

And I'm not standing in the Matrix chamber anymore.

I'm in Brooklyn.

Wait, no.

I look around again, blinking after-images from my mind. No wonder MiBs have really good sunglasses. If they didn't, they'd all be blind by now. I have this sudden mental picture of a bunch of blind MiBs trying to grapple your typical killer-lizard alien and flailing about all over the place, unable to do anything but tap at him with those white canes as he just waltzes right by them, only the canes shoot lasers. Yowza.

Regardless, just now at first glance I thought I was in Brooklyn. Now that my eyes are mostly recovered, though, I see that I'm not.

Not by a long shot.

I mean, a lot of it does look like Brooklyn, with the cute

little attached houses and the wide, tree-lined streets and something like a bullet train whooshing by overhead. But I don't think there are rocket-packs in Prospect Heights and Park Slope, I doubt they have hover-cars, and I'm almost positive the billboards aren't holograms. Also, I'm pretty sure none of the boroughs have residents in various shades of green, white, and orange with tufts of broccoli, cauliflower, carrot, cucumber, and other produce sprouting from their temples. Not unless there was a recent accident with a town meeting and a vat of Miracle Gro and this is the first I've heard of it.

So no, I don't believe I'm in Brooklyn. I can totally believe, however, that Ned is from this place. Without even having to strain at it. Looks like Tall owes me twenty bucks.

Speaking of Ned, I realize he's standing right next to me, also blinking and rubbing at his eyes. "Man, I hate that!" he says after a bit of mumbled swearing. "It just never gets any easier."

"You tried keeping your eyes open during the teleport, didn't you?" I accuse, and he jumps. I'm not sure he's recovered enough vision yet to see me, so it may have just seemed like my voice was coming from nowhere, or from some enormous, fuzzy, black-and-green blob. I wish I could figure out how to duplicate that for next Halloween! "Uh-huh. Close your eyes, they won't hurt as much." I only know this because of Mary, actually. She'd shown up one day—just appearing suddenly in the Matrix chamber itself and right beside the couch, talk about pinpoint accuracy!—with her eyes closed, and at first I thought she wanted to play hide-and-seek or was expecting a surprise party or something, until she explained.

Of course, we did play hide-and-seek after, just because. And let me tell you, that game's a lot more fun when groping's allowed.

"Yeah?" Ned laughs. "You're telling me you didn't try seeing it too?"

"Can't, remember?" I tap a finger on my cheekbone, just below my eyes. "Nictitating membranes—they automatically go into lockdown if the light's too bright. I can't see for crap while they're down." Though I have to admit, if not for those I'd sure be tempted. Who doesn't want to try watching a teleport in progress, just to check if you can see yourself disintegrating while it happens? Uh, yeah, then again, maybe I don't want to watch that any time soon.

I distract myself from those thoughts by rubbing at my bill as I look around some more. There's a kid with an oversized cap standing on a nearby corner, waving a newspaper. Huh. "So," I ask Ned, "what, is my brain doing that weird reprocessing thing again where it's seeing one thing but pretending I'm looking at something else I can understand? Because otherwise I'm not entirely sure what I'm looking at here." Unless somebody nearby is airing *Newsboys* on a wraparound hologram screen. In which case I totally need to buy one of those for the living room!

"What?" Ned lifts his ever-present baseball cap to a little old lady who's tottering past. She's the color of stewed spinach, and looks about as friendly, but does offer Ned a wintery little smile. Brrr, I think my tonsils just froze. "What can I say, people like me," he explains, smiling. "But to answer your question, no, this is exactly what Artelusia IX looks like. They—"

"Wait, what?" I point to a pickle guy on the next corner, with his vats of pickles all arranged in the cart, each one clearly labeled. And yes, he's got pickles coming out of his head too, which would certainly make me wary of sampling his wares! "You're telling me there is an actual guy over there selling pickles? Here? A million light years away from Earth? Dude, if you'd said it was some tentacled beastie growing extra limbs just for fun, I'd have believed you, but pickle barrels? Really? Is there some galactic homage to *Crossing Delancey* I don't know about here? Why do so many places we wind up look just like New York? I mean, I know it's the greatest city ever, but I didn't think the news had spread quite this far yet!"

Ned looks over at the pickle guy, who sees us staring and waves. Ned waves back. Then he shrugs. "Coincidence?" he offers in exactly the same tone you take when your girlfriend asks what you were just doing whispering in her former best friend's ear and you say "Catching up?" knowing full well that excuse is so see-through it's like clear or at least lightly tinted glass but still hoping against hope that she'll have a major brain fart at precisely that instant and decide "yeah, okay, I guess I can buy that." Of course, following up with "hey, the two of you *do* have a lot in common!" probably doesn't help with that.

"Uh huh, sure," I tell him, probably in pretty close to the same tone Sarah Cruise used with me back in college. But whatever. It's clear Ned doesn't have any idea why either, and it's not like he's to blame—this planet was here long before he came along. I think. Actually, I have no idea if that's true or not—for all I know, Ned's half a billion years old and shapes entire star systems for fun, and he built this whole place as some sort of recreational therapy and has been masquerading as one of its mortal residents just as a way to pass the time.

Wow, it's a good thing I can leave the Matrix building now, because I'm pretty sure I need to get out more.

The rumbling of my stomach brings me back to the business at hand. It also startles a woman walking by with her three kids, and they all take one quick glance at it, and at me, and hurry away. Hey, I want to call out, just because you look like walking celery doesn't mean I'm going to eat you! I don't, though, because that would just be rude. Also, I can't help wondering, if cannibals came here and ate these people would they use up more calories than they gained, just like when you eat normal celery? Would this be like the perfect cannibal diet then? "Now you can still eat people, and lose weight while doing it!"

I'd blame extreme hunger for giving me thoughts like this but, let's face it, I think this sort of stuff all the time. Of course, I *am* hungry most of the time, so maybe there's something to that theory after all.

Which reminds me. . . .

"You said something about a buffet?"

"Yep!" Ned's all smiles again, worries totally forgotten as he focuses back in on the prospect of food. "Come on, it's this way!" We start walking, nodding at people as we pass. Most of them nod back, or say hello, or wave, or at least smile. Friendly little place. A few growl, though, or scowl, or shake their heads, or just ignore us. Yeah, whatever. You can't have a society without at least a few curmudgeons—it's like Scrooge's Law or something.

One of those curmudgeons is driving a car that's hurtling down the road beside us with all the abandon of a small child who's just slipped his leash and has the hotel pool in his sights. There's a guy crossing the street, looks like a typical college student though I'm only assuming they have colleges here, and like most college kids he's not paying the slightest attention to anything around him, he's so busy playing on something that resembles a cell phone if it had been shoved into a dog's squeak toy and then mated to a handheld blender. He's heading right for that speeding car, or the car is heading right for him, and I know who's going to win that particular shoving match.

"Hey, stop!" I shout. He doesn't even look up. "Look out, dude!" Still nothing. "Whoa, check out the hot chick!" That does the trick—his head snaps up, scanning the immediate area, and he sees the car just in time to jump back out of the way. College guys are the same everywhere, apparently.

"You nearly hit me, you bum!" he shouts, shaking a singularly unimpressive fist at the car and its driver, who are already half a block past him.

But that's not the weird part.

The weird part is that, when this kid shouts that, everyone around him stops. Every single one of them. Ned, a young couple on the other side of the street, people driving past, the guy out sweeping the front of his store. Everybody.

And then, like they'd rehearsed it, every single one of them spits on the ground in front of them and shouts, "Dirty bums!"

After which they all go right back to whatever they were doing before.

'Cause that's normal.

"Yo," I say, grabbing Ned by the arm. "What the hell was that?"

"What was what?" he asks. And I know Ned well enough to know when he's fooling around and when he's being serious. Most of the time. He's not joking right now.

"That!" I gesture behind me at, well, everything. "The 'bums' bit. That kid said 'you bum,' and all of you—"

Which is, of course, when they do it again. Spit. Shout "Dirty bums!" Back to normal.

The hell? I really wanna try "Frau Blucher," just to see what that does to them.

"That!" I tell Ned. "What was that?"

"Hm?" He shakes his head, shrugs. "Just old habit, I guess. Now come on—Gus's is just around the corner."

Yeah? Okay, fine. I can sure do with some food right about now. Maybe it'll wash away the taste of whatever the hell that synchronized spit-take routine was left in my mouth. I traipse after him as we reach the corner, turn, and—

"Oh, no!"

That's Ned doing his best "Charlton Heston at the end of *Planet of the Apes*" moment. He's on his knees, arms raised to the sky, head turned up, wailing. I scan the area, and don't see what's got him so upset.

Except I also don't see Gus's All-You-Can-Eat Melva Buffet. Oh.

"Uh, Ned?" I nudge him as gently as I can with one foot—I have to be careful there, I've been known to shove parked cars aside that way. "Ned? Where's this buffet you were talking about?"

"There!" he waves one hand at a building on the corner across the street. "It's always been there, for as long as I can remember!" He peeks over there now, then wails some more. "This can't be happening!"

I study the building that *is* there. It's a good size, long and deep, and has big plate glass windows all along both sides, with an awning over the front door right at the corner. There are plenty of people coming and going, so business must be brisk. Which makes sense, really, at least according to the awning. It says:

WELCOME TO APOLLO'S!

THE NUMBER ONE ORAL-INTAKE STIMULANT PROVIDER

ON ARTELUSIA IX.

Wow, they really need better sign writers. I wonder if that's even a job.

Still, I don't need a dictionary to know what those ten-dollar words mean. All I have to do is look at the building again, studying its small awnings over each window, its bland color scheme, its tinted windows, the bar tables and chairs set up along them, the display case full of sweets right in front, the workers behind the counter, various pitchers and cups scattered about. And of course, most telling of all, the rows of canisters up against the back wall between the windows, labels plainly visible on each one, small, roasted brown beans filling each to the brim.

It's a coffeehouse. A chain, judging by all the banners and other promotional materials both inside and out.

Ned's favorite restaurant got taken over.

Guess I won't be trying the warab filet after all.

Chapter Seven
Nonconsensual reality

"Sorry, dude," I tell Ned, patting him on the back. "It happens, though. When I was a kid we had this place we always went, it was like our favorite hangout. Lots of space, plenty of old records and books and comics to dig through, privacy, and the best pies and cakes anywhere outside Manhattan. We'd go there all the time, me and my buddies, and just browse and eat and drink and chill." I sigh, caught up in the memory. "Then Old Man Taggert figured out what we were doing and boarded up the basement windows and that was that—no more hangout." I rub my belly. "Man, Mrs. Taggert's pies were good!" We never could understand why he got so upset about it. It's not like he was doing anything with his stuff anyway.

Ned's recovered from his angst enough to glare at me. "That ain't the same thing at all!" he complains, pushing himself back to his feet. "That was breaking and entering! This is the death of a local landmark!"

An older gentleman with a face like a wrinkled green grape—and for once I mean that literally—is just trying to sidle past us, and Ned turns on him like a hungry pit bull. "What happened to Gus's?" Ned demands of the poor guy.

"I-I don't know any Gus," Raisinhead stammers. It's clear he wants to run but Ned's focus is somehow holding him in place. Like a little personality-based tractor beam. That's so cool! I wonder if different emotions would give it more—or less— power? Like Ned could be annoyed and whoever he directed it at would barely slow down, but he could be colossally pissed and they'd get yanked clear across the room. Huh, guess I must be immune. But not Wrinklepuss—he starts to shrivel even more. Despite that, he insists, "Look, I don't know who you're talking about!"

"Not who!" Ned all but howls in the guy's face. "What! Gus's All-You-Can-Eat Melva Buffet! Been here my whole life! Where is it? What did they do to it?"

Before this, Grapeman was studying Ned as if he was just irritable and maybe mildly deluded, like those guys on the subway who're perfectly fine and friendly as long as you don't mention the one thing that sets them off. And it's not like they come with a "warning: trigger words are" card. But now he's looking totally terrified, like Ned's going to throttle him or dangle him out the window or something.

Which, in his current state of mind? I'm not putting it past him. Good thing we're on the ground!

"I don't know any Gus's," PruneDude repeats, dragging out that final *s*. "I swear!" He finally breaks free of Ned's tractor-beam gaze and takes off down the block at a dead run. Man, for an old guy he can really move! Ned just stares after him.

"This doesn't make any sense," I hear him mutter. "How could he not know Gus's?"

"Maybe he's new in town," I offer. *Or maybe he'd say any-thing to get away from you when you've got that crazed look in your eye,* I add, but don't say. I really am getting better about that—at least once a week I manage to not say something I just would've blurted out before. And about half of those times I don't even post it online afterward!

There's another guy coming toward us, this one with his lady friend or sister or something—they do have matching lettuce-head going on, and I have no idea if that's romantic or genetic—and I put a hand up to stop Ned from charging them. "Hey, how about I handle this one?" I say as gently as I can. He sort of shrug-nods—see, snods are catching on!—and I turn to the couple, giving them my best "no, really, I'm not out to sell you car insurance" smile. The one I patterned after Eddie.

"Excuse me," I call out as they approach, holding both hands up so they can see I'm not making a grab for their valu-ables. "I'm looking for Gus's All-You-Can-Eat Melva Buffet."

"Never heard of it, sorry," Mr. Lettucehead replies. He and the missus—they've got matching wristbands, so I'm thinking maybe that's like a wedding ring here, though it could just mean they both gave blood/V-8 or went to a rock concert—slow a bit but don't stop completely. Which is fair. I'm a New Yorker, I'm used to drive-by conversations. Sometimes even from so-called friends.

"Really?" I do my best to frown, which isn't as easy as Donald makes it look. "I'm supposed to meet a buddy there and I could've sworn this was the address he gave me." I glance around. "You don't suppose it closed or something, do you?"

Mrs. Lettucehead chuckles. "If it did, it must've been a long time ago," she answers. "I grew up right around the corner from here, and I've never heard of a Gus's."

"Oh?" Curiouser and curiouser, as Alice said. "Huh. So, let me ask you—where does a guy go to get a good warab filet around here?"

The Saladheads share a knowing glance. "Sal's," they say simultaneously. Which is creepy—it's like an entire tossed salad is talking at me now. "Sal's Green Tea Saloon," the mister clarifies. "It's three blocks up, on Core, and then over two to Eastern. It's the one with the green awning, you can't miss it."

"Core to Eastern, Sal's, green awning," I repeat. "Got it. Thanks so much!"

"Not a problem," the missus tells me. "Enjoy!" And they walk on.

I turn back to Ned, who's been watching the whole thing. "They seem nice."

"Sal's?" he says, though he practically spits the name at me. Good thing I'm still a few feet away, I'd hate to get alien saliva all over my shoes. Though around here I wonder if that would basically be vegetable juice? Or salad dressing? "Sal's? Really? Their warab's nothing compared to Gus's!"

"Maybe not," I say, "except that Gus's doesn't seem to exist and Sal's does, so I'd say Sal's sorta wins by default, y'know?" I scratch my bill. "Only, it's weird that they never heard of Gus's, and neither had that other guy. When was the last time you were there?"

"Just a few weeks ago," Ned answers. He's frowning now

too. "But I heard what that lady said, about growing up near here. How could she not know Gus's? Something weird is going on."

"Ya got that right! And here I thought we were just gonna have lunch!" My stomach rumbles its agreement, as well as its protest at the ongoing delays, and I rub it to keep it quiet. -er. "Whaddya say we head on over to Sal's, check it out, and, uh, see if they know anything over there?" I rub again. "And maybe grab a bite while we're at it?"

Unfortunately, Ned's not buying it. He's got that look in his eye, the one that says "Shhh, I'm thinking about something, leave me alone." I used to get that look a lot, but with Ned and Mary and even Tall I'm pretty sure they really are thinking about something important and not just "how do I get this weird guy with the duck head to stop talking at me?" At least, I hope so. Anyway, Ned's pulled out another of his odd little doohickeys and he's heading straight for this Apollo's joint at practically a full march. Uh-oh.

"Whoa, dude, what're you doing?" I ask, jogging after him and getting in his way. "Look, just 'cause they somehow made your favorite eatery disappear and possibly never exist doesn't mean you can go around destabilizing molecules or causing mini-supernovas or whatever." I glance over my shoulder. "Besides, their cupcakes look pretty decent." My stomach rumbles its agreement, and its offer to check into that claim more closely.

"What?" Ned focuses on me for a second. "I'm not gonna hurt nobody! I just want to check the energy readings, see if there's any sign of what happened!"

"Oh. Yeah, okay, you do that. But then we're eating!" I insist. He gives either a nod or just a shiver and keeps going, and I let him. The sooner he scans the place, the sooner we can grab lunch. Then maybe we can figure out what's going on, but I don't really think straight when I'm hungry.

Which may be why, when something moves out of the corner of my eye, I don't ignore it or pretend to until it's within taser range, the way a good little New Yorker should.

Instead I turn and look.

There's an alley just a little behind us, a narrow space between a drugstore—yes, it actually says Rex Drugs on it, though judging by the vials and everything displayed in the window and the dazed, happy looks of the people emerging every now and again it's more like a head shop than a pharmacy—and a "Gentleman's Tailer," which seems to specialize in fitting its customers with robotic tails in a variety of shapes and sizes. And somebody just slid back into the shadows in that alley. Somebody about my height who has very definitely been watching Ned and me, which explains why the little feathers on the back of my neck were standing up.

I thought there was just a breeze.

And now, to prove that I'm not thinking straight and that I haven't exactly mastered the whole "think before acting" routine, I waltz right over to that alleyway. "Hey," I call out as I do. "Who's there? Come on out, I know you're in there. Let's talk. Do you know where Gus's went?" My stomach rumbles. "And do you have any food on you?"

Nobody answers, which just proves that whoever it is must be a whole lot better at knowing when to keep quiet than I am. Of course, so are most toddlers, so that doesn't exactly mean a lot. The alleyway's narrow enough that you could maybe fit three people across if they didn't mind rubbing shoulders, but it goes back a good ways. And the buildings on either side are tall enough that, even though it's closing on noon and the two suns are both high in the sky, this particular patch is filled with shadow.

Just the kind of place you shouldn't walk into, especially on a strange planet when the only person you know is across the street nosing about in a coffeehouse.

So, naturally, I walk on in.

"Come on out, don't be shy," I say as I move from the light to the shadow, blinking to let my eyes adjust. "Look, I just want to talk, okay? Hey, maybe we can gab over lunch—there's this place called Sal's nearby, I hear they're decent."

I take another step in, then another, and suddenly the shadows have eyes. Two of them, up against one wall. And then two more, by the opposite wall. And then both sets are moving toward me. Quickly.

"Uh, hey," I manage, backpedaling, "maybe talking right now isn't such a good idea after all. Tell you what, why don't you give me your number and I'll call you later?"

But the eyes have caught up to me, and I'm still in shadow, here alone in this alleyway, and I'm just realizing how stupid this was when a big chunk of the shadows rears up like a dark tidal wave and swoops down on top of me. It wraps around me, all dark and close and tight, and I lash out but the shadows actually have substance now, and my hands and feet are immobilized just a few inches from my body. What the hell?

I try again, swinging and kicking, but again there's resistance. And it's closing in. It's getting hard to breathe, too, like the shadows are cutting off the air around me.

Which is when I figure it out. It's not the shadows. It's a sack. Somebody stuffed me in a sack!

"Hey," I try to shout, but the air's getting tight and my yell comes out as a whisper. "Come on, this is not cool." I can feel my eyelids getting heavy, same as my limbs, as my head gets fuzzy.

"At least you could've included a snack," I manage to mutter right before I pass out.

Chapter Eight
But I just *had* a nap!

"**Wakey, wakey, little** birdie."

This clever little rhyme rumbles forth from the mouth of a very confused-looking winged horse who could easily be part of the whole Littlest Horse line—the old version when they were cute and rounded, back before they all become anorexic supermodels. Who ever heard of skeletal horses with Day-Glo coloring and tattoos on their butts? That's not a children's toy line, it's the *Animal Farm* version of the Betty Ford clinic!

Anyway, this winged horse is talking to me again, more of the same. And at the same time it's speaking, it's kicking me in the forehead. Repeatedly. All while it's got this "don't ask me, I'm not the one driving this train" look on its face.

"Knock it off, horse," I mutter. "Lemme alone."

"Can't do that, pal," it replies, only just like in all the best martial arts movies its mouth isn't moving in time with its voice—a voice, I notice, that sounds like this particular winged horse enjoys long smoke breaks and lots of whiskey. Maybe this is Boozehound Horse? Or Barfly? Heh, that would actually work, and now I'm picturing a whole line of them with darker, more adult names, like Escort Horse and Methhead Pony and

Three-Martini-Lunch Mare. I have to remember to write these down as soon as I wake up.

Which is when I realize I'm dreaming. And open my eyes.

"There ya go! Now, wasn't that easy?" Okay, this is much worse than a rainbow cloud filled with saccharine-sweet starving miniature horses. There's a big guy leaning in over me, and his whole head is covered in little pockmarks that dimple his dark skin, sending pale lines radiating out in all directions, including his bare scalp, flat cheeks, and weak chin. In this light his skin actually looks green, it's so dark—a green that's almost black, except for those lines, where it's a light yellow-green.

Oh, wait. He's a cucumber. I remember where I am now—the Land o' the Salad People.

Still, it's pretty creepy. Especially when he's only a few inches away from me.

Picklehead is still wiggling his fingers at me—fingers that look like full-on dills of their own, they're that thick. "You with us, little birdy?"

"Dude, I'm a duck," I tell him. "Well, a guy, but with a duck head. Not a bird head. And definitely not a little bird—no sparrows or wrens or finches here." I glance around. "Love what you've done with the place   when do you tear down the rest of it?"

Because, apparently, I'm in an old warehouse.

Not just any old warehouse, either. No, this one is down on the docks.

You may wonder how I know that. See, here's the thing about me—I don't miss much. I notice all the little stuff, like the bare wood-plank floors, the wide open space, the rough wood walls half-hidden in shadow, the high ceiling with its supports right out in the open, the skylights that've been blacked out but still dot the ceiling in a pair of neat lines. I notice the dusty old pallets stacked in a far corner, the pile of old moving blankets in another, the scent of old machine oil and sawdust and years of sweat that still cling to everything.

I also notice the loading doors at one end, which're wide open and give a fine view of a short, wide pier just beyond, and the big-ass lake that spreads out from there.

Hey, a less observant person might've missed that!

"Bird, duck, whatever," Gourdface replies. "The important thing is, you're awake." He smiles at me, which is unsettling— his teeth look like cucumber seeds, pointy ends up. That's a whole lot scarier than you might think. "I'd hate for you to miss this next bit."

"Yeah, we don't want you to miss it," another voice agrees, and I twist around to see who's attached to that softer, almost squeaky voice, noticing for the first time that a) I'm sitting in a hard metal chair like they used to have in schools and police stations, and b) I am in fact tied to said chair, arms and legs and across the chest. I kinda forget all that when I see Ol' Gourdo's buddy, though.

He's an albino.

He's got white skin with an almost yellowish cast to it, his face is all lumpy as if he were breaking out big-time or got stung by fifty thousand bees at once, and his ears are just little nubs off to the side. He's got at least three chins, each one lumpier than the last, and his cheeks are all puffed out, too. I have no idea what color his eyes are, on account of the sunglasses he's wearing even though we're indoors and it ain't exactly bright in here, but I'm guessing they're either a pale pink or an arctic blue. The only part of him with any real color is his hair, which is a light green and curls limply atop his protruding forehead and floats sparsely behind his temples.

I suppose it makes sense, really. I mean, Ned's part broccoli. My new least-favorite alarm clock—also sporting sunglasses, now that I notice—is a cucumber. There's no good reason this place would restrict itself to green vegetables, right? And now I can't help wondering if they have race wars here, the radishes and turnips protesting for equal rights, the carrots writing angry poetry and leading marches, the tomatoes staging sit-ins, the pumpkins lobbying and going to court. Wacky.

But even so, being confronted with a cauliflower man is a bit disconcerting.

"Who are you guys?" I finally ask. Hey, I haven't eaten all day, I'm on a strange planet, I only know one person here and he's probably still stalking that poor coffeehouse, and I was ducknabbed and stuffed in a sack. I think I can be excused for getting to the point.

"Who are we?" Cukeman repeats. He glances over at Cauliflowerhead, and they both laugh. They aren't nice laughs. "Who do you think we are?" He tugs on the bottom of his suit jacket—yes, both of them are wearing suits, dark gray ones that look reasonably well made, certainly better than the one Gran bought me from JCPenny when I was twelve "and needed to learn to dress like a real man and not some demented Dennis the Menace ripoff." And yet neither looks quite right—their arms are bulging in the material, their shirt collars are tight around their necks, and I can practically see the outline of their guns through their jackets.

Okay, hang on a second here. Cheap suits, guns, an old warehouse, and vaguely threatening comments delivered in a half-joking manner?

When did I wind up in a Coppola film?

It doesn't look like the Veggie Brigade here is going to show me IDs, so I try a different tack. "What do you want with me?"

Picklebrain smiles again, like suddenly we're best buds. "That's real simple. We just wanna talk with you a bit, ask you about a few things, see what you know." That smile widens. "Then we'll let you go, I promise."

Uh huh. That smile says otherwise.

"And if I don't cooperate?" I ask. I've never been all that good at cooperation. In preschool whenever they'd tell us to cooperate and pair us off with another kid I'd steal his lunch money, use it to buy sweets from the vending machine—hey, if they're gonna put one of those out where kids can get to it they've got to expect we're gonna use it—and then stuff the empty wrappers into his backpack and tell our teacher that he'd been sneaking sweets. As my mom said in the parent-teacher conference that inevitably followed, "Well, you've gotta admit, that takes some smarts."

"You don't wanna do that." I wish I knew how some people managed that. One second he's fun-loving and a little inattentive, the next he's all business all the time. And when I say "business," I mean stone-cold killing. "If you won't talk," he continues, "I might haveta get . . . creative. And if it looks like you absolutely won't help us no matter what, well, then it's time to go, princess."

"Go? That's an option?" I strain against my bonds. "Fine, I won't help you, so untie me and let me walk."

He laughs. "Yeah, no, that ain't exactly how it works. If you go, you ain't walking anywhere. Ever again. Your feet'll be too heavy, on account of your new socks."

"New socks?" I know I'm probably staring at him like he's about to sprout horns, or in his case dill spears, but I can't help it. I thought I was the one spouting gibberish nobody else can decipher!

"Absolutely!" His smile is practically beatific now—if you could include cucumbers in the Heavenly choir I honestly think he would spontaneously sublimate and float out of here on a cloud of pure Happy. "You'll love 'em—they're the last pair of socks you'll ever own."

The last pair?

"Why, what're they made of, Egyptian cotton?" I ask. I'm running through fabric lists in my head. Wool? Naw, too itchy. Silk? You'd slide right out of your shoes! Same with satin. Gingham? Ugh. Rayon? Polyester? Double ugh.

"Nope." I didn't think his smile could get any wider—as it is, he's the most toothsome vegetable in existence—but somehow it does. "Watermint."

"What?" I'd stick my fingers in my ears to clean 'em out if

1) I wasn't tied up right now, 2) I still had external ears, and 3) Sister Mary Josephine hadn't taught me, repeatedly and with great fervor, that the Big Man Upstairs did not give us graceful digits and shell-like listening organs to have us rudely jab one in the other on impromptu fishing expeditions. Of course, it probably didn't help that I wasn't going after my own ears at the time. Or that, a few years later, she and I had the same conversation but about slightly different, ahem, portions of anatomy. Sending me to a Catholic after-school program was really just a bad idea for everyone concerned. Except for Ma, who claimed she'd needed the rest.

But right now, I'm wishing I could overcome the sisters' brutal behavioral conditioning because I'm sure I'm hearing something wrong. "Did you just say 'watermint'?" I ask. "Because if so I have absolutely no idea what that is. Is it like spearmint? Or watercress? Or a combination of the two? Which would work really well on a sandwich, if you ask me, and I'd be happy to taste-test something like that, especially if you had a few dozen of them laying about right now, but—" Their laughing stops my blather dead in its tracks. Which is impressive, because I've seen my blather mow down whole stadium audiences before. They should never have left the sportscasters' booth unlocked.

"You don't know what watermint is?" Cauliflower says to me, still chortling. He's laughing so hard he's practically wilting. "He don't know what watermint is!"

"Oh, it's a real peach of a material," Pickler promises me, laughing just as hard as his buddy. "Durable, heavyweight, lots of texture. Only comes in the one color, but hey, basic grey goes with everything, right?"

Okay, obviously I'm missing something here. Something they think I should already know. I wrack my brain. Heavy, textured, tough, gray, can be made into socks, called watermint. Then I remember to put it in the context of a Mafioso movie, and start playing with synonyms. Water. Liquid. Ocean. Sea.

Sea-mint.

Oh.

"Yeah," Cauliflower adds. "You'll be napping with the eels."

Yeah, that one I got, thanks.

Gourdo's about to say something else when all of a sudden there's this horrible rending, grinding sound like somebody's about to pull the entire house down.

Which is exactly what they do.

There's a crack like thunder and the warehouse's front doors buckle inward. The top hinge on the right tears free. My two new friends are doing their best to duck and cover, except all of the furniture's gone so there really aren't all that many places to hide. Except for behind me, which is exactly what they try to do. This really is a strange but oddly typical chain of events for me—one minute worshiped, the next about to be sacrificed, then kidnapped, threatened, and now in danger of being crushed, plus with two stereotypical thugs cowering behind me like frightened little boys. Actually, come to think of it, this is one of the less scary moments I've had since leaving my boring but sane old office job. Except that the front door's still getting slammed and still looking like it's about to break, and the entire building's still quaking with each hit, making me hope it isn't about to collapse and turn me into DuckBob paté.

Yes, right now everything is a food metaphor. I can't help it, even though this could be the end I'm still hungry. And I'd hate to die hungry. It just doesn't seem fair.

There's one last, horrific crash, and the entire front door flies inward like a morning commuter late for work. Standing outlined against the opening is a tall, powerfully built figure made even taller by the addition of cowboy boots and a trucker hat.

Hang on, I know that menacing and almost supernaturally fit silhouette!

"Tall?" I call out. "That you?"

"Hang tight, DuckBob," Tall—also known as former Man in Black Agent Roger Henry David Thomas, also known as probably my best friend in the whole universe—answers, his voice gravelly and gruff but still reassuring. "I'll have you out of here in a jiffy."

Which is, naturally, when Mr. Cauliflower perks up. He pops to his feet right behind me, pulls a piece out of his jacket from under his arm—it looks like a .45 automatic got peckish and ate a Buck Rogers ray gun—and points it. Straight at the side of my head.

"Back off or the duck gets it!" he shouts.

Of course.

"Put the gun down and walk away and you might get to keep all your teeth," Tall growls back, stalking across the wide, bare warehouse floor. They really should turn this place into an ice skating rink when they're not using it to torture people. Or maybe a dance club. It has such great space!

Cauliflower Boy isn't buying it, though. "You'll never take me alive!" he shouts, and shifts his gun so it's pointing at Tall instead. Unfortunately for him, he leaves his arm right beside me, mere inches from my face.

So I lean over and bite him.

Hard.

"Aaaggh!" he screams, dropping the piece, and starts punching me with his other hand. Too bad for him that doesn't work—he's hitting me square in the bill with each blow, and it's obvious someone did teach him how to throw a punch but nobody ever bothered to explain how hard a duck's bill is and how you'll only hurt yourself if you try hitting one.

Pickleface hasn't moved since the walls started shaking— he's curled up behind me doing his best "you can't see me" chant beneath his breath. Sadly, it isn't true, and he only has time to let out one little whimper when Tall strides past me and hauls Pickles to his feet by his shirt collar. Ow, like temple-going days all over again! Tall smacks Pickles in the jaw once, just once, and the wannabe gangster folds and crumples to the floor.

Which leaves Cauliflower Guy. Who is still screaming and still punching me in the bill. And yes, I'm still biting him.

"Mind if I cut in?" Tall asks, and my mouth pops open, though that might be from the corny one-liner. All the time I've known him, Tall's been one of the stiffest, most straight-forward, least funny people ever. Now he cracks jokes? I don't know if I should be relieved or frightened. But I do know that I don't want to make him ask twice, so I open my mouth, the guy drops to the ground, and Tall reaches over and hauls him back up again. A knuckle sandwich or two later and both thugs are passed out on the floor.

"So, what'd you get yourself into this time?" Tall asks as he whips out a knife and cuts my bonds. Always such the Boy Scout. Right now, though, I don't exactly mind.

"I have no idea!" I protest, pushing off from the chair and standing upright for the first time in what must be hours. I immediately sit down again. Maybe I should start slow and work my way up to walking. I hear crawling's good for the back, even if it's hard on the knees.

"DuckBob?" a second, somewhat less heroic voice calls through what used to be the front door. "You okay?" Ned steps carefully over the threshold, around the remains of the door, and ambles over to join us. "Glad we could get here in time!"

"Yeah, how'd you find me, anyway?" I ask, trying this whole "standing" thing again and managing it a bit better this time. As long as I don't try walking or take my hand off this chair I should be fine.

Ned glances down at his feet. "Oh, I, uh, noticed you'd stopped talking, so I turned around to see what was up and you were gone. That's when I called Tall." They exchange nods, very manly all the way around.

"Sure, cool," I say, "But that's not what I asked. How did you know where to find me?"

"Right, so—" Ned starts again, but Tall interrupts him.

"There's a GPS chip in your new headpiece," he tells me. That's one of the things I like about Tall. He always tells you the truth. Which can be inconvenient, embarrassing, and some-times even dangerous, but at least you know he's not going to lie about it.

"GPS? Really? Huh." Now I remember, Ned had actually mentioned that before, when he saved me from the MiBs yesterday. He still looks embarrassed about it, though. I guess he figured I'd be all pissed about being chipped, but how can I be when it basically saved my life? "Cool," I say, and he perks up. "Thanks, guys."

"No problem." Ned gestures back toward the door. "We should get out of here."

"Oh. Okay." I follow him, and Tall grumbles something but brings up the rear.

GPS. Right.

That's sure going to make sneaking out for donuts a lot more challenging!

Chapter Nine
Now in shadier gray

"**You really have** no idea who those guys were or why they grabbed you?" Tall asks as he marches me down the street, his Volvo-sized hand clamped onto my upper arm. Which is a good thing, since without some help I might fall down and then he'd just wind up dragging me along behind him. Though that does sound restful. Still, the street here is less what I'd call an actual street and more an old wooden dock, so I'd probably end up with splinters. I can't help noticing that the other buildings around us look just as rundown as my recent interrogation chamber, all peeling paint and warped wood and rusty nails. Between that and the dock itself I feel like I've stepped into a bad version of *Moby Dick*. I keep expecting to hear a foghorn and then a clanging bell announcing a whale sighting.

"Not a clue," I tell him yet again. "I wish I did—I'd smack 'em with a bill for time wasted." Just like I always want to do whenever I've got a doctor's appointment. Why is it that, if you show up a little late, they tell you you've missed your appointment time and have to wait for the next available slot, which is usually hours to days later, but if you show up on time or early you still wind up sitting for hours on end, well past the time you were supposed to be there? And if you cancel on them they charge you for the visit anyway, but if they tell you they need to reschedule they don't have to pay any kind of fee? The last time I went to a regular doctor I had a one o'clock appointment, got there at noon, and wound up sitting until three-thirty—then saw the doc for all of five minutes. He billed me a hundred and fifty bucks for the privilege. So I billed him two-forty, figuring he'd wasted four hours of my time and during the brief period where I was temping I was getting sixty an hour. I wrote off the half hour as an acceptable wait time, plus the visit itself. Not surprisingly, he didn't pay. Neither did I until that nice marshal showed up at my door and informed me very clearly and precisely that my choices were to cough up the one-fifty or get out of his way while he seized and then auctioned off all my worldly possessions. I decided the one-fifty wasn't worth the hassle. I did ask the marshal if he billed by the hour, though.

"What did they look like?" Ned wants to know. I guess he didn't get a good look from all the way back by the door, and it's not like he can go examine them now with half of the building on top of them. I'm not blaming him for hanging back, though. I know Ned's not a coward or anything—I've seen him face all sorts of tough situations, including the scourge of the galaxy and a zombified Tall. But Ned's not a fighter, and he's not stupid, so he let Tall wade in while he hung back in case Tall needed backup or a lookout or somebody to go on a coffee run. I'd probably do the same thing if I ever stopped to think twice before acting. Or once, even.

"A cucumber and a cauliflower," I tell him. "In cheap suits."

"Oh." You ever seen broccoli go pale? Like when you've been soaking it too long and some of the green has leeched out into the water, leaving it sort of a milky greenish white? Yeah, it's not appealing. Now put that on somebody's face. "They wore suits." Poor Ned—I'd say he looks like he's been hit by a truck but his face is always that flat.

"Uh, yeah. And they talked like bad gangster parodies—and not gangstas but gangsters, the old-fashioned kind from the movies." Which may not help Ned much, since I don't know how many Earth movies he's watched. Then again, we do keep helpfully broadcasting all of our shows out into space, which means unfortunately the rest of the galaxy has been forced to put up with endless reruns of *Knots Landing*, *Punky Brewster*, and *Manimal*, but on the plus side they also got *I Love Lucy*, *Mork and Mindy*, and *The Incredible Hulk*. I feel bad about all the home shopping networks, though, especially since it seems like every other civilization has decided these are a great idea. Back at the Matrix, where I get every channel ever, it's like every third one is somebody trying to sell me the greatest knife in existence or the niftiest backscratcher or the most comfortable seat cushion. And I tend to be very susceptible to sales pitches—I once agreed to upgrade my home's heating system from oil to natural gas and I didn't even own a home!

Ned's nodding, though, like he knows exactly what I mean. And apparently it's a really bad thing. "Wait, do you know these guys?" I ask him.

"What?" That startles him out of his little panic-trance. "Uh, no—not exactly. I mean, not specifically, but if they're who

I think they are . . . well, I don't know why they'd have kidnapped you like that." He scratches at his head and tugs at his toolbelt. "That's not really their style."

"We should report this," Tall declares with all the conviction of a career law enforcement official. We've gone a few blocks from the warehouse now, and he releases my arm and turns to face me and Ned. "People can't just go grabbing innocent bystanders off the street." He eyes me for a second. "Well, innocent as far as they know, anyway." Gee, thanks, Tall. You're a pal.

"Who would we report it to?" I look around as something dawns on me. "The entire time we've been here—which, admittedly, is probably only a few hours unless I was out for a lot longer than I realized—I don't think I've seen a single cop."

Ned visibly shudders at that last word. "We don't actually have police here," he explains slowly. "It's a little more . . . complicated than that."

"How is it complicated?" Tall demands. "Do you have a standing army that doubles as a peacekeeping force, instead? Or marshals, sheriffs, and deputies? Some sort of justice agency?" Ned just shakes his head.

"School crossing guards?" I suggest. "Wellness officers? Security guards? Bell captains?" Tall glares at me, which means I'm officially out of my "can't get in trouble because he was just the victim of a kidnapping" grace period. "What? They've got spiffy uniforms, they know where everyone and everything goes, and they can solve any problem in minutes as long as you tip them enough. Sounds like an effective police force to me!"

"It's not like that around here," Ned answers. "There isn't a whole lot of crime, see, and what little there is, well, it's sort of . . . allowed."

"Allowed? Who allows it?" Tall asks, his voice getting louder and deeper with every second of increased outrage. Any minute now he's gonna have steam start shooting out of his ears. I wish I had a camera. Or a sausage on a stick.

"There's no law, but there is plenty of discipline," Ned replies. "And yeah, sometimes there's violence. Kinda hard to avoid, right? People're people and get mad, have to blow off a little steam. So there's some allowances made. And some examples, too." He shrugs. "Nobody just whacks another person, though. Not without facing some pretty nasty punishment after." He shudders slightly, and I wonder if he faced some of that punishment himself, or knows somebody who did. And did he really just say "whacks"?

"What about kidnapping?" I ask him pointedly. "Is that allowed, too, or no? Because if so, I can't imagine that you get a whole lot of repeat visitors."

He shakes his head. "No, kidnapping's a no-no. Only certain people can get away with it, and only if it's sanctioned." He rubs at his nose. "Which I can't imagine yours was."

"So we're back to reporting it," Tall points out. He squares his jaw. "If there aren't any authorities we can tell here, we can always inform the MiBs. This isn't exactly in their jurisdiction, but they still might be able to send an agent or two to look into things and find out what really happened—and why." I'm impressed that Tall said "they" and not "we"—it's only been a

few months since he quit and went into business trucking with
Heidi instead. To be fair, though, I've never once seen him
regret that decision, or pine for his old job. Other than the whole
shooting things part, which I know he misses. That's why there's
now a shooting range off to one side of the Matrix chamber, but
Tall tells me it just isn't the same.

"No!" I've rarely seen Ned this worked up, usually everything just rolls right off him. "The MiBs are government, they'd
never fit in here." He chews at his lip, which only serves to
remind me how hungry I am—now I'm thinking about pasta
primavera, and if the rumbling at my waistline is any indication
my stomach is eagerly insisting we place that order, and pronto.

"Dude, we gotta tell somebody," I inform him. "Look, I've
only seen a little of this place so far but most of the people seem
pretty cool—I can't imagine they, or their council or whatever
it is, really want to get yanked off the street, stuck in a dark
warehouse somewhere, and then tortured until they're dead. If
you're saying any crime has to be approved by the higher-ups
first, either they're pissed at me without ever even having met
me—which is impressive, and means my dark powers are growing or my reputation precedes me or they simply have an unrea-
soning hatred for all waterfowl—or somebody's acting without
their say-so. If it's the first one we might as well just get it over
with, and if it's the second one they're definitely gonna wanna
know." Heh, I love it when Tall gives me that look, the one that
says "I always forget there's a real brain under those feathers
somewhere," coupled with that little "manly respect" nod. I'd go
for a fistbump but I don't want to push it.

Ned sighs. "Fine." He pulls out a little tube and pops it open, and a swarm of small, iridescent shapes dart out and begin circling his head. I worry for a second that he's being attacked by the smallest, cutest insect swarm ever, but then I remember—a little while back, during the whole crazed zombie thing, I called Ned and he wasn't holding a regular phone. Instead he'd had some new-fangled gadget he'd created, which generated a "sound-conducive dome" about him. He didn't have video capabilities at the time, though he'd said he was working on that next. Regardless, he half-disappears into this globe of low-end static, and I can see him dial a number and then start talking but the dome prevents us from actually hearing what he's saying. He talked for a minute before turning off his phone—he holds up the tube again and basically summons the little worker-bees back into their nest, and turns back to us.

"Okay," he says, though his face and posture and tone of voice suggest the opposite. "They want to ask you guys some questions about what happened. We're to wait here."

"We are? For what?" I ask. I wonder if I should find a more comfortable place to stand, or rather to lean against, because though I am feeling mostly recovered I'm not sure I'm really up to just standing still for long periods yet.

Turns out I don't need to worry about that.

Not even two minutes later, there's a loud whooshing sound overhead and a big, boxy thing the color of a good ale drops out of the clouds and hovers a few feet from the ground. It's like an old Cadillac had an affair with a jet plane and this is the result. I have to admit, it's a killer answer.

The hovercraft's side door opens, and we clamber in: Tall first, then me, then Ned. We're like a descending scale of violence, mayhem, and general physical activity, though there might be a really big drop-off after the first one. As the hovercraft lifts off again I imagine a bar graph of the three of us showing those stats, Tall towering way up in the stratosphere while Ned and I are basically skimming the pavement. Then I try to mentally convert to a pie chart, but it gets a bit muddled and instead I have this image of a big, segmented pie, with Ned and I stuck waist-deep and Tall dive-bombing like a crazed circus performer.

I'm still giggling a little at this one when our car stops moving forward, plummets for a second, and then opens its door once more, showing we're only a foot or so off the ground—

—and facing the entrance to what I'd swear was an honest-to-God old-school Italian restaurant, all smoky wood and awnings and hints of pasta sauce and olive oil in the air.

"We have to go in there?" I ask. Ned nods.

Man, this place is getting better all the time!

Chapter Ten
That's what I call pasta primavera!

"He's expecting you," is all the one guy says as he opens the door for us. That's enough. This guy is built like Tall if he'd merged with a support beam—tall, broad-shouldered, barrel-chested, tree-trunk-limbed, and so wide he literally has to stand aside so we can enter. Between his size and his suit—which must have taken whole bolts of cloth—you almost don't notice the bad complexion, the yellowish skin, and the sparse, shoot-like green strands of hair poking up from the back of his head and above his eyes. Almost.

There're two other guys just inside, and they check us over for weapons, taking Tall's knife and the gun he confiscated from Cauliman and Ned's whole toolbelt before letting us head deeper into the restaurant. They didn't bother removing anything from me, but I'm not exactly armed and dangerous. Hey, even I know better than to trust myself with a weapon, plus the idea of a guy with the head of a waterfowl carrying a firearm is just a little too ironic for my tastes.

Walking back, I wonder if we're veering from Coppola to Fellini. It's dark in here, so dark almost all the color's leeched out of our surroundings, so I feel like I've entered the world of black and white somehow. Then there's the whole veggie-head theme, which definitely has that surreal quality. On the other hand, the Mafioso element is still running strong, which is much more Coppola's bailiwick. What can I say? Film Studies was usually an easy class, all you had to do was watch a bunch of movies and argue with your classmates about whether something had artistic merit or not. Hell, I'd do that for fun, let along college credits!

It's weird being in a restaurant and having it so empty, though. There's a pair of guys off to one side chowing down on big bowls of pasta, but they're wearing the same cheap suits as everybody else we've seen so they're clearly part of the crew enjoying a lunch break rather than paying customers. The only other person sitting is the guy at the big round table in back, the one we're being steered straight toward. He doesn't bother to get up as we approach, but he does gesture us to chairs across from him. There's a huge spread on the table—pasta, some kind of chicken dish, some kind of seafood dish, bread, salad, what look like appetizers, a bottle of wine, a carafe of water, another that steams and is probably coffee—but only the one setting in front of him. Either this guy can pack it away to put even Ned to shame or he likes to graze and they just rotate dishes through as he gets bored. Of course, if he's the only one eating at the entire restaurant most of the time I can imagine the kitchen staff does these big elaborate meals partially to stay in practice and partially to thumb their noses at the boss, but it doesn't look like he's suffering any. And my stomach is happy to rumble out an offer to help with clearing the plates. If I go any longer without eating I'm afraid it's going to take up semaphore instead, using my other organs as flags.

"Sit," he instructs, and we do, both because he's got that kind of deep gravely voice you tend to obey and because his goons are lurking nearby and look fully prepared to shove us into chairs if we can't manage on our own. "Espresso? Zeppoli?" He gestures, and a waiter hurries over with plates and cups for us. Ned shakes his head, and Tall hesitates, but I'm starving and I was just kidnapped so I figure I can get away with a little breach of etiquette here. Besides, he offered!

"That'd be great, thanks," I tell him, and help myself to a zeppoli off the plate while a waiter pours a thick black liquid into my cup. "Cheers." I take a big bite of sugar-sprinkled fried dough and chew happily. Ah! That's the stuff!

Our host watches me closely, wearing that bemused smile I see a lot, the one that says "I can't decide if I should be amused by you or pissed off, and I may have to table it and decide later." He's a big guy, not as tall as his doorman but just as broad, with pale skin so light it's almost blue and a wispy little beard and mustache but a thick head of hair that's noticeably green and leafy. His eyes are freaky, red and white in a radial pattern, like a starburst dipped in pink, and his teeth when he shows them are clean and white and smooth. It takes me a second or two to figure out his lineage—I'm not really up on my veggies as much as I should be—but the hints of red and the beard finally tip me off.

The Big Cheese is far less of a cheese and far more of a . . . radish.

Well, I guess that answers my earlier musings about whether there's bigotry by color here.

"So," he says after I've had a chance to swallow my first few bites and take a sip of my piping-hot espresso, which is so thick it's practically sludge. "I hear there's been a problem?"

"Yes, sir," Ned replies. He's got his baseball cap in his hands, and is clutching the brim nervously. Tall took his off as well but has it tucked into his back pocket. I'm not wearing one—one good thing about being covered in feathers is that I really don't have to worry about sunburn anymore, and with the nictitating membranes it's not like the sun can blind me, either. "My friend here"—he gestures toward me, and I wave and take the opportunity to snag a second pastry—"was just abducted. He got taken to a warehouse down by the docks, and they were threatening to torture him when we rescued him."

"Hm." The Radish frowns at me, but it's not really directed at me, exactly. Trust me, I can tell. "You're not from around here, are you?"

What was your first clue, I think, the fact that I look like poultry and not roughage? I don't say it, though. Hey, maybe they're sensitive about that sort of thing, main dish versus side salad. Maybe there's a rival planet that's all meatheads and fishheads and lords it over them at the annual summer games. I don't know. Besides, my mouth's full of zeppoli goodness, so I just shake my head.

"And you say someone abducted you? Where?" Ned supplies the address, and El Radisho nods to one of his men, who turns and hurries away. No doubt placing a call to whomever's in charge of that district to ask if they've got anything on the slate today for kidnapping random strangers. Who knows, maybe it was a free period.

"And they took you to the docks?" the boss continues. I've finished and swallowed by now, so I can answer for myself again.

"Yeah," I tell him. "There were two of them, a cucumber and a cauliflower, same sort of suits as your guys"—his own is much higher quality, as befits a bigwig—"they stuffed me in a sack, tied me to a chair, and told me they were gonna ask me some questions and that things could go badly for me if they didn't like my answers." I'm eyeing the rest of the food laid out in front of me, wondering if I dare take some pasta and maybe some shrimp or whatever they are, but I figure I'd better not press my luck. At least my stomach's stopped complaining for the moment while it deals with those zeppoli. I know it's just biding its time, though.

"And what was it they wanted to ask you about so desperately, hm?" The way he says it, with his hands steepled in front of him, the tips of his index fingers resting against his chin, makes me wonder if he actually sent those guys after me and if this isn't just the carrot half of the "carrot and the stick" routine. You know, brute force and intimidation didn't work, let's try acting friendly and offering snacks. Which is certainly a better way to get me to talk—hell, give me food and you have a hard time shutting me up again!—except that he did look genuinely annoyed when he heard I was grabbed in the first place. Maybe he'd wanted me questioned but not quite so forcefully? Maybe it was some of his guys but acting on their own initiative, which every boss loves when it works out and hates when it blows up in their faces?

Regardless, I can honestly say, "I have no idea. Tall and Ned showed up before they could actually ask." I shrug. "But I can't imagine what they'd want from me. I'd only just gotten here, and we were only here for lunch. I don't know anything else."

"Lunch, hey? And where had you planned on dining?" The way he asks, it's almost like he's a food critic, waiting to either poo-poo or applaud my choice. But I know plenty of people who use the same "oh, that's not really important, is it?" technique, and I see right through it. He's really interested in our intended choice of restaurant. Maybe he owns a share in some local chain?

Anyway, I don't see any reason not to be honest about it, especially since anybody walking by could call me on a lie, so I tell him. "Gus's All-You-Can-Eat Melva Buffet."

Radish King's brow furrows for a second, and I think I see something in his beady little red eyes, but then he shakes his head. "Never heard of it."

Damn.

His gaze shifts now to Ned, who gulps and looks all washed-out again. "It's a real place, I swear it," he offers weakly. "I don't know why nobody but me seems to remember it now."

The Boss Radish nods noncommittally, and his eyes move to Tall. "You are not from here either, I think," he murmurs, "but your type I know well enough. You are a tough guy, yes?" All around him, his goons stiffen like they're about to be called on to test that claim. If that happens, I'm totally grabbing the plate of mozzarella sticks and diving under the table, because things are about to get really messy and I hate to see good food go to waste.

Tall just shrugs and offers up his "yeah, you think you can take me? Guess again, unless you're hiding the entire Macedonian army, complete with elephants, in that shoulder holster" grin. "I can hold my own," is all he says. "But no, I'm not from around here. Ned called me when DuckBob disappeared. I got him back." Tall's a master of subtext, so there's an entire "yes, I beat up two goons just like yours, and they were armed and I wasn't, and I also may have laid waste to an entire warehouse in the process" hidden within that brief recounting, and I can see Radish's eyes narrow and then widen as he parses the message and realizes that maybe this table and those goons won't be enough to protect him if he pisses Tall off. But then he smiles and gives Tall a nod, man to man or at least veggie to man, and the goons relax a little.

"Yes, you are a good friend to have, I think," he tells Tall, and smiles broadly. "I, too, am a good friend to have." The goons all laugh at this little joke, while Tall, Ned, and I make like Bobbleheads and nod our agreement to this incredibly obvious statement. Why yes, we'd like to stay on the good side of the local crime boss, thank you very much. Guess I won't be swiping his food after all. Shame, that.

The goon who got sent away returns now and leans in to whisper in the Radish's ear. It's totally unfair, by the way, that these veggies get external ears and I don't! I'm gonna tell the Grays that the next time I see them. Though then I picture myself just the way I am now only with my old human ears stuck on the side like broken windflaps and I reconsider. Maybe I'm fine just the way I am. I do still miss 'em, though.

"Those men who grabbed you," Señor Radish tells after he's waved his man away, "they were not working for me or mine. They used to, but recently they have strayed. We are bringing them in to find out why. I will learn who they are working for, and what they wanted from you." He leans forward, and I have to resist the urge to pull back in response. "I apologize for what you went through. Such a thing should never have happened. You have my word that you are welcome here in our city, and I hope you enjoy your visit with us. If anyone else should trouble you, you have only to say that you have my blessing to be here, and you will find that they leave you alone."

I feel like he's about to add something, but he doesn't, he just studies us a second with his hands clasped together like he's trying to shake with himself. Finally he nods and shifts back to recliner mode again. It's clear the audience is over.

Ned's the first one out of his chair. "Thank you," he says. "And I'm sorry to have troubled you. I didn't want to bother you with this, but it seemed best . . ." He trails off as the Radish gestures, waving away Ned's concerns with one hand to make it clear both that he wasn't offended by the intrusion but also that, yes, it's dealt with, bye-bye now, you're interrupting my afternoon snack. Ned gulps back whatever else he was going to say and quickly heads for the door.

Tall doesn't say a word, which is pretty much the norm for him anyway. He just nods at the boss, rises from his chair like a jungle cat rearing up into attack position, smiles, and turns away. I don't miss the glare he gives the biggest of the nearby goons, though, the one that clearly says "I could take you apart with one hand while spooning up ice cream with the other, and don't you forget it."

Me, I gulp down the last of my espresso, snag one more zeppoli for the road, and then say, "Thanks, it's been swell!" before turning to follow my friends toward the door. I can feel the Radish's eyes on me the whole way. Maybe he's still trying to figure out what those two ex-goons wanted from me. Or maybe he's worrying about why Gus's sounds familiar—or why it doesn't.

Or maybe he's just annoyed because someone actually took him up on his offer of food, for a change. I get the impression he's not really big on sharing.

But hey, like Ma always says, "don't put it out there if you're not willing to let it get bitten off."

Which applies to a whole lot of life situations, really. And explains why one of her cousins only has three fingers on his left hand. Pre-abduction, I definitely got my jaw strength from her side of the family.

Chapter Eleven
Is everyone doing the Jitterbug, or just me?

"So, that went well, right?" I ask once we're outside—no sign of the wacky hovercar sedan that brought us here so I guess we're on our own as far as making our way back wherever. At least Tall and Ned both got their stuff back, and I had time to finish off that zeppoli and snag a napkin, a toothpick, and an after-dinner mint. "I mean, he didn't order us killed or have a horseradish's head delivered to our beds or anything like that, and he said he was sorry and that we've got free run of the city, so I'm taking all that as a good sign. Too bad about the guys at the docks, but it's their own lookout if they've decided to walk out on a union gig, am I right?" I take a breath. "Whoa, I think that espresso is starting to kick in!"

"Clearly," Tall says, deliberately letting his drawl come to the front. I've never actually asked where he's from but I know darn well that, even if the drawl is real, he exaggerates it for sarcastic purposes from time to time. Like now, when he drags the one word out as long as any three normal words—or as long as it took me to say all that a few seconds ago. That's Tall for you, though—why use a second word when you can just milk a bit more out of the first one?

"It did go well," Ned agrees, wiping his brow with a bright red hanky that's seen better days and probably better years. "It still doesn't explain what those two guys wanted from you, of course, but at least now we know they were acting on their own." He breathes in a bit. "If the bosses had actually had it in for you, well, that would've been bad." The way he says "bad" is like when you've just been caught in an exploding building and have managed to crawl your way out of the rubble and the wreckage, getting dirt and ash and soot and who knows what else smeared all in your hair and on your clothes and skin and then afterward, as you're sitting there in the ambulance so covered in grime and filth they can't tell if they should try cutting things off or just subject you to an industrial-strength car wash and see what peels away, someone says to you, "you've got a little something on you." Which makes sense, I guess, seeing as how this is apparently MafiaWorld and so, no, you really don't want to piss off one of the dons.

"Maybe they were entrepreneurs," I offer, going back to the question of Cucumberhead and Cauliflowerface, "and they decided to start their own protection racket, shaking down hapless tourists and claiming it's some kind of entrance visa fee. Or maybe they spotted me and they're part of an amateur birdwatching group and thought my plumage might attract big bucks from crazy collectors. Or maybe they know about the Matrix and figured they'd ransom me back to the Grays, not realizing that my job could be done by a trained monkey as long as he'd been altered or, for that matter, that I was still doing my job even while I sat, bound and gagged, in a cheap motel room's bathtub somewhere. Or maybe—"

"Enough!" Tall reaches out like he's gonna clamp one of those dinnerplate-sized hands of his over my mouth, which would be a bad idea both because I might bite and because even his hands aren't big enough to cover my entire bill. We're talking acres of real estate, here! So instead he clenches his hand into a fist, then jerks it open again. "We won't know until the locals question them, unless we want to track them down ourselves." He shrugs. "I don't think that'd be a good idea, interfering with their operations, so I suggest we just leave it alone for now and wait to hear what the locals turned up." He eyeballs me for a second. "And you need to work all that caffeine and sugar out of your system."

Ned nods. "There really isn't anything more we can do." He glances around—other than the restaurant behind us there isn't a whole lot about, just what look like factories or warehouses or marshaling yards, none of them apparently active at the moment. "We should head back toward Gus's, whether it's there or not—I know that neighborhood, not this one. I can call us a cab—"

"We'll walk for a bit," Tall puts in, eyes still on me. "DuckBob needs to burn off some of this new energy of his."

Ned shrugs and I'm buzzing too much to argue so we set out, the three of us, just like old times. Back before everything went wonky. –er.

Both of them seem content to stay quiet while we walk, but that's never been me. "So," I say after we've been walking a few minutes. "What was with that guy, anyway?"

Tall just clenches his jaw a bit more—if most people just have the two settings for that, clenched or unclenched, Tall has like ten of them. He's the performance bike of chin movement, or something. Ned looks puzzled, and not by Tall. That we're used to.

"Whaddyamean?" Ned asks, peering at me instead of sweeping his gaze back and forth from side to side the way he's done since we headed out.

"Well, look, I like Godfather movies as much as the next guy," I explain, "and who hasn't done the whole 'you're wondering why I called you all here' bit at some Italian restaurant, waving a breadstick in your friends' faces and pretending it was a Tommy gun, but this guy took it about as far as anybody and he clearly isn't the only one. Those goons from the warehouse, they'd bought into the scenario, too, and if this is just one big live-action roleplay I wish somebody'd told me beforehand so I could've changed clothes."

Ned shakes his head, making the broccoli on either side dance like little green hula girls. "I've got no idea what you mean," he says. "What scenario? He's the local boss, that's all. He's just doing his job."

"That's a job?" I rub at my lower bill. "Huh. What'd he do, fill out the aptitude test in school and it came back 'Marlon Brando wannabe?' I wonder who I would've gotten on mine if that'd been an option? James Cagney, maybe—'you dirty rat!' Or James Earl Jones: 'Luke, I am your father.' Or maybe John Cusack: 'I'm really sorry your mom blew up, Ricky.' I've always felt I was more a Jimmy or a John, actually, but Ma insisted on Robert. She said it'd build character."

"You're a character, all right," Tall comments, drawl still in full effect, but there's that hint of humor to his words and I know he's just giving me grief. He's like that. He's doing the eye-darting thing too, though, and I'm starting to wonder if this neighborhood is a whole lot more dangerous than I realized or if both of them are just being a little bit paranoid thanks to what happened before.

Right up until Tall shouts "Get down!" and proceeds to grab me by the shoulder and forcibly hurl me at the ground—

—right before a shot rings out exactly where I was standing a second ago.

Okay, maybe not so paranoid after all.

"What the hell?" I shout, pushing myself back up to my knees and rubbing the front of my bill where it hit the pavement. I think I may've chipped it. The pavement, that is—my bill can stand up to just about anything, including one of those iron girder support beams in the subway. Don't ask. "Come on, you guys wanted to ask me stupid questions before! What happened to that? I can't say anything if you shoot me!" Which, actually, I probably shouldn't tell people, like, ever. There're way too many I can picture lining up for a gun once they know that's an option.

Ned is on the ground beside me, and he gestures frantically at me to shut up. Which, y'know, is about as useful as waving a hand at a runaway train to make it suddenly slow down. "Shhh," he cautions in a loud whisper. "They'll hear you!"

"So what?" I snap back. "I'm pretty sure they already know we're here, thanks to that bullet a second ago that had my name on it. We're in the middle of the sidewalk, it's not like they're suddenly gonna wonder where we went." Having said that, I suddenly realize it's just the two of us talking. "Hey, wait, where's Tall?"

I glance around and see the massive statue of an enraged Greek god striding toward the corner of a nearby building, practically radiating electricity from its ferocious glare. Only this god has cowboy boots and a trucker hat on. And instead of relying upon hurling thunderbolts, it has a large gun in its hand and is shooting toward the shadows there at that corner and beyond. Go get 'em, Tall!

Of course, with Tall taking the fight to that corner it occurs to me that Ned and I are left here all on our lonesome. What if there's more of them hiding on the other side, just waiting for our heroic protector to wander off? I search my pockets, but the closest I can find to a weapon is that toothpick. I pull it out and pinch it tight between my thumb and forefinger. First person to come after me gets jabbed in the eye, I swear it! Unless they're wearing sunglasses like the last two, in which case I'll settle for poking 'em in the nose. Then I spot something nearby, and stretch out my free hand to grab it. My fingers just brush against something long and stringy, and I manage to latch onto that and tug. I really hope this isn't a giant spider, because if it is I might just save those guys the trouble by up and dying from a heart attack. But no, as it hurtles toward me I realize the lumpy brown thing isn't a spider, or any kind of critter at all.

It's a shoe.

Yes, I'm familiar with the visual of having a shoe hurtling toward my face. Several people over the years have evidently mistaken me for an alarm clock, with the Snooze/Off button located smack dab in the middle of my forehead. And, admittedly, hitting me with a shoe there does shut me up for a few minutes, so I can't entirely fault their logic. I am still pissed at the one ex-girlfriend who decided this bit of news needed its own PSA, however. Complete with full-color video ad on the college website.

On the plus side, I made a pretty penny ransoming all those shoes back to their owners.

This particular one, though, I don't think I could sell for even a single penny, pretty or otherwise. It's an old work shoe, the heavy brown leather kind with the big rounded front and the thick, clunky sole—not quite a boot but every bit as sturdy.

Hey, at least it's a better weapon than the toothpick, which I switch to my off hand in case I need a backup.

Now that I'm armed, however badly, I stand up. No way I can throw this thing while lying prone! I spin around, but there's nobody coming at us from behind. And Tall's still keeping the shooters occupied, it seems. He's focusing in on an old Dumpster squatting against the alley between that building and the next, and judging by the answering fire coming from behind the big lump of rusted metal I'd say he's correctly identified the shooters' location. Unfortunately, it doesn't look like he can get any closer to them without getting shot himself, and, angry or not, Tall's not that dumb. Which means we're at a standoff.

I hate standoffs.

"Knock it off, you creeps!" I shout, brandishing my shoe at them. The new one, not my regular ones, though those'd be a lot more fearsome, probably, on account of their being large enough to double as a viola case. "Get the hell out of here and leave us alone!"

And then, because you should never wave a weapon and not use it or something like that, I throw the shoe at them.

I've got pretty decent aim—I used to kill 'em at Beer Pong—and it hits the Dumpster solidly in the side.

That isn't a surprise. Like I said, I've got pretty decent aim.

What is a surprise is what happens next.

Ever take a leafblower to a stack of papers, like, say, a teacher's carefully graded reports that she foolishly left on her desk with the window open while she went to investigate why her car alarm had suddenly gone off? You hit the switch and bam! What was an orderly little stack suddenly goes everywhere?

Or have you ever used one of those potato guns on a loaf of bread, shooting it out of your brother or sister's hand just as they were reaching to cut off a slice? Pow! The potato hits it full-force and the loaf goes shooting off across the kitchen—if you're really lucky, it pelts another sibling in the back of the head. Two for one!

That's about what happens here, which only goes to show that messing with my teachers and tormenting my siblings was in fact good training for surviving the real world. Take that, Ma!

Anyway, this shoe hits the Dumpster—and it goes flying! The Dumpster, not the shoe. It's like the Dumpster was made of cardboard instead of steel, and the shoe was brick instead of leather, and maybe got shot out of a small cannon to boot. Seriously, the whole Dumpster just leaps off the ground and goes slamming down the alley, caroming off the walls and leaving sparks every time it hits, before it impacts the back wall with a thunderous clang and a big cloud of dust and dirt and rust and, probably, shattered brick.

Did I mention that there'd been some guys hiding behind that Dumpster a few seconds ago? I don't think they're there anymore. Or, rather, they're still there, but probably in a thin layer across twenty feet or so. Talk about a veggie spread!

Yeah, they're not likely to bother anyone anymore. Unless someone tries walking through there and gets those guys all over their shoes. Ick.

I'm just standing there, staring. First at where the shoe still sits innocently on the ground by the corner, then down the alley where the Dumpster went, then down at my hand. Then all over again. Shoe, alley, hand. Repeat.

"What the hell was that?" Tall demands as he crosses back over toward me, making the gun disappear somewhere beneath the leather jacket he's wearing instead of his old black suit jacket. A definite step up fashion wise, if you ask me, which nobody ever does except for that one crazy guy on the subway and those people who were starting up that company called Loudshirts. Whatever, I like clothes that are as outspoken as I am. Especially the ones that require batteries.

"Uh, a shoe." I point over at it. "I threw it at them."

"Yes, I saw that." He's eyeing me like I'm hiding something, and I show him the toothpick just in case that's what he wanted. "What I meant is, how did it do that?"

"I have no idea." I scratch at my bill—not with the toothpick, though. "Is it because I've been working out?"

Ned laughs—he's gotten to his feet again and we're all back together on the sidewalk, right where this whole thing started. "Not unless your definition of working out is injecting yourself with nanites that rebuilt your arms into portable proton cannons."

"Ooh, you can do that?" I ask him. "Would it hurt? Would it look funny? Would I still be able to wear the same shirts? Would I be able to pick up an egg without it exploding?" I catch the warning in Tall's glare. "Yeah, no, I haven't done that—as far as I know."

Tall glances back where the Dumpster was, then down the alley, than at my hand. See, it's spreading! "Maybe there was something odd about the shoe?" he offers.

"What, like it was made from a dwarf star?" Ned counters. "He'd never have been able to lift it, then, much less throw it!" Hey, I've been working out, I said! He goes over to study the shoe, prods it with a gizmo, then returns, shaking his head. "Nah, it's normal. Just an old shoe."

Both of them look at me again, and I shake my head and throw up my hands in surrender. Oops, I'm still wielding the toothpick! "Look, I have no idea," I promise. "Really." I glance back at the alley. "But it was a good thing, right?"

Tall sighs. "Yes, it was," he admits. "I couldn't get to them where they were, not without taking at least a few hits myself." He nods. "Thanks."

"My pleasure. Was it the same two guys?" I ask him, pocketing my toothpick but making sure I can get at it in a moment's notice. I'm half considering grabbing that shoe again, too. Just in case.

"No idea," he admits, scanning the area again. "And it's not like there's enough of them left to identify." He frowns at Ned, or at least in his general direction. "I thought your friend back there said we'd be safe now."

Ned nods. "He did. And you'd have to be stupid or completely new around here to disobey him. Whoever this is, they've no idea the kind of trouble they're in if his guys catch them."

"Should we go back and tell him what happened?" I ask. I admit, I'm thinking about those zeppoli, and seriously considering making a play for the mozzarella sticks this time. "He's gonna want to know, especially seeing as how it's basically right outside his front door." We're actually about ten blocks away now, but close enough on the grand scale.

"No point," Tall says firmly. "Whoever this is, they're clearly not going to stop just because he tells them to."

"You don't understand!" Ned protests. "I know it's different on Earth, but here these guys are the law! Nobody messes with them!"

"They're not messing with them," Tall points out. "They're messing with us." He zeroes in on me. "Or, more precisely, with you. It's you they were shooting at."

"So I noticed." I shiver a little—I get like that when in close proximity to high-velocity lead. "If it was the same guys from before, maybe they just figured there was no way they were getting anything out of me so they'd better cut their losses and bump me off before I could finger them in a lineup? Or maybe it's a different group and there's some sort of warning out about me, but the first guys wanted to ask me questions and these new guys just want to rub me out? Or am I just the figurehead, like the masthead on a ship, and they're gunning for me because I'm the biggest, easiest target?" Yeah, I really am talking even more and even faster than normal, so much so that all my words are sort of running together. That espresso was seriously high-octane!

"No idea," Tall replies, grabbing my arm and starting us walking again, his eyes still searching every nook and cranny up ahead like he's got lasers installed in 'em. "And while I'd love to find out, we'd have to grab some of them in order to ask. Right now, let's just concentrate on getting out of here in one piece."

Ned scurries to join us, and the three of us set a brisk pace out of this area, which is fine by me—I'm still starving, the zeppoli notwithstanding, there's only the one restaurant around as far as I can tell, and it's all full up with gangsters. The sooner we get to a more populous area, preferably one with a good diner or deli, the happier I'll be.

"We have to do something, though," Tall continues after we've covered another block or two. "Because I'm guessing whoever's after you isn't going to stop just because the local boss warned them off or I returned fire or you did whatever it is you did back there with that shoe." He glances over at Ned, who sighs.

"There's not much else we can do here," he answers, not meeting Tall's glare but finding the sidewalk extremely fascinating instead. "We can go up the food chain, though," he adds a minute later, sounding about as happy about it as if somebody had just told him to go feed the sharks in the tank by strapping steaks to his chest and diving in.

But all I hear is "food chain." "Yes, please," I tell him. "Let's go up the food chain. I got zeppoli from the last guy. Maybe we can find someone who'll offer us sandwiches instead? Or a nice antipasto?" Tall hits me with one of his patented stares, the one that says "remind me why I don't just shoot you and incinerate the body?" "What?" I ask him. "I get hungry when someone's out to get me."

"You must be even more paranoid than I am, then," he mutters back, eyeing my admittedly robust figure. I think I liked it better when he didn't have a sense of humor.

Chapter Twelve
Don't make me cross!

"**Okay, explain this** to me again," I ask as we cross the street. Which, from what I've seen, is every bit as much taking your own life in your hands as dyeing your whole body red and leaping blindfolded into a bullfighting ring while wearing shackles about your ankles. Or, y'know, while trying to cross Queens Boulevard pretty much any time of the day or night. "We already saw the local boss," I point out, dodging a car that seems determined to plant its hood ornament in my sternum like an oversized metal bee stinger. "But now we're going to go see another boss, a different one, who's also here in the city. But who's not the local boss. But his boss. The boss's boss." Another car comes at me like a hungry dog and I twist to one side, letting it zoom past so close I'm pretty sure its hubcaps just creased my shins. Still, one more pirouette and I've made it safely to the opposite curb, where I collapse against a mailbox, panting. Who knew those ballroom dance lessons back in grade school would pay off so handsomely some day?

"That's about the size of it," Ned agrees. He didn't spin and twist and bob and weave the way I did, but just walked straight across without slowing or stopping. Hell, he barely even glanced around! But then, he'd shown me the little device he'd attached to his belt beforehand. "It's kind of like the monotony overlay," he'd explained, "except that in this case it's set to broadcast a concrete barrier, traffic cones, a gaping manhole, etc. Anything that'd make the driver swerve rather than pass through my space." He'd grinned. "It's the perfect pedestrian accessory." And it looks like he was right, too—cars had swerved around him instead of the other way around, and he'd made it across the street with a lot less effort than I had, and a lot less worry. The only reason he didn't beat me to the other side is that his legs are so short.

Tall, of course, treated crossing the street like going into battle, which it pretty much was. When we'd approached the curb on the far side he'd squared his jaw, lowered his brow, tugged down his trucker cap, and then nodded. "Okay, let's do this." Then he'd walked straight ahead—marched, really—as if daring cars to hit him. It was like there was a giant neon sign over his head saying "yeah, you can hit me, and yeah, you might win that match, but you'd better be sure I can't move after because otherwise I'm gonna come after you and wrap that car around your neck like it's a necktie and I'm your great-uncle trying to remember how to tie it right."

It's amazing what they can fit on neon signs these days.

It worked, though. Nobody hit him. Actually, I saw at least one driver zero in on Tall, tightening his chubby little hands on the wheel, his face lit with sadistic glee at the thought of committing another vehicular homicide—and then gasp, eyes going wide, face pale, mouth falling open, sweat popping out across the brow, as his brain took in that subliminal sign and started sending Abort signals through the body at breakneck speed. There was a loud screech as he slammed on the brakes, the smell of burning rubber as the tires melted from the attempt to stop, then the squeal as the car fishtailed, its back end twisting sideways and shimmying forward to catch up to and even pass the front. The driver was now desperately trying to regain control, yanking the wheel this way and that as he clipped cars to either side, sending them spiraling away as well, before finally coming to a screaming halt mere feet from Tall's side—right before getting flattened by another car it had bumped earlier, in a moment of poetic automotive justice.

So, final tally: Ned made it across the most serenely, I managed the most artistically, and Tall did it with the most incidental damage.

That's what I call teamwork!

"So why is the boss's boss here if there's already a boss here?" I ask, listening to the sirens and watching the flashing lights of the rescue vehicles approach through the smoke, flames, and gas fumes now ringing the street. "We should probably get moving."

"It's like D.C.," Tall's the one to answer, leading the way as we quick-step from the recent accident site. "You've got the mayor, but you've also got the president. The president's in charge of the whole country, he just happens to live in D.C., which the mayor's in charge of. And most of the time the president tries not to step on the mayor's toes."

"Oh." That actually makes sense, but then Tall's always

been good at cutting through the bullshit. That's part of why we make such a good team—I can spout my usual nonsense, then he'll summarize it into something everybody else can understand. He's like a Reader's Digest version of me, only not as snazzy a dresser. "So where is this Big Kahuna, then? Another restaurant?"

"Exactly!" Ned looks thrilled that I'm finally starting to get the way his world works. Sure, dude—you've got Mafia bosses in restaurants, killer cars on a rampage, kids hawking newspapers on the corners, and men selling pickles from barrels on a cart. I understand perfectly. It's like all my grandpappy's stories come to life. I'm just surprised there's no Prohibition around here.

"So we can just walk in to see this guy, though?" I try not to look back at the carnage behind us. "You don't have to make a reservation or anything?"

"Normally you do," Ned admits, "but if it's really urgent he'll squeeze you in. And since we already saw the local boss, if we tell him that I think he'll see us." He still doesn't look thrilled about the idea, but now he seems a lot less scared than before, anyway. I think part of it's that he's gotten angrier the more we've walked. He kept muttering about how nobody should treat a visitor this way, and how it was giving the whole planet a bad name.

It's nice to know that, wherever I go, I'm a major part of the tourism trade.

My stomach rumbles again, reminding me that it still hasn't been fed properly. "So where is this White House of Italian restaurants?" I'm actually picturing a restaurant the size of the

White House, which would be awesome. Especially if the food was all equally super-sized. Just imagine ordering ravioli and having them show up as big as your head! Garlic bread the size of a VW Bus! And the cannoli! I could curl up and die happy in a cannoli like that!

"It's just around this corner and across the street," Ned assures me, gesturing at the corner we're approaching. "Right—there!"

I swear, somebody is hiding in the bushes nearby and playing that choir music you always hear in films when they show Heaven. Because the minute we round the corner and it comes into sight, I hear an angelic chorus spring into song.

It's beautiful.

Now, I'm an unabashed foodie. I love food of all types, as long as it's good. And preferably plentiful. I don't care if the place you get that food is a palace or a dive, a handsome old home or a crappy hole in the wall, as long as the grub is up to snuff.

Having said that, though, this place is gorgeous.

It is huge, just like I thought—only two stories tall, but easily a New York city block in area. Most of that is the courtyard surrounding the actual building, though. It's old, rough paving stones, the kind you saw a hundred years ago or more, well worn from the passage of feet over the years. The building itself is stone for the first floor and old brick for the second, with wrought iron balconies above and green striped awnings below. Small tables dot the courtyard, white tablecloths upon them, and unlike the last place, most of the tables are full. Plants in large pots ring the space, and waiters glide between them and the tables carrying trays of food, pitchers of water and wine and coffee, napkins and silverware, and of course, the ubiquitous little leather wallets that hold the checks. I guess the local government dines while it works, a job plan I can wholeheartedly endorse. I wonder if they have open elections, say, in time for supper?

"Nice," I whisper, out of respect, awe, and ravening hunger. "So where's the big guy? Inside?"

Ned shakes his head. "Naw, he always eats outside as long as the weather's decent. He's right over there." He points toward a table smack dab in the center of the courtyard. It's a bit bigger than most of the others, which have only four seats around them. I count eight at this one, six of them filled, and five of the diners are clearly deferring to the big man in the sixth chair. He's not as broad across as the local boss but either he's got a stack of phonebooks under him or he makes up for width by being seriously damn tall. His face is long and thin, a definite Lincoln type right down to the green ruff that lines his chin and jaw, and he's got a strong brow and deep lines around his eyes and mouth. His suit's top-notch, I can tell that even from here, and it's a deep greenish gray that nicely sets off the orange of his weathered skin.

That's right. The Big Boss is a carrot.

I'm so glad it's a colorblind crime family here on Ned's world.

Anyway, there's something about this guy; we're still half a block away but I can already see that aura about him, the kind you get from true leaders. This guy's the Big Boss for a reason.

He's clearly listening intently to his subordinates, and it doesn't even look condescending. He's actually interested in their opinion the way a proper boss should be, not just "sure, yeah, blather on all you like, my mind's already made up and I'm just thinking about my vacation on my new yacht that I got with my company bonus last month while you slaved away pulling overtime for nothing but a nod and a 'guess you can stay another month.'" This is the kind of boss who cares.

"Okay, then," Tall says, and I can tell by his tone that even he's impressed. And that ain't easy to do. "Let's go meet the man, then."

"Heck, yeah!" I agree. "And order some real dinner while we're at it!"

Ned can't argue with that, so the three of us check carefully, start across the street—

—and get tossed back onto the curb like leaves on a stiff breeze as the very air ripples toward us and over us.

"What the—?" I start, clambering back to my feet. I stare out across the street the way the wind came. "Awww, come on!" I can't help but cry out.

Because that awesome, awesome restaurant? With the awesome, awesome Boss?

It's not there anymore.

In its place there's now—an arcade.

Yeah, that kind. The cheesy 80s type, the blocky building with the ugly stucco siding, the tinted windows covering the entire front, the word "Arcade" in big flashy letters over the door, the parking lot stretching out before it like the beach before the ocean, and inside the building, the glare and blink and flash of a hundred video screens, all showing their garish little images and enticing you to spend your hard-earned quarters on a chance to shoot down the bad guy, stop the invasion, save the princess, etc.

Don't get me wrong, I love places like that. I spent a lot of my childhood—and a decent part of my high school and even college years—in places just like that.

But right now? Right now that is really not what I wanted to see.

"What the hell just happened?" Ned demands. He's on his feet again too, and staring at the same thing I am. "An arcade? What's that doing there? Where's the trattoria? Where's the boss?"

"Somebody is messing with us," Tall growls. Leave it to him to take this personally.

Me, I just have one question, and I wail it at the top of my lungs:

"Why is it the universe wants me to starve to death?"

Chapter Thirteen
Sometimes it really *is* all about me

"**What do we** do now?" I grouse after I'm done crying about how all the good food keeps disappearing right before I can get any of it. Tall hands me a PowerBar to shut me up, which only works for a few minutes and then only because it basically glues my bill shut. Stupid peanut butter flavor. And yes, it quiets my stomach's protests down from full-on mob riot to angry town hall meeting, but it's still not happy. And neither am I.

"I don't know," Ned admits tugging at the broccoli on either side of his head. Maybe it's harvest season? "That trattoria was the seat of the entire planet's government! And now it's gone!"

A few people walking past eye us strangely—what, you never saw an angry country-western trucker, a despondent duck-headed man, and a panicking veggieheaded plumber before? But on a hunch I call out to them, "Hey, what happened to the state capital restaurant thingy that was just here, any ideas?"

"Restaurant?" One of them, a stringbean of a fella—literally!—scoffs. "The nearest decent restaurant is Sal's, over on Eastern. I wish there was one closer!"

"Sal's again," I mutter, ignoring Ned's conniption fit about the guy's answer. "What is it about that place? Hey, maybe this is all just a marketing takeover on Sal's part! You know, kill off the competition, corner the market, all that."

"What is this Sal's?" Tall asks. That's right, he wasn't with us for the start of all this.

"Sal's Green Tea Saloon," Ned answers, practically spitting the name. Funny, he did the same thing last time. Maybe it's like that "bums" thing with him? "It's a decent place," he admits after a second of obviously getting himself back under control, "but that's about it. No way I'd choose it over Gus's, or here, or a half-dozen other places I can think of."

Aha! "We should check on each of those other ones," I point out. "And fast, just in case they disappear, too. You know, go in, ask around, order a sampler platter, that sort of thing. All in the name of science, of course." My stomach loudly seconds this motion and offers to be the official tester, which is very considerate of it, really. But that's my internal organs for you, always putting other people first.

Tall is rubbing his jaw. I've often wondered if that's because it hurts from being squared so often, not to mention all the tooth-grinding he does. It's gotta be sore after that! "Is Sal's involved in the local government at all?" he asks Ned. Ned shakes his head. "What about Gus's?"

"Naw, Gus's was strictly apolitical," Ned insists. "They had the best warab in town and everybody knew it, and all their food was top-notch, but that was all they did. They didn't care who you were as long as you didn't cut in line, didn't destroy the table, and paid your bill."

"So why target Gus's and then this place?" Tall asked,

glancing back at the video game parlor across from us. "What do they have in common?" His gaze switches to me like a searchlight swiveling around and then latching onto that one little rowboat bobbing along in the middle of the choppy ocean. "Except that you were heading toward both of them."

"Sure, but I went to that other Italian place too, remember?" I point out. "And we got in and out of there just fine—I still have the powdered sugar on my shirt to prove it!" I brush at the telltale white splotches, but of course they don't go anywhere. I've often thought that powdered sugar was secretly some sort of universal binding agent—the second it gets even a little damp it's impossible to get off anything. It's a good thing today's shirt includes a cloud pattern. You can barely tell the sugar wasn't there the whole time.

I'm getting that one look from Tall again now, the one that says "So your brain does sometimes work after all!" "You're right," he admits, grinding out each word. See? This is why his jaw hurts! "If somebody is just eliminating each food place before you get there, why didn't they take that one out, too?" He shakes his head. "Maybe because they knew you wouldn't actually get any real food there, whereas you and Ned were going to Gus's for lunch and you wanted to order a full meal here as well?"

"So this is just the universe's way of putting me on a diet?" I glare up at the sky. "Thanks a lot, universe! Couldn't you start off small, like making pink Sno-balls disappear at lunch one day or getting rid of all the broken pretzels in a bag or something?"

"Hold on," Ned insists. "This is crazy. Even if somebody did decide to keep DuckBob here from eating—sorry, man—how are they doing this?" He points to the video game parlor. "They didn't just blow the trattoria up, you know! It's gone! Like it was never here! Nobody else remembers it! And the same thing happened to Gus's! Who can do that?"

That's a darn good question, actually, and I scratch my bill, thinking about it. Who could make someplace disappear like it was never here? I do come up with one answer immediately, but I *really* don't like it. And judging by the looks on my friends' faces, they had a similar thought and aren't any more fond of it than I am.

"No way," I whisper. "That's not possible, right? They're gone. I made them all go away. And the Matrix keeps them out."

"It should, yeah," Ned agrees. "And it's running perfect, no hiccups or nothing." I decide not to mention all the times I've snuck away for a smoke break and left a metal guitar string bridging the gap in my place.

"We'd know," Tall agrees, though he sounds less like he's sure of that and more like he just really wants to believe it. We all do.

We're talking about the invaders, of course. The ones from outside our reality who took out the Matrix so they could break through and start transforming our universe into someplace more compatible with them. The same guys the Grays sent me to the Matrix to stop, which is what got me out of my crappy old life and into this one in the first place. But we stopped them, reactivated the Matrix, repaired the wall between our realities, and that was that. Wasn't it?

"What if one of them was still here somewhere?" I say

slowly, thinking it through as I go. Which is a big step up from my usual "say it first and think about it later, if at all." "And he's cut off from his reality now, trapped here for good? And he's out for revenge? And he's decided to get that revenge by making me starve?" I shake my fist at the empty air all around. "Damn you, you sadistic bastard! How could you?"

"It's possible," Tall says slowly, tugging on the brim of his trucker cap. "It would explain why it's happened near you both times. And they were able to bend reality—they might be able to alter things so that everyone else assumed the universe had always been that way." He nods. "Your time in the Matrix might make you immune to that, and Ned and I have both been hooked up to it as well, which might be why we can remember the way things really were." Tall and Ned and Mary have all stood in for me in the past when I needed a quick break—the Matrix is willing to tolerate other, nonattuned people as its living component for half an hour or so at a time as long as you don't overdo it.

"Okay, I'm really not liking this explanation," I tell him, leaning against a nearby lamppost. The invaders are crafty little buggers, after all, and they'll do anything to achieve their objective. Plus they can take on any shape they want, or be completely invisible, so this guy could be anywhere or nowhere. I jerk clear of the lamppost, just in case. "It fits, though." I sigh.

"At least, if that's what's going on, it's a localized effect," Ned points out. "Not an attack on my whole planet." Okay, yeah, good job looking on the bright side of things there. And he's right—better there's some crazed alien invader out to get me than that somebody's going after Ned's whole world. I think.

It's just bad luck, then, that the second intended stop on our list happened to be the center of his world's government, and now instead of a world leader and a top-notch restaurant they've got their planet's equivalent to Pong and Donkey Kong and Spy Hunter. Sorry, man.

Still, there are probably worse ways to figure out planetary problems than to challenge your opponent to a game of Centipede or Zaxxon. Imagine all the zoning issues you could solve that way!

"What do we do about it, though?" I ask again. Isn't this where the whole conversation started? "We can't see the guy unless he wants us to—we don't even know for sure that's what's going on, exactly. So do we just wait for him to come for me directly and then jump him or something?"

"I can try something," Ned offers. A second later two of his little widgets are in his hands and he's rubbing them together like they're a cross between chopsticks, a knife and a whittling stick, and a cricket's forelegs. "If that is what's going on, there'll be some kind of disturbance in the fabric of our reality. It'll be faint, but I might be able to pick up traces of—aha!"

"What, you got something?" I demand, immediately moving over beside him. "Is it the invader? Or a leftover salad bar? I'll take either, though if it's a dessert station that'd be even better."

"There's something right nearby," Ned replies, fiddling his widgets again. I think I'm imagining the little humming and crackling noise emanating from them, but maybe not. It's hard to tell sometimes where my imagination leaves off and reality begins. Especially on Disco Night. He frowns. "It's actually bigger than I'd expect, given how these guys work—they're not usually this sloppy. But it's definitely a hitch in the fabric."

"Maybe because it's just one guy and he's gotten careless," I suggest. "Or tired. Or just too angry to care." I know how that is—that basically explains my approach to housekeeping, or the lack thereof. "Where is it, exactly?" Maybe we can nail this guy right now, and even get him to give us back Gus's and the trattoria. And they'll be so grateful they'll both let us eat for free! Ah, the benefits of saving people in the food industry!

"Over this way," Ned replies, not looking up from his tools. He starts walking, and I hop to it right beside him—unfortunately, our current heading takes us over the curb and out onto the street, and the cars whizzing past don't seem as keen on investigating this problem as we are. Good thing Tall is here— he immediately throws himself into the role of crossing guard, striding out in front of us and putting up a hand that dares cars to cross him. None of them do, and there's a loud squeal of brakes all around.

"Hurry up," Tall hollers over his shoulder. "I don't know how long I can hold them!"

"On it," I yell back, but of course there's no hurrying Ned when he's like this. I know—I still remember the time I asked him to sort out the wiring so I could hook a new game system up to my big-screen TV back at the Matrix. Four hours later he was still tracing conduits and muttering about better linkages. I'd already given up and patched the new system in two hours before. Admittedly, it later turned out I'd plugged it in through the audio ports, which resulted in some really weird game play, but hey, I just figured synesthesia was some kind of challenge mode! I got really good at the whole "hearing impending danger" thing, too. Turns out it involves a lot of deep bass.

Fortunately, our path does finally lead us across the street and to the side of where the trattoria's courtyard was and what is now the video game parlor's parking lot. Which is good because, judging by the way the honking and shouting was escalating behind us, the natives were starting to get restless and it was only a matter of time before somebody decided to ignore Tall's hand signals and try driving around him. Which would probably have resulted in his shooting out their tires, and then things would've gone all kinds of crazy.

I'm just about to shout at Tall to catch up to us when Ned lets out a sound that's somewhere between a laugh, a giggle, and a burp. Yeah, he's got mad skills. "There you are!" he adds, raising his crossed widgets like he's dowsing for water and just spotted one of those big cherub-headed fountains. "There's some kind of block on the frequency," he mutters, "but I think I can clear it. Hold on."

"Hold on? What do you mean, hold on?" I demand, grabbing his arm. "Do you mean 'wait a second while I check this out,' or 'grab hold of something because this might hurt'? Well?" Yeah, I'm not the only member of this crew who can sometimes act without thinking things through. Especially if Ned's caught up in a technical problem—he sometimes forgets there can be real-world consequences. This is why it was a bad idea that time I asked him if there was a way to reconfigure the traffic lights near the Matrix so the annual local parade could pass right by my front door. They did eventually get the street cleared again, and most of the vehicles were still usable, but the locals opted to detour around the Matrix anyway, just to be safe.

Ned opens his mouth to reply—which is right when the entire universe decides to tilt sideways, then start spiraling inward like it's caught up in a massive drain. And lucky us, we're the little bits of leftover food getting pulled down with it.

Oh, I manage to think as I'm squeezed and twisted and wrung about like a wet hand towel about to be used in locker room hijinks. He meant option two.

Chapter Fourteen
No wonder Alice was cranky!

"**Oh. Ow. Okay,** whoever's using my head as a foosball table, knock it off. I concede the match." I grab my head in both hands, trying to hold it still or at least stop it from ringing quite so loud, only to discover it's not shaking in the least. All the jittering must be on the inside instead, which is lovely because right now it feels like my innards are right in the middle of a big Limbo contest and fiesta, and I think my lungs are about to swing for the piñata while my kidneys have decided just to give up and crawl under the bar the easy way.

Yeah, there might be some pain and disorientation involved. Or it might just be another Monday morning.

No, wait, I don't do that anymore—both because I'm older and more mature now, with a cool job and an awesome girlfriend and the glimmerings of self-awareness and some inkling of responsibility, and because I've discovered all kinds of funky alien substances that can give me similar effects while partying, but with far less severe or at least more entertaining consequences. Like that one thing, I think it's actually meant for delinting insect wings or something, but it makes you feel all happy and floaty and everything around you looks iridescent like the whole world is made of soap bubbles. And the only downside is for a few hours afterward you still see shimmers and your tongue tastes a little like soap. Also, any insects in the area think you're the best thing since fresh flowers.

But if I'm not epically hungover, why do I feel like this?

When I hear the groan beside me, I remember. Right. This time it actually isn't my fault.

It's Ned's.

"What the hell did you do to me, man?" I ask. It's meant to be an outraged roar but comes out more like a plaintive bleat—figures I go for lion and get lamb and there's not an Annie Oakley in sight.

"I didn't do it," Ned manages to gasp back. I'm guessing from the pain evident in his hoarse whisper that he's in as much agony as I am. Serves him right.

"What? Of course you did," I tell him. "Remember? 'I think I can clear it, hold on'?" Yeah, it's all coming back to me now. "What did you clear, and what happened to us? And why is it so dark in here?"

Which is when I realize I've got my eyes closed.

Oh.

I blink, shudder, turn away, blink again. Nope, still there.

"Bad news, man," I whisper. "There's some kind of localized inferno bearing down on us. I think we're toast."

There's a pause. Then: "Uh, I think that's the sun."

What? I look again, squinting even through my membranes. Oh. "Yeah, well, it's not usually so . . . menacing!" I argue. Wait a second. Sun? Singular? I look again. "Hang on, I thought you had two suns?"

"We do," Ned agrees. "Well, actually we have three, but the third one's a tiny little thing on an elliptical path, there's a school of thought says it's really a comet that got sucked into the others' orbit and ignited when it passed too close, it only shows up once a year. That's when we know we're hitting swamp season, all heat and humidity and nasty-ass storms. Why?"

"Because," I tell him slowly, sitting up and then asking myself what made me think that would be a good idea but feeling too darn stubborn to just lay back down again, "unless somebody's made off with one of them, we're not on your planet anymore." I look around, which is a lot less painful than staring up at the sky. "In fact, I think we're back on mine."

Ned's sitting up too—it's amazing what you can learn when your eyes are open and you're looking around!—and he nods. "I think you're right. This is Earth. Weird." He frowns. "It kinda looks like home, though. In a way."

I study our surroundings. We're on the sidewalk, which is good because even though apparently it's not rush hour there are a few cars driving past and I'd rather not get run over if I can avoid it. Right next to us is a four-story brick building, the kind with no front lawn or porch or even stoop, just a single step up to the front door and windows alongside that for the first-floor apartment, a rusty fire escape on the floors above, no ornamentation to the building, just solid construction. The building next door is similar only it's three stories, has the front door in the middle rather than by one corner, and there were some attempts at decoration above the window frames and just under the roof gutter. To the other side is a smaller building, only two stories, the brick painted beige, a small awning over the front door and a steel gate over the big windows to the side. This one and the next are right up against each other even though they were obviously built at different times—there's a small space between this building and the three-story one, closed off by a locked gate with razor wire above it. The other side of the street's similar, small houses and apartment buildings all jammed up together, nothing really fancy but some little touches here and there, especially on the older ones, that keep them from just being cookie-cutter homes or bland new apartment complexes. This all looks real familiar to me.

"I don't think it's just that we're on Earth," I tell Ned slowly, studying everything. "I think we're back in New York. In fact"—I lever myself to my feet and wobble my way over to a car parked near us, an old Jeep— "I think we're down in Brooklyn somewhere."

I guess Ned doesn't want me showing him up, because he hauls himself upright, too. "Oh, yeah? How do you know that?" he asks. "Is it something about the sidewalks? Or the streets? Or the air quality?"

I shake my head. "Naw, it's this." I reach over and swipe a flier from under the Jeep's windshield wiper. "It's for Coney Island." Hey, not everybody would've seen that there!

"Don't know that one," Ned admits, and I stare at him like he's got two heads. Which, y'know, could happen. Maybe that's what his people do when they hit old age. Ugh, imagine a bunch of cranky retirees but each with two heads. They could argue with themselves about who's cheating at canasta and whose turn it is to hobble over and change the channel on the TV. But of course Ned is an alien. I keep forgetting that—despite his coloring and vegetation, he really does sound like he's from Brooklyn himself.

"Coney Island," I explain to him, "is the awesomest of the awesome. It's basically the bottommost edge of Brooklyn, and it's like one big amusement park. But it's old, so instead of all crazy digital screens and laser lights it's like old-school neon and banners. It's got roller coasters and sideshows and carny games and the Cyclones baseball stadium. And it's the original home of Nathan's Hot Dogs. Awesome."

Ned's gotten more and more excited the more I've explained. "And we're near there?" he asks. "Can we go?"

I think about that for maybe half a second. Possible alien invader running around zapping places out of reality, maybe out to get me, we just got tossed from Ned's planet to Brooklyn somehow, Tall's probably freaking out and taking Ned's planet apart inch by inch looking for us—"Yeah, sure. Why not?"

"Nice!" Ned rubs his hands together and looks around. "Which way?"

That is an excellent question. Fortunately, it's one I can answer. Turns out ducks have an excellent sense of smell, particularly for things like salt and fish. In other words, I can taste the ocean. "That way!" I point, and Ned and I immediately start walking.

Of course, Brooklyn is on an island, so technically there's

ocean all around, but I decide not to mention that unless it turns out I was wrong and I need an excuse.

"So how did we get here, anyway?" I ask Ned as we stroll down the sidewalk. It really is nice to be back, even if I never lived in Brooklyn myself. I had plenty of friends who did, so I was out here semi-regularly. Plus frequent pilgrimages to Coney Island—one of my old frat buddies wound up working for the Cyclones for a while, and got us into games for free, so we'd always come down, hang out, wander the carny area, watch the game, ride the Cyclone, etc. Good times.

Back to the topic at hand, though, I add, "Even if there is an invader around, why would he have sent us here? That makes no sense."

"I don't think it was an invader," Ned admits. "Remember I said whatever I was picking up was bigger than I'd expected? It also didn't feel recent, if that makes sense—my instruments were picking up signs of long-term wear and tear in the fabric, like it's been that way a while." He scratches at one ear. "I think it was a wormhole."

"A wormhole? Seriously? Shouldn't that have, like, sucked your entire planet into it or something?" Hey, I admit, a lot of what I know about science comes from old Disney films. *The Black Hole* for the win!

But Ned's shaking his head. Way to burst my bubble and stomp all over my childhood memories, man! "No, a wormhole is just a tear or twist in the fabric of space-time," he explains as we stop for a light. Typical New York drivers race past, shouting at each other as they weave in and out of lanes, but really it's no different than it was on Ned's world. "It can be big or little, localized or far-reaching, and yeah, a big wormhole could pull in a planet or a solar system but this one's not like that. It's a baby on the cosmic scale of things, barely a pinprick. And it was sorta locked, too." He grins sheepishly. "Guess I shouldn't've unlocked it without checking it out more first."

"Eh, no harm no foul," I tell him, patting him on the shoulder. Hey, I'm feeling fine again and I can afford to be magnanimous. "All that happened is you found a way from your world to mine, so that's actually kind of cool."

"It *is* cool." As we cross the street, Ned studies the area. "It's funny, though. Everything really does look familiar."

I look around, too. It's typical Brooklyn, little old shops and a few restaurants mixed in with small houses and apartment buildings, all of them older and a little worn but still in decent shape. Not the best neighborhood but not terrible either. Ned's right, though. I kept thinking his home world was like a bad mob movie set, and a lot of that synchs up with our current surroundings.

"Hey, check it out!" Ned shouts excitedly, his eyes lighting up. That is still so weird. He's pointing at a drugstore, the old-fashioned kind. It's clearly seen better days but it's still here and apparently still open, so that's something. But what Ned's homed in on is an old tin sign in the window that says "We have egg creams!" "Man, I could really do with an egg cream," he says with a sigh.

"Okay, hold up, time out." I turn on him. "What do you mean, 'you could really do with an egg cream'? How do you even know what an egg cream is? You know it's got nothing to do with either eggs or cream, right?"

"Uh, yeah, of course." He's looking at me like I'm the one growing two heads now. Gee, I really hope the Grays didn't program in anything like that—what if it was on a time-delay and is only just now sprouting? Ugh! Though it would be cool to be able to carry on a conversation over a meal and not have to worry about spraying everyone constantly. I've gotten really good at eating through straws and at tossing food deep into my gullet like flinging fish at a seal. "It's chocolate syrup, milk, and seltzer," Ned explains slowly, like I'm an idiot. Which I get a lot, but not usually from him. "You gotta use Fox's U-Bet for the syrup, though—anything else just ain't quite right."

I can't stop staring at him now. "This is crazy," I tell him. "Fox's U-Bet? There's no way that exists exactly the same on two different worlds independently, is there?"

Ned considers that. "No, probably not. Why, you have U-Bet too?"

"Of course we do! This is where it's from!" I'm practically shouting in his face now. "H. Fox & Company created it in 1895!" Did I mention I've got a really good memory for anything involving food? I can tell you pretty much every product Hostess ever made. In order of release date.

I force myself to calm down. Ned's my pal, he's not deliberately messing with my head—not this time, anyway. But egg creams on his world and here? That's an awfully big coinkydink. And then you add in all the other stuff and it's just too much. There's no way.

Which gets me to wondering.

"How long's your world been like that?" I ask him. "I mean, the delis and pickle guys and corner drugstores and the whole bit?"

"Oh, ever since the Wise took over," Ned answers. "Maybe two hundred years now?"

"The Wise? So they brought all that with them? The chocolate malteds and egg creams and zeppoli and the whole schmear?"

"Exactly." Ned shrugs. "At least, I think so. Before that it's a little hazy, there ain't a lot of history left. We had a lot of wars, I think, and the Wise put an end to them all. They brought us peace."

"Yeah, and bagels, apparently." I frown, thinking of something else. "When we were on the street and that kid shouted 'dirty bum'"—Ned stops like he's run into a wall, shouts "Dirty bums!", shakes his fist, spits on the ground, then continues on— "yeah, that. You have any idea why you do that?"

He shrugs again. "Just a habit, I guess."

"I think it's more than that, man." I'm starting to get excited as the idea takes shape fully. "Do you know who the Brooklyn Dodgers were?"

"No, but I know what a 'dodger' is," Ned tells me. "It's somebody who'll stab ya in the back, turn on you, all that."

"Ha, yeah, so here's the thing," I say slowly. "There was this baseball team, the Brooklyn Dodgers. Big deal back in the day, won the National League pennant a bunch of times, were the first ever to include a black player in the major leagues, won the World Series back in 1955. The whole city loved 'em. Then, in '57, they moved out to California, became the LA Dodgers. And all of New York took it personally." I've heard about this plenty of times from my dad, who was in high school when it happened. "Whenever anybody here talked about 'em, they wouldn't say the team's name anymore. They called them"—I take a preparatory step back from Ned—"'dem dirty bums.'"

Sure enough, he does the routine again. Bleh.

"So what're you saying?" Ned asks me when he's done. "That somebody on my world heard that story somehow?"

"Naw, it's more than that." I gesture all around us. "Look, you said it yourself—it looks familiar. Only, your world doesn't look quite like this. It's more like Brooklyn used to be. Back in the fifties and sixties, I'd say. When there were still pickle guys and corner drugstores—and the Dodgers were still verboten." Another piece of the puzzle falls into place. "And those gangsters who run things—that's from here, too. It's classic New York, man. Wiseguys and all."

Ned stops and looks at me, his eyes wide. "What'd you just say?"

"Uh, it's classic New York?" Then I get it. "Wiseguys. The Wise. That's it! Somehow, a bunch of wiseguys wound up on your world, probably through that same wormhole! And they took over! They made everything look the way it was back home! No wonder there are so many similarities!"

Ned's nodding now. "That actually makes sense," he says. This is one of the things I love about Ned, and for that matter about Mary, too, and even Tall. They may call me on it when I spout nonsense—especially Tall—but when I offer a suggestion they do take it seriously, no matter how crazy it sounds. It doesn't hurt that I've actually nailed it a bunch of times, and saved all our butts in the process. "The wormhole's right next to the trattoria because they set up their headquarters right where they first popped. But it looks like the wormhole doesn't open all the time, I had to force it for us, so once they went through they couldn't get back anyway. They had to just stay and make the best of it."

"Do you know what these guys looked like, the original Wise?" I ask him.

"Are you kidding? Everybody learns about the Wise in school!" He pulls out something that looks like an origami fortune cookie or maybe a wadded-up napkin, tugs it this way and that, and turns it into a small screen the size of his hand. He taps in a command or two, and a series of faces pops up— literally, floating a few inches above the screen and rotating slowly. "That's Vinnie Lamanna," Ned tells me, pointing at the first head, "and that's Al Nuzzi, and there's Luigi Pacelli, Dante Spataro, and Aldo Cassone."

I scratch my bill. Man, those names sound familiar! I was never all that good at history, but I do have a prodigious memory for movic trivia, and I feel like I've seen films about these guys. Only one way to find out. I pull out my own phone—trying not to feel self-conscious about it compared to Ned's nifty hologram screen thing—and type in a search for the first name, Vinnie Lamanna. Aha! "It's the Phantom Mob!" I practically shout, which gets an old lady across the way to turn and stare at me, then stare some more, then scream something and run back into her house. Yep, definitely back on Earth—out among the stars I'm not even close to the weirdest thing anybody'll see in a day. Hell, sometimes I'm the blandest, most boring person they've encountered all week!

"Who's the Phantom Mob?" Ned wants to know.

"They were five big-deal wiseguys back in the day," I tell him, reading off the entry. "They disappeared right before the cops and the Feds could haul them all in for racketeering, murder, tax evasion, the usual fun stuff. Literally disappeared, not a trace of them—tons of stories about what happened to them, from being shot and buried by the Feds to skipping out to South America to being abducted by aliens." I glance over at Ned. "I guess that last one wasn't all that far off, huh? Only maybe they didn't get abducted so much as taken in after they stumbled into that wormhole and got whisked away to your world."

"That is so weird," Ned says, crumpling his screen back up and putting it away. I've got to ask him to get me one of those. "So the Big Bosses of my world were criminal bosses here?"

"Yep." I grin at him. "And now I finally know why you sound like you're from Brooklyn! That's been driving me nuts since we met!"

I feel much better now that we've figured all this out. Not that it changes anything for anybody, really, but at least now we can enjoy our Nathan's hot dogs without wondering how Ned knows to order them with fried onions instead of sauerkraut. It's stuff like that can really effect your appetite.

Chapter Fifteen
Hello, Evil, have some pie

We're almost within sight of Nathan's—I can see the Cyclone peeking above the houses from here, and the banners along the Cyclones' stadium—when my phone rings.

The Imperial Death March. Again.

How the hell does she do that?

"I swear, Ma," I say as I answer, "we only just got back into town like ten minutes ago. I was gonna call." I really want to know if she has one of those clocks like Mrs. Weasley, with different hands for each of us to show when we're within local call range or something. In which case mine's got to have been going nuts for the past year.

"That's fine, dear," she tells me, and something in her voice makes me stop walking and shift to hold the phone closer. Look, you grow up around somebody you get to know a lot about 'em, right? And despite the fact that I can literally walk right into a street sign because I didn't notice it the whole time I was heading straight for it, I'm pretty observant when it comes to people. I know my own mom, that's for sure. And I can tell that right now she isn't mad at me, or trying to set me up with some neighbor's cousin, or planning to guilt me into helping Harold empty out the furnace and install all the window AC units.

No, what she is right now is worried.

And maybe a little scared.

"Is everything okay?" I ask her.

"Why wouldn't it be?" is the best answer she can manage, which definitely has me concerned. Especially since it's followed by: "It's just that your friends are here, and they want to know when you think you'll be back."

"My. Friends?" I glance over at Ned, who shrugs. "Which friends, Ma?"

"Giuseppe and Mario and Tony," she says. Then she adds in a hoarse whisper, "there's something a little funny about them. Are you in some kind of trouble, sweetie?"

"No, no trouble," I promise her, though I'm not sure if that's really true. Actually, I'm beginning to suspect it may not be even remotely close, but since I don't know for certain it's not technically lying, right? More like being aggressively optimistic? "Tell them I'll be right over, okay? I'm grabbing a cab now."

"Oh, that's fine, sweetie," Ma assures me. "I just set them up with some iced tea and the leftover brisket. They should be good for now." She drops her voice again. "Just get here before they finish eating, hm?"

"On my way," I repeat, and hang up. I immediately start looking for a cab. We're almost to Surf Ave and I'll have better luck there, so I pick up the pace until we're practically sprinting.

"What's going on?" Ned demands through huffs and puffs. No matter how out of shape I am, he's moreso, poor guy. Maybe I should suggest to Tall that he help Ned get fit instead of hounding me all the time. Torture/exercise regimens are the least of my worries right now, though.

"I don't know exactly," I tell him, spotting Surf Ave up ahead. "But it sounds like three guys from your world may be camped out at my mom's house, just waiting for me."

"That makes no sense," Ned argues. "How would they even know you were here on Earth? And why would they be looking for you in the first place?"

"The same reason those other two lunkheads were?" I suggest, stopping right beside the curb and hailing the first cab I see. Fortunately even though it's a weekday there are always cabs near Coney Island, and one pulls up in front of us a few seconds later. I give him Ma's address. "And step on it," I order, which is all the encouragement our cabbie needs. Next thing I know, Ned and I are both being slammed into the back of our seat as the cab practically hits escape velocity. "All I know," I add, getting back to Ned and our conversation as soon as I can inflate my lungs again, "is they're bothering my Ma. And that's gotta stop."

Ned nods. "Agreed. We'll figure out the rest as we go."

Despite my worries, I grin at him. "Leaping into danger without a plan," I say aloud. "Sounds like just another day at the office for me."

We're maybe halfway to Little Neck—it's actually only about forty minutes by car, straight up the Belt Parkway to the Cross Island, and I think this cabbie's going for under thirty in case there's a land-speed record he still needs to cross off his list—

when it occurs to me that, even with Ma and Bernie VIII, us against three goons isn't great odds. Fortunately, I know a way to even them a bit. Ned doesn't say a word as I pull my phone back out and place a call.

"Yo, Jimmy?" I say as soon as he answers. "It's Du—it's Robert. Yeah, your cousin Robert, the one you just saw at dinner? Listen, there's trouble at Ma's. Grab everybody you can and meet me over there ASAP." I hang up before he can argue, ask stupid questions, or try negotiating a day rate. Some people.

I can see it's killing Ned not saying whatever it is he's thinking. "What? Go ahead, spit it out." Not literally, though, because we're back to notions of V-8 as a bodily fluid and uck, that's enough to put me off Bloody Marys forever.

"Not to cast aspersions on anyone," he replies slowly, "but exactly how much help do you expect your cousin to be?"

It's a fair question, of course, given that Ned's met Jimmy. Still, "you'd be surprised," I tell him. "Jimmy's a screw-up, sure, but he's loyal as all get out. And he'll spread the word, too. There's no way he'll walk into trouble alone."

Ned doesn't argue that one, and we share the rest of the ride in silence. When we do finally screech to a halt outside Ma's house, however, I'm pleased to see I was right. Standing there waiting for us are Jimmy, Frank, Dolores—who, in a fight, is probably worth both of the other two put together—my brother Grant, his son Andy, and my sister Bonnie.

And now it's nine to three. I'm liking those odds a whole lot better.

"Hey, Bobby!" Grant engulfs me in a hug the second I'm out

of the cab—I handed the cabbie one of my credit cards at random and it apparently went through fine, seeing as how he takes off just as fast as he did when he picked us up, barely giving Ned time to clear the door before it slams shut behind us—and I know I'll probably wind up with grease stains as a result but I don't care. "Good to see you, little bro!" Grant's technically my stepbrother, the older of the two kids Harold had with his first wife, but he and I have always gotten along. He was the sibling I most wanted to be like when I was growing up, with his slicked-back hair and leather jacket and cool attitude. It's a little funny that, for all his coolitude, Grant wound up becoming an auto mechanic, but the job really does suit him. And he's easily the coolest mechanic you'll ever meet. He's got his work coverall on, but he's thrown the leather jacket on over it—still fits him, too, which makes me jealous, that and the fact that he still has all that awesome hair—and I notice he's got a monster wrench in one hand. Nice.

"Good to see you too, man," I tell him back, and mean it. "This is my buddy Ned." Fortunately Ned thought to use that same stuff he'd had on before while we were in the cab, so he looks perfectly normal again. "Hey, Andy, how're you doing?" The kid—he's Grant's eldest and probably at least twenty-five now but still a kid to me—nods back. Andy's never been a big talker, but what he lacks in his dad's smooth moves he makes up for in being rock solid and the size of an old Plymouth. He had a promising career in football but gave it up to work with his dad, which I consider a sign of real character. That and maybe some concern over what would've happened if talent scouts had learned he was part of our family. "Bonnie." She gives me a huge hug as well, though with a lot less risk of grease and oil. Bonnie's one of the ones that made my count for Ned confusing the other night. She's not technically related to me, since her mom and my dad hooked up for a while after my mom and dad split up but never actually got married, so we don't share any blood or any legal tie, but she's been part of the family since I was a kid and even after our parents went their separate ways we still included her in family gatherings. Mainly because she's awesome, and always has been. She and Grant bonded the second they met and have been thick as thieves ever since—I honestly think that, if not for their almost sort of being kind of related, they might have wound up together, but instead they're just best friends. Whenever I had a choice, growing up, I hung out with them.

"Looking sharp, little man," Bonnie teases after she releases me. Seeing as how she's always been taller than me—she's built like a true Amazon or Valkyrie or something, tall and broad and blonde—I figure she can still get away with calling me that. "So, what's going on exactly? Jimmy hit Defcon 1 but all he said was to meet you here." She's unarmed, as far as I can tell, but that doesn't make her any less dangerous. Bonnie's weapons were always her looks, her wit, and her mouth, and I doubt that's changed any. Especially since she's a lawyer now, and uses all three on a regular basis.

"There are three guys in there with Ma," I tell her, raising my voice so everybody can hear me. "I don't know who they are for sure, but I think they came looking for Ned and me. Ma called to tell me, and she sounded worried." That immediately has everybody on high alert, since Ma withstood all of us, even all together, practically without blinking. "I'm hoping we can just go in there and tell them to leave and they will, but I want to be ready in case they get uppity."

"No worries," Frank assures me, lifting the baseball bat he brought and banging its tip into his other palm, then wincing. "Uppity we can handle."

"Right." I choose to ignore the wince. "Let's go, then." And I take point, heading up the walk and onto the porch to the front door. I consider banging, or even kicking it in, but Ma wouldn't appreciate either so I just ring the doorbell.

It's like she was waiting right on the other side, because I swear the door yanks open before I've finished pulling my hand back. "Right on time, Robert," Ma tells me, giving me a hug. She glances around at the others arrayed behind me and nods, and I can feel the tension lift from her. "Come on in—your friends are just finishing their snack."

I squeeze past her as best I can, gesturing for the others to wait outside for the moment, and head down the hall to the dining room. And there, arranged around the table and polishing off what looks like another brisket the size of a rhino, are three goons. None of them are the two who grabbed me earlier, which fits with what I'd thought, that those two had been behind—and then under and on and all around—that Dumpster, but they're all cut from the same cloth. One's another cucumber, I think, or maybe a zucchini, but something similar, with the same sort of dark green skin and radiating marks. Another looks to be spinach, also dark and really weathered but with wild hair, and the third I'm guessing is a turnip, big and broad and pale with pink blotches and little tufts of hair. They're all wearing the same sort of cheap dark suit, and all still sporting sunglasses even though they're indoors. Typical.

And all three of them rise to their feet when I enter the room. What manners!

"I hear you're looking for me," I tell them straight out. "That's fine. I wanna talk to you, too. But not in here. Outside."

They look at each other and nod, with those little half-smile smirks you see on bullies' faces when they think they're about to administer a beating. I don't bother sticking around to see what other facial expressions they can make but turn and head back toward the front door.

I do turn around once I'm outside, though, so I can see their faces when they follow me out and realize just how badly they're outnumbered. I always loved that part. Like I said, there are advantages to coming from a big family.

"So," I say after I'm sure the situation has sunk in. "You wanted to talk. Let's talk."

The turnip reacts first. He sort of snarls and shifts, hauling back his right arm like he's gonna punch some sense into me. Except that, the way he's aiming, he's going for my jaw, which means he'll just learn the same lesson Cauliflower did back in the warehouse—don't chin-tap a guy with a duckbill. It never gets to that point, though, because Andy steps up and punches the guy full in the gut, doubling him over and dropping him to his knees.

At the same time, Grant taps Spinach on the wrist—the

same wrist that was just disappearing into his jacket. Taps with the wrench. Spinach grunts, though not as loudly as Turnip did, and pulls his hand back out, empty.

And Frank, not to be outdone, levels his bat like a sword, with the tip right under Zucchini's chin. "Don't even think about it," he says, and whether this goon believes Frank's tough-guy impression or just sees how things are turning out he nods and holds both hands well out in front of him.

Man, it's times like this I remember how much I love my family.

"Okay, that was fun," I say, because it kind of was. For our side, anyway. "But playtime's over. Who sent you and why?" All three of them just glare at me. "Aw, come on, guys," I tell them. "Look, you can talk to me or we can play another round of 'hit you with heavy things,' it's all the same to me, but I'm guessing you'd really prefer Option Number One. Whaddyasay? Conversation or target practice?"

"You will not stop us," Zucchini finally volunteers. His voice is funny, high-pitched and scratchy like an old record, with lots of hisses and pops. "You will be eliminated."

"Eliminated? Aw, but then I won't be able to catch up on all my shows," I bluster back, but inside I've got a chill. I knew they were after me, of course, but having it confirmed still smarts—and knowing they want to off me is kinda scary, even if we are talking about basically a dip tray with sidearms and pretensions. "Who's us, exactly? Just you three or are there more in the veggie crisper back home?"

I catch a brief frown from Dolores and Frank, more a "what's he saying now?" than a "why is he still talking?", which shouldn't be all that surprising. Some of my kin, like Grant and Bonnie, always got me. Others, like Frank and Jimmy, not so much. I am surprised, however, when Ned sidles over to me.

"There's something funny going on here," he murmurs for my ears alone. "Did you get a good look at these guys?"

"Sure," I answer as quietly as I can—subtlety isn't exactly my strong suit, and bills weren't made for whispering, as it turns out. "A zucchini, some spinach, and a turnip. So?"

But Ned's shaking his head. "Look at them again," he urges. "The rest of your family isn't seeing anything weird, which is strange all on its own. But these guys, they're not normal."

I study our trio of uninvited roughage. Ned's right, now that I'm eyeballing them more closely. They're not like the others I saw back on Ned's homeworld. Something's a little off about them.

I'm not exactly sure what it is at first. Then I see it. "Their angles are all wrong," I tell Ned, who nods. And it's true, these guys' limbs are all hanging a little funny, too sharp and too stiff and too pointy, like somebody broke all their arms and legs and other joints and then reassembled them but couldn't get the pieces back exactly so none of the seams are quite perfect. I know what that's like—it's why I gave up on model cars. There's more to it than that, though. There's . . . it's almost like a smudged edge around them. Like their auras are visible and they're made of charcoal, all dark and hazy. I mention that to Ned, and he nods again.

"Yeah, I see it too," he agrees. "I think it's why the others don't see them as aliens. Something about them is clouding people's minds."

"Like the Shadow?" I blurt out, getting more funny looks. "Sorry. But what does that mean? Are they like your world's version of supervillains or something?" Though, given that the Mob basically runs his world, wouldn't they be superheroes there instead?

But Ned's shaking his head. "I've never seen anything like it," he admits, "or heard of it, neither. Maybe it has to do with their passing through the wormhole, I don't know. But that didn't happen to us."

"No, it didn't, maybe for the same reason we can see them better—the Matrix and all that. But if it was the wormhole we're about to find out if going back the other way reverses the process." I nod to Grant and Andy and the others. "Okay, boys, wrap 'em up, I'll take 'em." They don't even bother to question me, just produce ropes and duct tape and, in Bonnie's case, a pair of handcuffs—I'll have to ask about those at our next get-together—and quickly disarm and then bind the trio. Who glare and hiss but don't otherwise resist. Not such stupid veggies after all.

"Where're you taking 'em?" Frank asks once they're all trussed up like three Christmas geese, or at least their side dishes. "And what's this all about, exactly?"

"Corporate espionage," Ned answers smoothly, which is good because I was probably about to launch into a bastardized version of *A Muppet Christmas Carol* and his answer makes marginally more sense. "This other company's been trying to horn in on ours' operations. I guess they figured they could bully Duc— Robert and I into giving up secrets or something."

"Yeah, ain't happening," I assure him, and them, glaring to make sure the goons get my double meaning. "We'll haul 'em back to our people, hand them over to security, let them clean up the mess. Thanks, guys." I administer hugs and fist bumps and backslaps all around, then go over to Ma, who's been standing on the porch watching the whole thing but not interfering. Just like when we were kids—she was there in case anybody pulled a weapon or the cops came but let us fight our own battles otherwise.

"Sorry about this, Ma," I tell her, giving her a hug. "I had no idea they'd drag you into all of it."

She shrugs. "Not like it's the first time." Her half smile turns into a scowl. "It had better be the last, though, eh?"

"Yes, ma'am." I mean it, too. Whoever these guys are, whoever they work for, they crossed the line when they involved my mom. And I'm going to make sure that doesn't happen again.

Even if it means I've got to get the biggest can of onion dip the world has ever seen.

Chapter Sixteen
Time for a change

Our street isn't exactly a hotspot for cabs, and I'm not entirely sure how we'd explain the three trussed-up veggie goons anyway, much less fit them in the back seat. Fortunately, Grant comes through for me again. He offers to drive us wherever it is we need to go, and he's got his beat-up old pickup parked right in the driveway. You can always tell a good mechanic by his own car, which should look one of two ways: either it's been tricked out all to hell and back, with chrome everything and neon and spoilers and so on, all glitzy and snazzy; or it looks all beat to hell but is solid as a cement pylon and runs smoother than a cheetah on speed. Grant's is the latter, and I know from experience that his pickup can drive on pretty much anything, outrun just about anything, and endure darn near anything. So I'm happy to take him up on his offer, and Ned climbs into the extended cab's back seat while I claim shotgun.

The goons we stuff in the flatbed. Still tied up. And under the tarp. Which just makes them look like the start of a vegan casserole, and makes me wish I had some olive oil to splash over them.

No, I still haven't eaten properly today. And these guys ate up all of Ma's leftovers!

We drive back to Coney Island, me and Grant swapping stories and Ned mostly just listening. Of course I stick to the same cover with Grant, which I hate having to do, but if there's any holes he doesn't point them out. Mostly we talk about what Andy and the rest of Grant's kids are up to these days, and how the garage is doing, and family gossip in general. Grant says he was sorry to miss dinner the other night, one of the kids had a thing at school, but it's fine, and I promise that if I do wind up moving back I'll come over for dinner some night soon. That's a promise I'll be happy to keep—being able to see Lizzy, Grant, and Bonnie on a regular basis again would almost make losing the Matrix gig worth it. Almost.

"Sure I can't just take you straight in?" Grant asks as we reach Coney Island and direct him away from the main drag, back the way Ned and I had walked.

"I wish, man," I tell him truthfully. "But they're kind of nuts about security right now, what with all this espionage crap going on. Better if you drop us off over here and we have them come pick us up for the last leg."

He doesn't look completely convinced but does what I ask anyway, and a minute later we're dragging the goons out of the flatbed and perp-walking 'em over to the side of the building Ned and I appeared beside. "Take care, little bro," Grant tells me as he hugs me good-bye. "And call as soon as you're free." He waves at Ned, hops back into his truck, guns the engine a little just for fun, and pulls away.

"Cool guy," Ned comments, and I nod proudly. That's everybody's take on my big brother.

"Okay, pop this puppy open and let's drag these guys back," I tell him, returning to the task at hand. Ned's got his gizmos out in a flash, and after a few seconds of fiddling, waving, rubbing, and clicking, he nods.

"Hold on!" He grabs one of the goons so I grab the other two, a hand clamped on each one's shoulders. The world twists in on me, and again I feel like a quarter that was left in the clothes dryer, bounced all around and tangled up in a whole heap of sopping-wet underwear. It doesn't feel as amazingly, gut-wrenchingly awful as it did before, though, whether that's because one direction is easier than the other or because having done this once already I'm better prepared to handle it, I have no idea. I'm just glad for small favors. I still stagger as we pop out, though, and lurch to the side like a punch-drunk zombie who's just realized one of his feet snapped off half a block back.

The only good news is that the veggie trio looks even more afflicted than I feel. I suspect if their mouths weren't duct-taped shut they'd be puking right now. Too bad for them, that's what they get for messing with Ma—and for eating all the brisket.

I'm not exactly unscathed, though. My head is splitting and there's a massive ringing in my ears, loud and harsh like somebody's running a buzzsaw directly over my skull. Or maybe up against it, seeing as how each crescendo matches a painful pulse all through my head.

Then I realize the sound is real. And it's coming from my head—or right on top of it.

"Ned! Ned!" He's on the ground, curled in on himself like a leafy green doodlebug, but glances up dazedly as I stagger toward him. "I think it's for you."

I can see it when his eyes clear and focus, his senses starting to come back to him—and then they widen as I guess he registers what I said and also the ear-splitting cacophony coming from my snazzy new headgear. "Oh, crap." He holds up a hand and I grab it, tugging him to his feet.

"'Oh crap' doesn't sound good," I point out. "In fact, I don't think I've ever heard it used to mean something good. What's going on? Why is it telling me I'm late for school? And where's the Snooze button?"

"Working on that," is all Ned answers, already with three of his little devices in his hands. He pulls out a fourth one and now it looks like he's either trying to knit double overlapping scarves using invisible yarn or practicing for a marionette show or maybe getting ready to sign something in triplicate simultaneously. Or prepping to eat Chinese, with chopsticks, double-fisted. Whatever it is he's doing, the noise is getting worse, louder and more shrill and the beats closer together—

—and then it stops.

Ahhh!

It's that sudden silence after deafening noise, like all the pressure's suddenly lifted from your head. In my case, literally. I almost fall over, I'm so relieved, but I flail about and manage to stay upright. "What the hell?" I ask.

"It was a shutdown alert," Ned explains, down to two gizmos now but still working them like mad. "It's only supposed to go off when you've been disconnected from the Matrix for too long and the system's at risk of shutting down."

"I thought this thing kept me linked in twenty-four-seven?" I reach up and feel it, making sure it's still there, though I know it is—even though I've kinda gotten used to wearing it, I can still feel it there, like the band-aid you've had on for days and don't really notice anymore except when it catches on your sleeve or rubs against something.

"It does," Ned agrees, stepping in closer and tapping the headgear with a widget, then studying the widget's tip. "Looks like going through the wormhole disrupted that, though. You're back online now."

"So the wormhole cut us off, and the Matrix freaked?" I rub the tip of my bill. "That's awfully needy of it—usually it allows a little leeway." I know because, especially right after I got the gig, it took a bit of fumbling whenever Ned or Tall or Mary took over for me. Hey, "pass the weird, cobble-together, wired-in headgear without pulling the wires loose or tripping and landing face-first in the Matrix or getting swallowed up by the couch or getting freeze-dried by the computer" isn't as easy as it sounds!

Ned nods absently, still studying the widget. "I can see why," he answers after a minute, and his expression is one I've seen on him before, halfway between intellectual curiosity and impending panic. "Apparently we were gone a bit longer than we thought."

I almost don't want to ask, but I know I gotta. "How long, exactly?" I have sudden images of myself as Rip van Winkle, complete with beard. Hey, Uncle Scrooge managed to get sideburns!

"Three days," Ned replies. There's a beep from along my head, and he sighs. "Ah. Okay, I've got it reset. Good thing, too—any longer and the Matrix might have gone into lockdown to prevent tampering. Which would mean we'd have to go back and reset it by hand."

Yeah, glad we don't have to do that—I still remember the shock I got when I reset the system the first time. My fingers tingled for days afterward, and not in a good way. Plus there was the whole "with the Matrix down the invaders could—and did—come swarming through to start remolding our reality into their idea of a cozy weekend retreat." Not eager to run that gauntlet again! Then my mind catches up with my hearing. "Did you say three days? But we were only gone a few hours!"

He shrugs. "Seemed that way to us, yeah, but wormholes can warp time as well as space. Looks like this one does both."

I think about that. "But when Ma called, she said she'd served the goons the leftover brisket. And in my house, brisket won't last more than a day, tops. So we didn't lose any time going from here to there. It must've all been on the way back."

It's nice when Tall gives me that "okay, you're not that dumb" look, but even cooler when Ned does because he's such a brainy guy himself. Not that Tall's stupid or anything, but Ned can be a bonafide egghead sometimes. Right now, he's nodding to what I just said. "There could be a discrepancy in one direction," he agrees. "So going from here to there is basically instantaneous, but from there to here takes ten, twenty, a hundred times longer. It might not be a constant, either—sometimes it could be in one direction, sometimes the other, sometimes faster, sometimes slower."

"That's why they've been here so long," I blurt out. "The Wise. You said it'd been a couple hundred years, right? But they only left Earth fifty years ago. When they came through the wormhole, because it messes with time, they wound up getting thrown back a few centuries local time." Which has me looking for a hot tub or at the very least a call box. No such luck—the closest I find is a parking meter, and those don't usually give you time back so much as steal time, especially when the meter maid is within sight and you're racing them to drop that last, saving-grace quarter.

"Makes sense." Ned frowns. "Which means we shouldn't mess around with the wormhole too much—we don't know exactly when we'd show up if we went through again." He raises two gadgets and crosses them, then lowers them again. "I've locked it up tight," he tells me as he stows his tools in his belt, which is like the geek plumber version of Batman's. "This way nobody's gonna just wander through by accident. In either direction."

"Cool." Speaking of wandering through, I look around. The three goons are still slumped against each other over by the edge of the parking lot. None of them have even tried to stand up yet, let alone escape or call for help or whatever. "So, what're we gonna do with our friends here?" I ponder aloud. "There's no cops, the Head Honcho's gone—back to the local boss?" I wonder if those zeppoli are still sitting out?

Ned sighs. "I guess so. We've gotta take 'em somewhere, and this is his city."

"Right." I grab the Turnip and shake him a little. "Rise and shine, big boy. You don't want to miss Homecoming." He glares at me but doesn't actively prevent me from helping him to his feet. I need to be careful—we're back on their home turf now, and I still don't have a clue who they're working for, or how many others have it in for me. But the local boss seemed genuinely surprised and pissed off at the whole kidnapping thing, so I'm hoping he's still on our side.

Between us, Ned and I get all three upright again and point them in the direction of that first Italian restaurant. I consider calling Tall—I already glanced around and didn't see him anywhere, and if it's been a few days I'm thinking he might've gone back to the Matrix to look for us there, or be canvassing the local galaxy and roughing up people in bars or whatever—but right now I've got my hands full. I'll call him after we've handed these three over.

Only, it turns out, that could be something of a problem. Because twenty minutes later we reach the restaurant—

—and it isn't there.

"Are you freaking kidding me?" I ask the universe at large, staring at the office supply depot now sitting in the restaurant's place. It's typical for that type, big and blocky with digital signage all over the wide front windows, and doesn't exactly match the local motif. It isn't the break from the prevailing visual aesthetic that's getting to me, though. "I can't even have zeppoli anymore? This is cruel and unusual punishment!"

"Uh . . ." Ned has slowed to a stop, as have I, but now he reaches over and tugs on my arm. "I think we should get out of here. Fast."

"Why, in case we get warped out of existence too?" I wail. "At least then I might be wherever they put all the food!"

"No," he answers, tugging harder now. "Because of them."

Looking where he's staring, I see a handful of guys come pouring out of the depot. They're all big and burly, they're all wearing suits and sunglasses, and they're all heading right for us. And, when I squint a little, I see that they've all got the same weirdly sharp joints and splotchy black aura as our three hostages here.

Oh.

"Right, going now," I agree. Hey, it's not like I can call my cousins from here! Besides, it was just luck Frank didn't hit anybody with that bat last time, and by "anybody" I mean "me or another family member." There's a reason when we have family reunions and decide to play baseball or volleyball or even Frisbee he's relegated to being water boy. "What about these three, though?"

"Leave 'em," Ned urges. "With any luck untying 'em will slow the others down. Come on!" And he starts edging backward.

"Fine, fine." I glare at the three, then lean in close to Spinach. "You boys owe me a brisket," I warn him quietly.

Then I thrust one foot out in front of him and give him a good hard slap across the shoulder blades, sending him flying forward.

He hits the ground hard but still rolls to one side—and knocks down Spinach and Zucchini in the process. A strike!

Even if the others don't stop to untie 'em and everything, they'll still serve as makeshift speed bumps.

Then Ned and I are hauling butt in the other direction.

I swear, the next food place I see, even if it's just a gas station sip-and-go, I'm carting off as much food as I can carry. Just in case.

Chapter Seventeen
Putting the band back together— with a staple gun

Luckily for us, the modified goons turn out to be shamblers rather than sprinters. Probably because their joints are so funky now— they walk like they're wearing casts and braces, all lumbering and stiff. It's like being pursued by an entire squad of angry Nutcrackers, only with a Five Families motif. That makes it easy for us to outrun them, even at Ned's speed, and ten minutes later Ned waves for us to stop near a small butcher's shop. While we both catch our breath I eye the sausages and hamburger patties and steak cuts displayed in the front window. I wonder if they'd cook something up for me on the spot if I asked nicely?

"I think we lost them," Ned says finally, still huffing a bit. Hey, at least this latest crisis is giving him some exercise!

"Cool." I'm in much better shape, which is why I'm barely panting at all anymore. I'm just breathing quickly to demonstrate heightened anxiety, that's all. "So, what now? We can't go to the authorities, seeing as how there aren't any left. But I don't think we can take on even the remnants of a criminal empire all on our lonesome, especially these new 'made more evil' types."

"We need help," Ned agrees. He pulls out his phone canister

and sends the tiny little buggers floating all around him in a glittering cloud. "You call Mary, I'll call Tall."

Well, that makes ten kinds of sense and I wish I'd thought of it sooner myself. Of course if we need help we'd call Tall and Mary. Who else saved the universe with us? I get out my phone and hit the speed-dial for Mary. She answers on the second ring, which is sweet—nobody answers on the first ring unless they're expecting a medical diagnosis, a job interview, or a lot of money, and the fewer rings you wait the more you care about either the person or what you think they have to say. Since Mary has no idea what I'm about to tell her—I doubt anybody could have seen this one coming!—it has to be me she's picking up for. Awww!

"Hey, babe," I tell her when she answers. She's just as lovely onscreen as in person, which is saying a lot. Let me put it this way—if Mary went to beauty and charm school she'd be the entire "cool kid" contingent, class president and homecoming queen and all. "Uh, you busy right now?"

"No, I am currently at liberty," my lady love answers, batting her baby blues at me. "I have just finished an assignment, and now I have been given time before the next task." Yeah, this is how she always talks, which can be hella sexy. It's like being with Marian, Madame Librarian, if she was also a genius astrophysicist and a Playboy bunny.

"Great!" I see that cute little blush starting along her neck, and hastily add before she gets too excited, "because Ned and I've kinda stumbled into something and we could really use your help."

Her eyes flash—not literally, because even though the Grays

did mod her they only did stuff to her brain, not her eyes or her looks, which amazed me when I first met her and found out she actually looks this hot all on her own—but it's not anger, it's just her switching gears from girlfriend to partner in crime. Though I'm pretty sure all those warrants've expired by now. "Where are you?" she asks. She knows there's no point my explaining everything over the phone—far better if she gets her lovely derriere out here and then we tell it to her live and in person. Besides, even Ned's fancy-shmancy new phone can't let you cuddle long-distance! I'll have to get him to work on that.

"Ned's homeworld," I tell her, glancing around. "We're next to Auto's Fine Meats." I realize I didn't mangle that sign, somebody else did, and take a closer look at the window display. The food isn't real, I realize. It's all made of metal, specifically from old car parts. That figures—the one food place the invader hasn't touched yet and it isn't even real food! I can't even figure out why you'd open a place like this. What is for, junkyard dogs?

But Mary's already nodding. "I will be there in an instant." Funny, when most people say such things they're just using hyperbole—it could take a few days to get here by even conventional interstellar transportation—but I know Mary and she isn't onc to make idle promises or give empty looks. If she says an instant—the ground bucks in little waves in front of me, like I'm suddenly in the middle of a concrete river to match the usual jungle and the tide is coming back in, and the air directly ahead starts to shimmer and darken into a certain familiar, curvy silhouette—an instant is exactly what she means. Sure enough, a second later the ground settles back down and the air clears and there she is, standing right beside me. Mary.

"Are you injured?" she asks immediately, wrapping both arms around me in a hug strong enough to realign my spine. Her sapphire gaze sweeps around to include Ned, though her arms stay locked around me for now.

"Naw, we're fine," I promise her, though the sound comes out a little squashed on account I can't inflate my lungs fully until she loosens her hold some. Ned gulps and nods. There's another disturbance forming in the air just behind him, and as I watch a tall, strapping figure begins to materialize there.

Along with what looks like a helium balloon hovering over his shoulder.

Well, this ought to be interesting.

Sure enough a second later Tall is stomping toward us. And Heidi floats along right behind him.

"Where the hell've you been?" Tall demands as he closes the distance, and it's a good thing Mary's still holding me tight because otherwise I might flee just on reflex. "One minute you were right across the street and the next you were gone. I've been looking everywhere!"

"He really has been," Heidi agrees, shifting from concerned red and black to a calmer blue, though with veins of purple showing through. "Another dozen years and he'll have this quadrant totally canvassed—and half the good bars broken or closed down." He focuses on me. "Yo, glad you're okay, though."

"Thanks." Heidi's actually a pretty good . . . guy? Sentient mood-ring aquarium? Spherical floating viewscreen? Tall and I met him a little while ago when we stumbled into a plot to use

CampGirl cookies to take over the world. We needed a lift to this other planet, and Heidi was the one who offered. He proved to be a big help, and he and Tall really hit it off, so after Tall decided to leave the MiBs he took Heidi up on an offer to partner with him in his interstellar trucking business.

The only thing that makes any of this weird, of course, is that Heidi's basically a floating bowling ball that changes color like a mood ring and contains something suspiciously similar to Jabba the Hut's snack. I'm actually pretty sure the thing floating inside and occasionally bumping up against the glass is the real Heidi and the ball is just its version of a car or a barcalounger. I've never asked outright, though, because that just feels like it'd be awkward, saying "so, which is the real you and which is just the nifty pet or accessory?"

Mary relaxes her grip finally, keeping one arm wrapped possessively around my waist but letting the other loose so I can turn and survey my campadres properly. It's good to see everybody all together like this. Mary's met Heidi a few times since he and Tall became partners, and nods hello now, but she and Ned don't know the guy as well as Tall and I do. I get the feeling that's about to change.

"Sorry we were out of touch," I tell the rest of them now. I'm assuming Tall told Mary what'd happened before we vanished, and considering she doesn't frown at me now I'm guessing I was right, which means at least I don't have to rehash any of that because it's all starting to blur a bit for me, even though from my perspective it's all happened today! "But turns out the wormhole sent us back the long way around, basically.

Took three days instead of a few seconds or minutes." I sigh. "Anyway, here's the sitch," and I fill them in on the black-edged goons and the local boss and the depot and so on. I even mention Ma's brisket again, just because I'm still ticked about that. She couldn't have fed them some leftover mock-oyster stuffing or something instead?

"That is indeed worrisome," Mary agrees when I'm done. "And it does sound as if one of the invaders could be to blame, as you surmised."

"Invaders?" Heidi asks. "Somebody wanna catch me up on those, then?" So then we have to tell him about how the rest of us first met, when the Matrix went down and the inhabitants of another reality decided to gatecrash and then stay and rearrange all the furniture. Reminds me of one summer back in school. But hey, that house was begging to be redecorated! Our reality's still shiny and new and had big "Hands off, private property!" signs posted everywhere!

"Wow," is all Heidi says when we're done recounting all that. "So you four saved the whole universe? Color me impressed." I never knew what color "impressed" would be before, but I do now. Apparently it's an eggshell white with hints of green and blue marbling throughout. Cool and classy, actually, and now I wanna paint my bathroom "impressed" next time I go home. I figure you ought to be pretty pleased with yourself every time you do your business, right? "And it's one of these guys coming after you now?" he asks.

"Looks like," I answer. "I haven't seen the crafty little bugger yet, but it all fits. Though messing with my food supply is new, and something I'm really not happy about. I don't suppose anybody thought to bring a snack?" Everyone ignores that, though I really wasn't kidding. I don't think clearly when I'm this hungry—all I get are mental images of takeout menus and brief daydreams of pie-eating contests with me as the star contestant.

Mary is frowning, though. It's amazing how she can make even that look sexy. "Although I agree with your analysis of the possible culprit," she offers, "I am not convinced this is strictly a vendetta against you. If it were, surely the invader would have struck at you directly by now. Instead, although he has certainly sent minions to harass your family and distract you, the main thrust of his activities has instead been toward the leadership of Ned's planet."

"She's right," Tall agrees, which doesn't surprise me. He and Mary are the strategists in the group, just like Mary and Ned are the eggheads. Me, I'm more of the motormouth and impulsive-action guy. Not action hero, mind you, that's still Tall. "This can't just be about you. It'd be way too much of a coincidence for that to be the case and yet all the leaders here to have been taken out."

Oh, fine, just keep me from feeling special! I don't say that, though. In all honesty, I'm a little relieved. I'd been feeling really guilty about how some guy with a grudge against me has taken out every authority figure here, like the guy who sets off the sprinkler system strictly for fun and gets the entire rest of the shopping mall soaked in the process. Even if it was July and everybody really needed to cool off a bit. So it's nice to know this time the invader *was* actually aiming for Ned's leaders and not just catching them in the crossfire.

"Why's he targeting people here, though?" I ask. "It can't just be revenge, since we haven't heard of anybody going after the president or the U.N. secretary or the late-night talkshow hosts back home. Why pick on Ned's world?"

The others all nod, that "okay, that was actually a fair question" head bob I get every once in a while between all the "why would you even ask that?" shakes.

"Maybe it's this wormhole thing you were talking about?" Heidi suggests. "It's a real doozy, alright—it's been messing with all my arrays since we got here."

Ned frowns at him. "You're picking it up right now?" he asks. "We're a good ten blocks away and I could only detect it within twenty meters or so." He's got that look in his eye like he wants to take Heidi apart and see what makes him tick, or at least float and change colors. And while that could be fascinating, and a great boon for the camouflage hovercar industry, I don't think Tall would appreciate it if his partner got disassembled for the sake of technical curiosity.

Heidi turns a little blue, which I know means he's confused. Ever since partway through that first ride I could figure out his emotional state from his coloring. It's actually a lot clearer than reading facial expressions, and allows for more emotional shades. Ha ha. "Ten blocks?" he asks. "Are you sure? I'd have guessed the range to be no more than two, and probably a whole lot less."

That has Ned blanching like an uncooked shrimp and gizmos practically leaping into his hands. He raises a few, waves them like he's summoning rain or signaling a landing aircraft, and then checks their sides and tips and fingerholes. "You're right," he says finally. "It's only forty meters, give or take a few." He frowns. "That doesn't make any sense, though. Not unless it doesn't have a fixed endpoint."

"It's gotta," I argue. "We figured that's why the trattoria was there, remember? Because that's where the Wise first came through. And on the other end it was in exactly the same spot when we popped out as when we ducked back in."

"I know," Ned says. "But Heidi's right, too. It's a lot closer than it was before." He starts to walk away, gadgets held out in front of him, and me and Mary and Tall and even Heidi quickly take up flanking positions, guiding him by gentle touches and not so gentle "Steer left! Now right!" shouts to keep him from running into lampposts and fire hydrants and storm grates and the like. A minute later, he stops. "It's just up ahead," he tells us.

"That's what I'm getting too," Heidi agrees. "Maybe ten feet and a step to the right."

Of course, me being me, I pace it out. "Right about here?" I ask. There's a loud beeping from my head, and the scene starts to distort, everything elongating and running together like the whole world got caught in a taffy pull, and I feel myself beginning to get stretched out and scrunched up.

Whoops.

Then a powerful hand like an enormous armored vise grip clamps onto my arm and hauls me backward with all the force of a monster truck. The world snaps back to normal, the beeping cuts off, and I find myself looking up at Tall, who's wearing his customary "Are you a complete flippin' moron?" look.

"Hey, thanks, man," I tell him. "I think I found it."

"No shit, Sherlock," he mutters. His hand's still on my arm, like he thinks if he lets go I'm going to try again. Come on, that only happened that one time! And then those other few as well. Oh, fine.

Ned's alongside me now, checking his doodads. "Good thing he pulled you back," he tells me. "Because now I know why this isn't the same place as before." He sighs. "It's a different wormhole."

"A different wormhole? What're they, sprouting?" I ask, glancing around a little nervously. "Is one gonna show up right on top of me next?" That sounds handy if I need to get somewhere in a hurry, but not if it's gonna throw me somewhere else and mess up my personal timeline and so on.

"I don't know," Ned admits. "This one's definitely newer than the other one. And a whole lot worse." He's still really pale. "The other end isn't in our universe."

"Oh. Crap." We all exchange looks, which is a lot easier than exchanging gifts and doesn't leave you worrying whether you were right about them loving candies shaped like famous people's heads. If it's from outside our universe it really *is* the invaders. And not just one who got left behind, either, but possibly a whole slew of them again. "But wait, I thought the Matrix kept them out?"

Mary shakes her head. "The Matrix prevents other realities from willfully permeating the barrier between us," she explains, all her sexy science talk making me shiver even in such dire

circumstances. "But wormholes are naturally occurring phe-
nomena, random tears in the fabric of reality. The Matrix was
never designed to prevent such a thing, or even to detect it."

"So you're saying the Matrix locked all the doors and windows but the invaders've found a spot where the roof's naturally
pulling up, and they're slipping in there?" Wow, the "so your
brain does sometimes work after all!" look from all three of
them at once, and the "impressed" color from Heidi at the same
time! I'm on a roll! Too bad it's about something so amazingly,
craptastically bad for our entire existence. "Well, what do we do
about it?"

"I can recalibrate the Matrix, I think," Ned offers slowly, "so
that it sends out an alert when a wormhole like this opens. Not
sure I can set it to prevent them entirely, but I can try. I'll have
to do that on-site, though."

"Okay. I'd better go too, check all the locks and make sure
nothing's gotten into the pantry." And yes, I might make myself
a quick snack while I'm there. Hey, I'll share! I'm just trying to
be a good host!

"I will accompany you as well," Mary adds. "I may be able
to assist if there are calculations required." I love it when she
calculates with me, but I don't say that. She can read my looks
pretty well, though, and there's that blush starting again. It's
adorable.

"We'll keep an eye on things here," Tall volunteers, and
Heidi goes green in agreement. "They'll have to go through me
to get in, and I'll make sure that's an expensive proposition." I
have this image of Tall manning an impromptu tollbooth and

charging so much to cross that the invaders can't afford it, but somehow I don't think that's what he meant. Still, if anybody can bodily block an entire wormhole's worth of angry space aliens, it's him.

"I'll look after him," Heidi promises. "Not sure I can keep him out of trouble, mind, but I'll try to minimize any collateral damage, at least." I don't bother wondering how an animate bowling ball could stop anything or anyone. I already know that Heidi's pretty darn resourceful—and that he's got a few tricks of his own up his sleeve or in the corner of his fishbowl or whatever.

"All right, sounds like a plan," I say instead. "Now we know where they're coming in and some of what they're up to—time to gum up the works." Hey, screwing things up is something I'm really good at—it's about time that talent toward chaos worked in my favor!

Chapter Eighteen
I didn't invite all of you
and I don't have enough to share

Ah, home sweet home—at least for now. It's funny, I think as we materialize in the main Matrix chamber, how quickly I've gotten attached to this place. And that's not even counting the time with the glue gun—I just wanted to hang some holiday decorations, I didn't expect to turn myself into a cross between an anthropomorphic fables frieze and a piñata! But the first time I saw this place, I won't lie, I thought it was pretty darn weird, all pink and glittery and oddly curved.

Then I found out it was actually some ancient, giant skull. Which only made it weirder—I mean, I know the Catacombs are partially constructed from bones, but those are a whole lot of regular-sized bones, not one really, really big one.

Though I guess this way saves on the cost of mortar.

Anyway, it was kinda creepy at first, being stuck inside an old skull. I felt like I was somebody's miniature psychosis, a tiny little voice whispering "Hey, I'm real, too!" and "Go ahead, nobody'll mind!" Admittedly, I've always wanted to be the devil on somebody's shoulder—ask any of my old frat brothers and they'll tell you I got lots of practice—but this was going a little too far, even for me.

But the longer I lived here, the more comfortable I got with the idea. Hell, in a way everybody lives in old bones anyway, right? Stone is the Earth's bones, wood is the trees', and brick is made from sand, which is crushed shells and the like. This was just the more direct route, honesty in building materials or something like that. Besides, lots of cultures used to make their homes out of skins and furs and bones. They'd have thought I was awesome if they could've seen my version of that.

Now, looking around at the smooth, curving walls with the sparkle deep within their almost-glowing pink luster, I have a hard time imagining living anywhere else.

And it terrifies me that I may have to do a lot more than just imagine it, very soon.

Now's not the time to worry about that, though. First things first—I set out to fix myself a snack.

"Anybody want anything?" I call out to Ned and Mary, who've gone to inspect the Matrix itself. "Sandwich? Lasagna? Braised longtufted spearkshark poppers?" Those last are amazing—they taste like a cross between really good tuna and marinated steak, light and flaky and clean but also just a little sharp and spicy. Plenty of iron, too, at least the meteoric kind—good for the bones but plays hell on compasses, lodestones, and watch batteries.

"No time for that right now," Ned warns me. "Check the door first, make sure it's secure." He usually has the Grays teleport him to the front stoop and then knocks, but this time we appeared inside—not sure if that's because it's urgent or because he figured it's my house so there's no need to ask if we can come in. Either way I guess he's right, so I head down the hall to the front door. One of the things about this place is that, despite several apparent openings, it only has one actual access point. That's the lower front, where the mouth was. Other spots, like the former eye sockets and nasal passages, let in light but have some kind of screen over 'em to stop anything else from wandering through. Even when the invaders were holed up here themselves the front door was the only way in, so I'm assuming that still holds true.

Also, I don't really wanna go climbing around all over the place checking that the windows are shut and the blinds drawn when I could be chowing down instead.

"Door's still closed," I call out as I approach it. It's a big sturdy thing, made from some wacky metal that comes close to matching the walls in sparkle and sheen, and curved at the top like a hobbit-hole door but squared on the bottom. I check the locks and they seem fine. "Still locked, too!" I add.

Then I peek through the peephole.

Nothing but darkness beyond.

"It's too dark to—" I start, then stop. Frown. Look around. Back up about ten paces and glance up, where the nasal passages form a pair of skylights.

Through which the suns—the collective light of hundreds of galaxies, fortunately filtered through the artificially induced atmosphere of a bubble containing the Matrix and the small town that's sprung up around it so that the combined radiance doesn't instantly fry us to a crisp—all beam merrily down upon us.

Crap.

"We may have a problem!" I shout instead. Seconds later, Mary and Ned are barreling toward me. Both of them are breathing heavily from the run. On Mary that looks good— really good. On Ned, less so.

"What's wrong?" Ned demands as he skids to a stop just in front of me. Mary slows more gracefully, which is a shame because she's welcome to bodycheck me any time.

"It's dark through the peephole," I answer, waving toward the door behind me. "I think somebody's blocking it."

Ned slumps a bit. "Crap." Yeah, that's what I said!

"We must ascertain if there are threats massing beyond this portal," Mary warns, and I sigh. Because I know she's right, because that means more work for me, and because I may never make it to the kitchen. But because she's right I turn and start up a narrow, twisting staircase that starts just a few feet past me, maybe ten feet from the door proper. The staircase takes me up, up, up, until finally it lets out onto a medium-sized platform that's a balcony on one side and a sloping cliff on the other.

This was the giant's left eye once. Ironic that even now, easily millions of years past his death, it still makes a great place to scope out the competition.

I step to the edge and look down. And there, right outside the door, are more of those black-edged goons.

Ten of them in all.

Ouch.

I wonder, briefly, if I can bribe them with CampGirl cookies. I still have a case or two tucked away.

Then I consider, even more briefly, surrendering on the condition that I get to eat those cookies before they haul me off.

After that, slowly, grudgingly, I claw my way back to reality.

No way these goons would ever share!

"How bad is it?" Ned calls up, and I hurry back down the stairs to them.

"Ten of 'em," I answer. "All just as freaky as those guys at Ma's."

"Was there any indication that the invaders themselves might also be present?" Mary asks.

I shake my head. "Didn't see 'em, but you know how sneaky those little buggers are." I scratch my bill. "Still, you'd think if they were along they'd have already warped their way in somehow."

"I suspect they are not in attendance themselves," my lady love agrees. "Proximity to the Matrix should significantly limit their influence over our reality, leaving them far more vulnerable."

"Yeah, so they sent a goon squad to shut it down for them," Ned adds. Which is about what I figured, too. Back on his world the guys outside are just mooks, minions, stooges, patsies. Looks like they haven't exactly climbed the ladder any—all they did was trade one boss for another and get some funky new perks.

Well, if they think they're getting anywhere near my cookies—I mean, the Matrix—they've got another think coming.

Which is right when they start banging on the door.

Hard.

"I don't suppose the door'll hold all on its own?" I ask Ned.

He shrugs. "No idea. It's not part of the original skull, of course—if it was I wouldn't even worry. But they added the door when they set this place up. I'm sure it's strong and all, but against ten of 'em, with whatever enhancements the invaders gave 'em?" He frowns. "I wouldn't wanna bet my life on it."

Which is exactly what we'd be doing, of course.

"All right, new plan," I announce. "We grab the Matrix and get the hell out of Dodge." I know full well that won't work, of course—the Matrix takes up most of its room, which is roughly the size of a football stadium. And it doesn't exactly fold down for easy travel.

"Right, *new* new plan," I correct. "We give these guys what for and teach 'em that even here at the Galactic Core, you don't mess with New Yorkers!"

Ned and Mary both nod. "If we don't stop 'em cold, they'll eventually force their way in," Ned agrees. "And then they'll shut down the Matrix—"

"—and that'll be the end," I finish. "Yeah, got it. Only question is, how do we stop 'em? There's ten of them and three of us. They're bound to have guns, and the best we've got is my pool cues, darts, bar stools, etc." I brighten for a second. "I could challenge their leader to a duel, winner takes all! You know I totally rule at foosball!" They don't even have to say anything. "I know, I know. Okay, other ideas? How do you stop a bunch—is there a word for ten, like 'quartet' for four? A dime? A dime of goons?—without any weapons of your own?"

"We are not completely unarmed," Mary corrects, and hauls what looks like a telescoping silver wand from her cleavage. Okay, I know for a fact that wasn't there last time she visited! I'm not complaining about its presence now, though, especially when she extends it to full length, waves it like a conductor preparing for a recital, and sparks shoot from the tip. I'm actually glad to see she's got something to defend herself with, just in case she's ever in a bad place and I'm not around to lend a hand. Though I suspect, between me and the Glo Stick o' Doom there, it's the much handier in a fight. And of course, Mary can mop the floor with me even barehanded. Oh well, I'm secure enough in my masculinity to admit my woman is the tough one in the pair.

"Yeah, I've got a few tricks up my sleeve, too," Ned agrees. He extracts one of his gadgets and, near as I can figure, rips it in half right down the middle, splaying it wider than a hipster's legs on a subway seat. A second gadget gets hauled out and inserted into the gap, which is then folded back up around it. Then a third is added to the mix, jammed in below the first two, and suddenly Ned's holding what looks an awful lot like a ray gun if it had been built from metal sculptures of praying mantises.

"Got a second one of those?" I ask them both at once. They both shake their heads, and I sigh. "Right, so you're both armed and I'm not. I guess I know what that makes me."

You guessed it:

Bait.

Which is why, a few minutes later, I shout, "Hold your horses, I'm coming!"

The banging stops immediately.

"Who is it?" I ask, stepping up right beside the door.

"We have an urgent message for you," one of the mooks replies.

"Yeah? From who?" I can almost hear Mary struggling against the urge to correct me, "from *whom*?" somewhere nearby. I know, I'm terrible.

"Not out here," is his answer. Smart. "Let me in and we'll talk."

"Talk and I'll let you in," I counter. Yes, I'm dragging this out. I don't want him to think it's too easy and get suspicious. But the plan does actually involve letting him and his buddies— the other nine cents—inside, so after a few more seconds I sigh, shout, "Okay, fine." And unlock the door.

Then I take off running.

I'm not even halfway down the hall when the door bursts open and the mooks start pouring in.

Fortunately, even though none of them is as wide as my big duck head they're still too broad to squeeze inside any way but single file. Which means they can't just mob me. Not until they've gotten past the door.

I'm almost to the end of the hall when I hear Ned's gun go off with an odd whooping sound like an old noisemaker. It's followed almost immediately by a hiss-and-pop combination a lot like the noise a radiator makes as it heats up. And then there's the thud of two bodies hitting the floor.

Clearly Ned and Mary, firing from their hiding places just around the bend of the stairs, nailed two of the goons.

Which only leaves eight more to chase me down.

Whee.

"Come on, boys, party's this way!" I holler over my shoulder as I hit the end and skid around the corner. I want them focused on me, not on Ned and Mary behind them. I need to keep the mooks occupied so my pal and my girlfriend can pick off more of them.

Provided they don't pick me off first.

I'm flying past the opening to a good-sized room with lockers set into the far wall. I've never bothered to do much with it because Tall and I were tortured here back when the invaders held the place. We turned the tables on 'em and eventually drove 'em all out, of course, but still—bad associations. That means, though, that when we scoured the whole building clean we didn't empty this one completely—we tossed anything that looked rotten, radioactive, or rayon (the three Rs) but left the rest.

I grab hold of the doorframe and bootleg myself into the room, heading straight for the lockers.

There's gotta be something in here I can use!

Problem is, whoever worked here before me clearly wasn't from Earth. Go figure, a whole universe of people to choose from, they hire aliens. Right now Texas is screaming. Anyway, that means I don't know what my predecessors' home culture was like. I don't know what could be a deadly weapon and what's a video game and what's a jar of Auntie's best homemade preserves. Most of the stuff in these lockers I don't recognize at all. And what I do seems useless right now—how is a parka or a small metal thermos or a bag of marbles going to help me any?

Hm.

Thirty seconds later, the first mook comes barreling around the corner—

—and slips on the marbles I've scattered on the floor there.

Heh. Just like living in the frat house.

His feet go out from under him as he sails up into the air, then crashes down on his butt and back.

Hard.

Next I step in and quickly bash him in the head with the thermos—which is something we didn't do to our frat brothers, we usually just videoed their spectacular wipeouts and posted those on the college website, with buttons so people could rate their degree of klutziness. This guy, however, gets a slightly different coup de grace. And it works nicely, because upon impact he shudders, stiffens, and then collapses, out cold.

One more down.

The next one trips over the marbles *and* over his unconscious playmate, and I nail him in the back of the head before he can even lift his face to whine "but I just wanted a late-night snack!"

Two down.

Assuming Ned and Mary have managed to take out two more, that's six so far.

Out of ten.

Oy.

Number seven apparently either saw what happened to five and six or just guessed it from the sounds up ahead because he actually leaps over them and the marbles, landing just beyond that whole mess.

I hurl the parka over his head like a matador's cape, cinch it tight and both blind him and bind his arms to his side, and slam him in the head with the thermos a few times until he goes completely limp.

Three to go.

Eight doesn't even bother to come around the corner. Instead he stops shy of it, peeks around, and takes a shot at me. Fortunately I was half-expecting that—and half-expecting pizza delivery, because hope springs eternal, especially when I have coupons—and dodge into the locker room. Not sure what I can do to take this guy down, since all my new toys are between him and me, but at least I'm keeping him busy.

And judging by the shots coming from behind him, Ned and Mary are doing the same with nine and ten.

Only problem is, we appear to be at a stalemate. Shots continue to rattle back and forth, meaning everybody must be using cover. And eventually more goons'll show up, pinning Ned and Mary between them. Then they'll crush me by sheer force of numbers, and—

That's it!

Stepping over to the lockers again, I yank open the one farthest to the right and start rooting through its contents. I'd noticed this thing back when I first went digging around in here, but Tall made me put it back. I guess he figured the fewer things I messed with the better.

But right now I really need to mess with something.

At last my hand closes around a thin metal bracelet, really just a beaten-flat piece of copper twisted or even cut into a circle. I haul it out, careful to use my hankie to keep from touch it directly, close the locker again, and hustle back to the corner.

"Still there?" I call out, risking a quick peek.

The answering shot that skims across my bill confirms that.

"Okay, catch!" I toss the circle around the corner, under-hand. I don't hear it clatter off the floor, so I'm guessing he did catch it on instinct.

A few seconds later, I hear a muffled grunt. Followed by a short scream. Then a heavy thud.

I have no idea why whoever used this place before me had a bracelet or wristband or whatever that got exponentially heavier every few seconds you were in contact with it. But right now I'm really glad they did.

Because, unless I counted wrong, there shouldn't be more than two of them left.

And there are three of us.

I wish I could retrieve the bracelet but I don't dare step out into the hall just in case somebody is watching, ready to take the shot. I'd be a sitting duck—and I'd hate for a pun that awful to be my last thought, so for now I'm staying put.

Which leaves me without weapons again. Why couldn't the previous tenants have been avid gun nuts who just happened to leave a whole fleet of weapons behind when they skedaddled?

Or bondage enthusiasts who'd just gotten in the new spring collection and hadn't had a chance to unpack them? Or at the very least a hockey team who'd left behind their sticks, pucks, helmets, brass knuckles, and so on after their last game.

But nope. Nothing. Not even a pointy stick. The only things left in the room at this point are me and the lockers themselves, and I'm not nearly strong enough to toss one of those at the goons.

At least there're vanity mirrors inside two of 'em, so I can make sure I look pretty for when the last two goons shoot me.

Just then my phone goes off. "Yeah?" I answer. "If you're calling to demand my surrender, forget it. I won't give up without a fight. Or at least an impressive wail of protest. Possibly a yodel, I've been working on one that—"

"DuckBob!" It's Ned. "Where are you? How many of them are left?"

"Locker room, and that depends—how many did you take out? I got four."

"Five here," he answers. "Which just leaves one. But he's got a clear line of sight down the hall, we can't get a shot without him taking us out."

"I don't have a weapon, or I'd offer to shoot him in the back," I reply. I creep forward, using one of the fallen mooks as cover, and peek around the corner. Sure enough, there he is, crouching to provide less of a target, watching the hallway. I pull back as quick and quiet as I can to avoid his turning his attention to me, and nearly stumble as my foot catches on the nearest goon's arm.

An arm that ends in a hand that's still clutching his gun.
D'oh!

"Belay that last bit," I tell Ned, squatting and setting the
phone on the ground so I can use both hands to pry at the
goon's fingers. It takes some doing—for a squash he's got one
helluva grip!—but finally I get the gun loose. It looks a lot
like the one Tall confiscated from those two in the warehouse
earlier, and the shape's familiar enough I don't think I'll have
any problems using it. "Okay, I'm armed," I report. "I'll shoot
at him from here—if I take him out, great, and if not, well,
he'll probably turn toward me and give you the opening. On
three?"

"Sure," Ned answers, and says something else but I'm
already counting.

One.

Two.

Three!

I shoot the guy in the head.

Hm. It definitely connects, and punches him back a step,
almost knocking him down, but he rights himself, swivels, and
glares at me. Uh, maybe there's an intensity setting on here I
missed, and the guy I took it from was a closet pacifist so his
was on Tickle or Mildly Annoy instead of Kill and Rend and
Dismember? Or maybe the black edging gives this guy some
kind of deflection quality, like mirrored paint. Either way, he's
still up and now he's pissed.

So I shoot him again.

At this point, I figure I don't have much to lose.

Another hit, another growl of pain, but still up.

Yikes.

He raises his own gun, grinning at me in that way dogs do right before they take a bite out of you and sharks do all the time because they're always about to take a bite out of you and school teachers do when they call on you knowing full well you weren't paying attention and were in fact asleep and drooling right through their lecture.

And then a shot hits him from the other side, staggering him sideways.

He's looking a little dazed but he still manages to aim at me—

—and gets hit again. Twice.

That's enough to make him snarl and turn back that way—

—so I shoot him. Again. Twice.

It's gotten to be like a game of tetherball now. The ball comes my way and I pound on it, sending it sailing back around, where Ned and Mary pummel it until it swings my way again, and so on.

A half dozen shots later, Super Mook finally collapses.

"What the hell was he made of?" I demand as I straighten, stick the gun in my fanny pack—in case I need it again later—and round the corner. Mary wastes no time running to me and wrapping her arms around me. Not that she was scared for her life or anything, probably she's just relieved I didn't do anything stupid and potentially fatal.

"No idea," Ned says, stepping up and holding out his fist. We fist-bump, very manly. Mary is kind enough not to roll her eyes, and her smile is genuinely amused rather than condescending.

That's one of the great things about her—despite being brilliant and gorgeous, she doesn't look down on anyone. She's cool that way. "Maybe he'd been altered more extensively than the others," Ned continues. "Or he just had a natural immunity to energy weapons. Or something." He takes a breath. "Important thing is, we stopped 'em."

"Yeah, but for how long?" I ask. "What's to stop them from sending a couple dozen more?"

Ned squats down by the Super Mook and starts waving his gizmos over the guy. "Okay," he says finally, "I think I can isolate the frequency of this energy around them." He grins at me. "Which means I can not only set up a proximity alert in case that same energy shows up again, I think I can nullify it. Anybody attacking this place will wind up just being a normal shmoe again."

I nod. "Cool. Normal shmoes I can handle." I look down at the bodies all around us. I feel like I'm on the site of some ancient, historic battle—or, given how they're all wearing suits, like I'm standing in the men's department at some store in the aftermath of a major holiday sale. I almost wanna check the mooks' sleeves for Clearance tags. "What about them?"

"We should return them to their homeworld," Mary insists. "Let the local authorities mete out punishment. We can provide holding facilities—permanent ones—in the event they require such assistance."

"Works for me," I assure her. I don't want these guys in my house any longer than necessary. "You tie them up tight and we'll haul them back in. Ned, see what you can do about getting that interference field up and running. And don't forget to set that wormhole alert, too." I'm already edging out of the room and back down the hall. "Me, I'm gonna whip up some food for us to nibble on the way." Hey, fighting off a home invasion is hard work!

Chapter Nineteen
Hands inside this reality at all times!

"Glad to see you're still in one piece" is how Tall greets me as I rematerialize near the arcade that was once Ned's planet's capital building. He's leaning against a lamppost, looking all cool and hypervigilant, with some big-ass rifle thing cocked back over his shoulder. I have no idea where he found that— maybe he had it delivered while we were gone? I'm sure there're places that'll deliver guns for the right price, and on a world like this that was crafted by mobsters maybe that's even the norm. Maybe it's easier to get gun delivery than pizza. Maybe when you order a gun they send along a pizza just as a thank you, like the cans of soda you get when you order Chinese. And maybe Tall didn't eat all of his pizza yet, and there's still a few slices around somewhere.

Maybe I didn't eat enough back at the Matrix building before we headed out. I wanted to order some food but Ned and Mary said it'd take too long. I should've had the Grays order it for me—they can teleport us across the galaxy in an instant, there's no reason they couldn't pick up some crab rangoons and moo shu shrimp at the same time!

"Yeah, thanks for the concern," I tell Tall, doing my best

manly swagger as I cross the street to him. Let me just tell you, it's really hard pulling off a manly swagger when your head is the size and weight of an industrial air conditioner. Try balancing one of those on your noggin and see how cool and hip *you* can walk! "We're fine, they only sent ten of 'em after us."

Ha ha, I love it when Tall gives me Stare Number Eight: "Okay, that's actually really impressive but your head's already the size of Jupiter so I'm going to downplay my admiration and settle for a raised eyebrow and a comradely nod." I don't get it very often, so I savor it when I do.

"Ten?" He says, and looks past me to Ned, whose confirming nod I see out of the corner of my eye. "Not too shabby." Then, because it's Tall, he smirks. "What'd you do, talk 'em to death?"

"Actually, I shot about a third of them," I tell him, "plus I bashed a few over the head with a thermos. Piece of cake." There's a mailbox not far from his lamppost, and I lean against that. "How's it been here?"

All levity instantly vanishes from his demeanor—it's like one of those doodlepads and somebody's just lifted the little sheet on the front, resetting Mr. Graniteface back to his usual stony demeanor. "Not good," he says, like I couldn't guess that from his expression. "We've lost a few other places in the area, like the dry cleaners down on the corner and the appliance store across the street. Worse, though, are the ones that're still here." He points with his free hand. "Like that one."

Naturally, I turn and look. Yes, I'm the kind of guy who falls for "Look! Air!" Which still isn't as bad as my roommate freshman year, who literally fell for it every single time—even if those times were only seconds apart. I always thought it was amazing he could put one foot in front of the other, or breathe, but you gotta love autonomic responses. And of course he wanted to be a teacher "so he could help educate the youth of tomorrow." The mind boggles.

Anyway, the place Tall indicates is another Rex Drugs, like the one I saw across from what should have been Gus's back when all this started. Only, that place was all trippy and dopey and mellow. This one definitely . . . isn't.

For starters, it looks like Goths took it over with a vengeance. There's black curtains in the windows, spiked bars along the windowbox and doorframe, heavy chains dangling from the roof. Candles must light the interior because the glow leaking through the curtains is dim, red, and flickering. The vials and jugs that would've looked right at home in a head shop have been replaced by a mad scientist's kit, all angular and sinister, and there's a Jacob's ladder arcing electricity across the doorframe, like if you're above the recommended height you can enter but you'll get one hell of a static charge on the way through. I sure as hell wouldn't go in there, and I'm betting their stock is now way light on the psychedelics and really high on the poisons and depressants.

"There are places like that all over," Tall explains quietly, his voice as somber as his look. "And it's definitely spreading. Heidi's out trying to get a sense of just how far. I'd say the invaders are consolidating their hold, remaking as much around them as they can so they've got a stronger beachhead."

"Yeah, sandbagging to prevent the tide from washing them

back out to sea," I mutter, and despite everything almost laugh when that earns me a Number Six. "What? I grew up on Long Island, remember? Trust me, tides and flooding and that stuff I definitely understand."

Ned's been quiet this whole time, which isn't like him—normally he talks even more than I do, especially if you count the running near-murmur of him thinking aloud, wondering about various new projects, debating the merit of any new tech he finds, and pondering the nearest place to eat. "Hey, you okay, big guy?" I ask him.

"I think I better go get my family," he answers. "If it's as bad as you said, I should take them somewhere safe."

"Yeah, sure, man." I hop up from the mailbox. "I'll give you a hand. Tall can mind the beachhead or whatever. Are your parents still around? You got siblings, cousins, crazy old aunts?" Everybody's got a crazy old aunt, it seems to me. It's really not a question of "do you?" so much as where they fall on the range from "delightfully kooky" to "scarily apocalyptic" to "eerily robotic."

But Ned shakes his head. "Naw, my brother and sister are both older'n me, they can take care of themselves," he says, and I remember he mentioned them before. "And my folks passed a long time ago. No, I mean my family. My wife and kids."

"Wait, what?" Tall's staring too, and this is one I've never seen before, a look of complete and utter shock like somebody just told him mustaches were actually made of candy and penguins were poodles in fancy bird suits and if you licked your own eyebrows enough you could fly. I'm sure I've got a similar expression. "Okay, hold the phone, Charlie. Hell, hold the whole goddamn network! You're married? With kids?"

He nods. Doesn't look embarrassed at getting found out or amused at catching us so flatfooted we might as well be nailed to the floor, just matter-of-fact, like it's every day you pull a jaw-dropping surprise on your closest friends. "Sure. There's Nessa and then there's Nellie, Neil, and Naomi."

"This is unbelievable." I'm still staring at him. So is Tall. Even Mary is, and she's usually really careful about her manners. "You've got a wife and three kids! Why didn't you say anything? Were you *ever* going to say anything?"

He shrugs. "It never came up."

"It never came up? Come on, man! It's not like we haven't hung out together for months and months! Not like we didn't go to prison together—and escape! Save the universe! Save Earth! Watch tons of crappy TV! Eat tons of crazy-ass food! All this time, not once when I said 'so, what's going on?' did it occur to you to say 'oh, so my wife and kids who I've never mentioned before just did X, Y, and Z'?"

And he shrugs. "I don't really talk about them much."

"No kidding!" I'm practically dancing circles around him now, I'm so worked up. "Well, let's go! I wanna meet 'em! I want to see what kind of woman can win my pal's heart, or at least earn some kind of partial stake in it anyway, and whether his three kids are twigs off the old stalk. Let's get this show on the road!"

He nods and holds up a hand, another little doohickey in it. A second later one of his planet's wacky aircabs descends to the street right in front of us. "Come on." He tugs open the door and hops in. I glance back at Mary and Tall, who both gesture me to go on.

"We've got this," Tall tells me. "Help Ned get his family out." Mary nods.

"Okay. Back soon with the whole passel of Nedlings." I slip inside, pull the door shut behind me, and the cab immediately shoots up and then jets forward. I don't know if I'll ever get used to these things—and I can only imagine what would happen if the NYC Taxi and Limousine Commission ever got their hands on one. It'd be like catching a ride in a fighter jet. With a meter.

"So, how long've you and Nessa been together?" I ask Ned as we cruise toward the address he fed the cab. "How'd you meet? What's she like? Does she ever wonder why you never talk about work or bring any of your work buddies home?"

"Fourteen years," Ned answers, gazing out the window at the buildings streaking past below. "We met in a tech class—I'd gotten my degree and was earning some dough as a teaching assistant, she was taking the class and was completely hopeless at it." A sweet little smile crosses his face. "She still is. As far as bringing people home, no, she doesn't. I'm actually not home much."

"What does that mean, 'not home much'?" I ask. Yes, I should've been a therapist. Or a talk show host. Let's see Dave or Jimmy or Conan compete with a duckbill, baby! "Every other weekend? Once or twice a month?"

He shrugs. "I come back a few times a year."

I study him. "Did you just say 'a few times a year'? As in,

you only see your wife and three kids every few months?" He nods. "Dude, what is wrong with you? That's not a family, it's a time-share!"

"I don't like being tied down," is all he says.

"Tied down! Come on, man, this is your family we're talking about," I tell him. "Yeah, it ties you down, but it's the bonds of love and all that jazz."

Ned turns to look at me. "You're real close to your family," he points out. "And that's cool. But I was never like that. I need to be able to go where I want, when I want. Nessa gets that. I call at least once a week, so the kids see me regularly. I'm just not actually there in person much."

I shake my head but there's not much point arguing. Obviously Ned's got some very different ideas about family from mine. I guess as long as it works for him and her and them that's fine, though I can't imagine his kids wouldn't like to actually see their dad in the leafy green flesh a bit more often. Though maybe vegetables just aren't as clingy? I really have no idea—I don't eat a lot of salad.

The cab drops—leaving my stomach up somewhere around skyscraper level—and comes to a halt, a chime indicating we've reached our destination. I haul the door open and hop back out onto solid ground as Ned pays, and then once he's out and the cab's gone we turn together to admire his family's home.

It looks like an igloo with a bad case of the mange.

That's my first thought. My second is, "Why is there a giant grassy mound here and shouldn't Ned get out the weed-whacker and really have a good go at it?"

My third is, "The people're all vegetables, it would've been cool if the houses were all meat!" Though admittedly that was partially just because, if that had been the case, I would've snuck off around back and devoured Ned's garden shed.

No such luck, though, as he heads straight for the grassy mound. "I've been calling," he says over his shoulder as he walks, "but Nessa isn't picking up. Which isn't all that surprising for her, exactly—I'm not sure she really understands mobile phones—but of course all three kids are tech-savvy like their old man, and they'd have answered by the third ring normally. It's weird." It's weird enough seeing Ned as a family guy, but seeing him all serious now is also just bizarre for me. It's upsetting the natural order of my personal cosmos, and I plain don't like it!

Closer in, I can see that the house is a giant dome and does have some sort of ivy growing all over it. There're plenty of windows along the front but only a few higher ones in back, most likely because it's easier to see trouble coming from in front. It looks nice, even cozy, and with the multiple antennae poking up I'm confident the whole place is wired to the gills.

What's weird, though, is how quiet it is. I know there were an awful lot more of us than most families, but even so if he's got three kids they should be running around in there, slamming doors in each others' faces, banging on the windows to get his attention, digging out escape routes to India and beyond.

I'm not seeing any of that. Not even a stray scream or a muffled squeal or the twitch of a curtain.

"Uh, you've got a key, right?" I ask as we reach the front door.

"Naturally." He produces a small, blunt square and flicks it toward the door with his thumbnail. The square floats forward, rotating lazily as it closes the gap, and finally melts against the door like butter on a hot day. A second later there's a pop and a hiss and the door opens.

"Nessa?" Ned calls as we enter. "You here?"

No answer.

We scan the house quickly, splitting up to cover more ground. "I got nobody," I report back finally. "No wife, no kids, no English sheepdog with lovable mannerisms. You?"

"No." Now Ned doesn't just look concerned—he looks downright petrified.

"Would she've told you if she decided to take the kids someplace?" I wonder out loud.

"Absolutely!" Ned pivots, taking in the whole of the empty house, and frowns. "I don't like this," he tells me. "I don't like it at all."

"Yeah, definitely not getting a good feeling," I reply, An extremely unpleasant thought hits me. "The invaders know who I am and how to find me," I state slowly, hoping to hell I'm wrong like usual. "Could they've figured out who you are, too? Mary once said the Greys protect her, probably same with you, so the invaders and their goons can't get to you. Not directly."

We both turn to look about the empty house again.

If the invaders wanted to take Ned out of the picture, but couldn't get to him easily, going after his family would be the next best thing.

Chapter Twenty
They were here just a minute ago

"Nobody takes my family and gets away with it!" I've never seen
Ned pissed off before. I didn't actually know broccoli could turn
that wine-dark, but it kinda works for him. "Let's go!"

"Uh, sure, yeah, okay," I agree, skipping along after him as
we head out of his house and back out onto the front walk. I'm
not actually skipping, of course—this is way too serious for that.
More hopping from foot to foot. Hey, it's a lot of weight to put
down on those things! "But how're we gonna do that, exactly?
Do you have a 'Family Recall' button somewhere?"

He grins at me. "Close," he says, pulling out a little round
jobbie that looks an awful lot like one of those car-alarm key
fobs, only with a little screen in it. "I got them on CPS."

"Really?" But of course he does. And I can't say I blame
him, either. CPS is Cosmic Positioning System, the galactic
version of GPS back home, and if Ma could've had us chipped
she would've done it in a heartbeat. She actually tried once,
until they explained that a) it was only for dogs and cats and b)
it didn't actually let you locate them, it just showed the owner's
name and address if you ran it under a chip reader. She wasn't
worried about other people knowing we were hers—usually

she was tempted to deny it!—but being able to track our every move all the time? She'd never have to leave the recliner! "Well, fire it up then, man! Let's locate this family unit and bring it home!"

Ned taps a command into the jobbie and the screen lights up, showing a grouping of four dots plus a fifth one I assume is us. It zooms in, clearly reorienting itself, and by crowding in next to him I see a city map overlay the image. They're still in the city, then—that's a good sign. But then the image goes fuzzy like Grandma's old TV from the 50s that she refuses to get rid of because "who needs all that newfangled color anyways?"

"What's wrong with it?" I ask him. "Low battery? That happens to me all the time."

Ned frowns. "Naw, it draws off ambient energy, never needs to recharge. Something's interfering with the signal." He taps it off then on again but it gives the same result— clearly within the city but fuzzy after that. "Shouldn't be, though. The signal's on a subatomic frequency, cuts through any material anywhere. Only thing could mess with it is a black hole."

"Or a wormhole?" Wow, I'm getting "that's right, you do have a brain!" looks all over today! If this keeps up I could get a swelled head, and the thought of my head getting any bigger is a scary one even for me. I'd only be able to ride in convertibles from now on! I'd need open-air stadium seating everywhere I went! My bathroom would have to be like an opera house!

Anyway, Ned's already signaling for a cab, and only a few seconds later one lands. Maybe it's the same one as before, I really can't tell, though that might make sense—it could've lingered to see if we needed a return ride. New York cabbies are never like that, but there's sure a lot less traffic here even with all the reality-bending going on. I wonder if the invaders have their own set of traffic laws, and if they're gonna start imposing those as well? Maybe there'll finally be a consistent "right turn on red" rule, because I know that's always irked me—sometimes it seems like the law-makers just tossed a coin over that one, heads for "yes," tails for "no," and on its side for "not usually but we'll allow it at random times or in specific locations just to really confuse you."

Ned's already placing another call as we hop into the cab and tell it to head back toward the arcade. "Tall?" he says—yes, we all call him that now. "Listen, is there a place near you with a whole lot of mooks guarding it? Oh." He glances up at me. "The arcade. Right." Well, that figures. "Great, we're on our way. Explain when we get there."

"You think they're in the arcade?" I'm already nodding even before he does, like a weird time-delay. "Yeah, that makes sense—it's right at the wormhole, so it'd be where they holed up. And where they'd keep high-value hostages." Hey, I watch a lot of *SVU* and *CSI* and all those other acronyms! My favorite is *PAW*, Passive-Aggressive Widowers, which is a bunch of old guys sitting around making backhanded compliments at each other, but that's not really applicable here. "So what's the plan, then? How're we gonna do this?"

In answer, Ned pulls out his three-in-one ray gun—I guess he never disassembled it after the fight at the Matrix, which makes sense. "The plan," he tells me without even a trace of humor, "is to go in there and get my family back."

"Whoa, whoa, Dirty Ned," I reply, pushing the gun down so he doesn't accidentally shoot me or the cabbie or anything. I've seen too many movies not to worry about that sort of thing, it's a wonder with all those films that anybody wants to drive a taxi anymore. "I admire your gusto and all that jazz, but don't you think we need a little more of a battle plan that that? Look how well 'charge!' worked at the Alamo. Or Omaha Beach. Or the OK Corral." I pause. "Wait, hold on, it did work on some of those, didn't it? Never mind."

Ned's still not laughing, not that I blame him. It's his kids, after all. "What do you suggest?" he asks instead. "We sneak in around the back?"

"Ooh, sneaking—yeah, good idea! I'm all in favor of a good sneak!" I glance at my reflection in the ubiquitous privacy shield between the passenger section and the cabbie's seat up front, which doesn't really provide much privacy seeing as how it's usually transparent plastic. "Oh, right, I don't sneak. I stick out like a thumbless man at a hitchhiker's convention. Never mind. You sneak, I'll distract." I scratch my bill. "Tall can provide cover."

"That could work," Ned admits slowly. He rubs at his nose with the tip of his gun and I'm really glad I didn't try that because I'd have bifurcated my bill. Trust me, there's a reason in Shop class I was usually relegated to sweeping up. But at least I still have all of my fingers, unlike a few of my classmates. Clumsy but intact—I'll take it!

"Cool." I feel much better now that we have a plan, even if it does involve me serving as bait again. Oh well, at least I get to be useful.

We're back with the others a few minutes later, and quickly explain the situation: "We think the invaders took Ned's family and they've got them in there." Told you it was quick!

Tall, of course, immediately pushes off his perch and hefts his gun. "Let's go get them back, then."

"Absolutely, big guy," I agree, " but let's not go off half-cocked, right? We've got a plan. I'll distract them, you shoot at them, and Ned goes around the back."

Tall nods. "Fine. Let's do this."

Mary stands as well—she was sitting swami-style atop the mailbox, which would look silly on a lot of people but she makes it work, like a surreal Victoria's Secret ad. "I will accompany Ned," she offers. "I can move without drawing undue attention, and will protect him from sudden assaults while he searches for his family."

"I'll let Heidi know what we're doing," Tall offers. "He can keep an eye on things out here once he's back from his reconnoiter."

"Right, it's a plan." I slap my hands together, then extend one in front of me. "Team Rescue Ned's Family on three—and, one, two, three!" Fortunately they don't leave me hanging—wouldn't that be embarrassing, it'd be like junior high all over again!—and we all put our hands in and then raise them up at "three." Ah, it's just like being back on the college football team again.

And, just like then, my job is to get pummeled a lot while the QB runs in with the ball.

Go, team.

Chapter Twenty-one
I've got quarters and
I'm not afraid to use them!

"Don't shoot, don't shoot!" I shout as I hurry across the parking lot, arms held high. "I'm here to talk!"

One of the modified mooks opens the tinted-glass door—revealing a brief look at the flashing lights of the arcade games behind him—and steps out. "What do you want?" he demands. He's got a gun in his hand but his arms are folded across his chest so right now if he pulled the trigger he'd probably perforate his own armpit. Which I'm okay with.

"World peace," I tell him, slowing now that I'm only about twenty feet away.

"What?" He glares at me. "No, what do *you* want?"

"I just told you—world peace."

"You can't have that."

"Whaddyamean, I can't have it?" I hop a little closer. "What, are you the guy in charge of doling out world peace now? Because if not, I wanna speak to the one who is! Trot him on out here and let's get this settled. I gotta tell ya, you're being a lousy host so far—you haven't offered me a seat or a nosh yet, you ask me what I want and then you tell me I can't have it? My gran would be spinning in her grave right now if she wasn't probably at spin class instead."

He blinks at me, the kind of twitchy blink you can see even behind dark sunglasses. Interesting side note: you know that vein in the forehead, the one that throbs a lot more noticeably when I talk to someone for an extended period of time? I've named Tall's Yurso, by the way. Yes, I'm a Carly Simon fan, what of it? Anyway, whatever the invaders did to mod these guys didn't change that vein any. It's still there, throbbing away. And glowing faintly through this guy's greenish skin. I've never seen Ned's do that. Maybe I haven't talked to him for long enough yet.

Anyway, after blinking the mook goes straight back to glaring. "What. Do. You. Want. To. Talk. About?" he grates out through clenched teeth. Sorry pal, if you were hoping to be intimidating I've been dealing with Tall's clenched mutterings for months now. You might as well be smiling and offering me coffee cake.

"Really, you're gonna make me say it again?" I ask him. "Fine. World peace. Seriously. What's it gonna take to get your new bosses to bug off back where they came from and leave this world in peace?"

Ah, the light dawns, as his glare changes to a smirk. "Leave? They ain't leavin', birdface. Not now, not ever. You got a problem with that?"

I get right up in his face, so close my bill is practically scraping his chin. "Me? Have I got a problem with that?" I pause to consider. "Well, some, but it's not really my place to say." This time I'm the one smirking as I step to one side, revealing Tall standing right behind me where he crept up while the guard was busy with all the glaring and vein-popping and so on. "Now, my buddy here—"

"I've definitely got a problem with it," Tall growls. Then his fist flies forward like a guided missile, nailing the mook right in the jaw so hard he'd have slammed into the arcade door if not for Tall's other hand lashing out and grabbing the guy's tie and hauling him forward again. A muffled groan escapes the mook's lips as he shudders and goes limp, falling at my feet like somebody chivalrous just tossed a cheap suit jacket across a puddle that was in my way. Only the suit jacket still has a body in it. I guess knights can't afford to be picky.

"So, hey, that worked," I say, nudging the guy with one foot. He doesn't move.

The look Tall gives me this time is one I haven't seen before, equal parts confusion, admiration, fear, and possibly constipation. "What?" I ask him.

"I'm just a little concerned," he tells me as he reaches down, retrieves the mook's gun, and shoves it into his own waistband before straightening back up, "that you've managed to turn your talent for talking people into incoherent rage into an offensive weapon. Impressed, but a little concerned."

"That's me," I agree, hauling out my own captured gun and stepping over the mook so I can reach for the door. "Most people aspire to talk others under the table. I can actually talk them into the wall and onto the floor immediately after. Though I'm pretty sure that punch helped." I grab the door and haul it open. "Shall we?"

Tall hoists his Macho Man supergun. "After you."

"Yeah, I was afraid you'd say that."

We step in, and it's like I'm instantly transported back to 1983. I actually stop and look back behind me, past Tall to where the door is just sliding shut, to make sure that hasn't happened. Hey, we're dealing with wormholes and stuff here, it's not completely unreasonable! But no, the world past the parking lot is still Ned's—at least, the newly twisted version—so it's just nostalgia and not actual time travel. Shame, because I could've used a good hot tub soak right about now.

The door shuts, I turn around and take a deep breath, sucking in that never forgotten aroma of coins, candy, spilled soda, and teen sweat, and—

—faceplant onto the cheesy black-light carpet. Courtesy of the hand that just shoved me from behind, though it felt more like I was hit by a forklift.

What the hell?

"Stay down, you idiot!" Tall hisses as he crawls up beside me. "We don't know how many more of them there are, and standing around with your mouth open like that you're a sitting duck!"

"Really?" I ask, lifting my head enough to turn and glare at him and not coincidentally spitting out rug fibers. Yuck. "You had to go there?"

He has the decency to look abashed about it for a half a second. "Just stay low and follow me," he growls and begins doing the classic military "I'm crawling on my knees and toes and elbows while holding a big-ass rifle and still somehow look all cool doing it" maneuver.

I follow with my own unique version, "I'm a pudgy, out-of-shape guy with an oversized head and an even bigger bill crawling along behind him holding out my little pop gun and trying not to shoot my pal—or me—anywhere we might need later."

Even from down here, this place brings back memories, though. We're inching past stand-up arcade games like Joust and Pac-Man and Spy Hunter, basically eye-level with the little blinking Insert Coin slots. The carpet is dark blue or black with glowing stars and planets and moons and asteroids, there are spacey ceiling fans overhead trying to keep the air moving but not making much headway given the large space and surprisingly high ceiling, and their lights aren't enough to counter the dark carpet so the whole place feels like it's permanently twilight and sparkly vampires would probably fit in just fine. I'm really hoping we don't encounter any of those, actually, but if we do I plan to start a debate about "books vs. movies" and hopefully make their little sparkly heads explode. I know mine nearly did back when Lizzie went through that—thankfully brief!—phase!

Beating down on us from all sides is the standard barrage of competing game theme songs, complete with "Are you man enough?" and "Who will survive?" and "Ultimate victory!" and so on, all in those deep and distorted announcer voices like World Wide Wrestling meets Dragonball Z. But aside from that, the whir of the fans, and the crunch of our limbs on the carpet—which does crunch, just like the old arcades I went to did—I'm not hearing anything.

"I don't hear anyone!" I shout at Tall. You have to shout to be heard at all in a place like this, and although he glares at me about it there's no way anybody who isn't standing right next to us would be able to hear us at all.

I can see the need for stealth warring within him against the desire for a strategy session, and at last the latter wins out. "I don't either!" he agrees, "but that doesn't mean they aren't laying in wait for us. They've got to have Ned's family stashed somewhere, and they can't have left only the one guy guarding them!"

"They could have if they were a bunch of total vegetables!" I holler back. Come on, I had to! Naturally my efforts are wasted, though—Tall just rolls his eyes at me and moves on. I start to follow, but my elbows and knees are killing me, and my back and neck already have dibs on ending my next life, so finally I just groan and get to my feet. If they're gonna find me I'd rather they did it when I wasn't doubled over in pain and pretending to be the world's most feathered inchworm.

Now that I'm back on my feet I scan the area. The machines are all taller than I am, of course, but not by a lot and since they're grouped in aisles you can just dart from aisle to aisle and peer down each one in turn. Which is exactly what I do.

"Nobody else out here!" I lean down to shout at Tall, having skipped past him two aisles back. Hey, even the best crawler can still get beat by a guy with a long stride.

More glaring ensues, but Tall does rise back to his full stature again. Even he's not tall enough to completely see over the machines, though. "Are you sure?" he asks.

"Yep, nobody here but us ducks. And friends."

Tall frowns and leans against the nearest machine, ironically a shoot-'em-up with a pair of bulky plastic six-shooters slung down by the coin slots—and suddenly those guns whip out of their holsters and wrap around his legs!

"What the Galaga is going on?" I shout, rushing forward and wrestling one of the guns free. It turns on me next, winding its cord around my wrist, so I snap up the gun with my bill and bite down hard.

Crunch!

The game's coils go limp, allowing both Tall and I to pull free, and I spit out broken pieces of plastic. Yuck.

But I don't exactly get time to congratulate myself on my quick thinking—or to search my pockets for a Mentos—because with a whole bunch of loud screeches and groans all of the other machines in our area start turning toward us.

"Oh crap, it's Night of the Living Arcade Games!" I shout to Tall. "They're gonna start shoving quarters up our butts and jabbing us in the nipples!" The idea of them button-mashing makes me wince, and thoughts about yanking hard on the joystick almost make me break down and cry.

"They have to catch us first!" Tall replies. He swings his gun around to his back—that's how he was carrying it before!—and wraps his hands around the top of the Galaga like he's going to give it a head squeeze, but instead he plants a foot on its buttons and clambers up onto its top. Then he reaches down and grabs my hand, hauling me up beside him. The game shudders and twists about, trying to figure out where we went, but I'm guessing its screen is its only sensory input and there's no way it's spotting us up here.

"Nice one, bro!" I tell Tall, holding up my hand for a fist bump. He nods instead, but I don't miss the little smirk now gracing his granite face. From up here we can see the whole room, of course, and I quickly do a one-eighty, careful to keep both feet firmly planted. The top isn't all that big, and Tall steps over onto the Joust next door to make more room. "Hey, look!" I point toward a door at the far back corner of the room. It's says "Arena."

"Aw, don't tell me," I half-mutter, half-whine. It makes sense, though. Most arcades back then had a PhaserTag arena if they could afford it. A place where teens—and younger kids, provided nobody was paying too close attention—could run around and shoot at each other with no repercussions beyond damaged reputations and the occasional skinned knee or bloody lip? It was the arcade equivalent to printing their own money! And of course if you were holding somebody prisoner in an arcade you'd really only have three places to put them: the office, the bathrooms, or the arena. All three of which would be behind that same door.

Tall nods, clearly having reached the same conclusion I did, and jumps from Joust to Spy Hunter on the next aisle. I follow his lead with a resounding thud and wobble but manage to stay atop Asteroids. Take that, 250 lives!

Next he moves to Tempest and I stick the landing on Donkey Kong. Ha ha, who's jumping now, Mario? From there it's Dig Dug for Tall and Centipede for me, and then we're hopping down and rushing past the grasping arms of nearby games to grapple with the doorknob, throw the door open, and rush through.

"Don't shoot!" someone shouts from down the hallway as we appear, and Tall raises his gun toward the air just in time to avoid drilling Ned and Mary. That would've been awkward! "Any sign of 'em yet?"

"They're not on the arcade floor," I tell Ned as we converge in the center of the hall. Both of them look fine, no signs of recent enemy contact. "Any problems getting in?"

Ned shakes his head. "There was one guy standing guard by the door. Mary distracted him." Mary smiles and the ZZ Top song "Legs" immediately goes through my head. I'll just bet he was distracted! "What about you?"

"Same, one guard out front," I answer. "I don't have Mary's legs so I talked him into a stupor and then Tall hit him." Tall nods, evidently still a little discomfited by just how well that tactic had worked. "Nobody else in the main area, but the machines themselves just attacked us. We had to go rooftop-jumping, Tick style, to get over here."

Tall's been studying this hall while we were comparing notes. "Office and bathrooms on this side," he points out, "Arena on that one." At the far end is a glass door that obviously leads out back—I guess Ned and Mary were being more cautious because they must have only just gotten in. "Let's check the office first."

We don't bother with stealth at this point—Tall kicks in the door and pretty much cartwheels into the room while the rest of us crowd around the doorway. But it looks just like a cheesy arcade office would, one big wooden desk in the middle of the small room, one smaller, crappier wood-and-metal desk up against one wall next to some battered file cabinets, and a table fan and a mini-fridge perched atop them. There's nobody in here. The mini-fridge is empty except an opened container of yogurt and some wilted celery, which around here might just count as a voodoo doll. I leave 'em both, though it takes some effort on my part.

We check the bathrooms next, setting aside any squeamishness to check both as a group, and they're exactly what you'd expect—standard tiling, basic sinks, metal stalls around basic toilets. Nobody in either of 'em.

Which just leaves the Arena.

"All right," Tall announces, stopping the rest of us back out in the hall by the Arena door. "If this is set up following the usual pattern there'll be a sign-up area just past here. From there you've got the armory where you suit up, then the briefing room alongside it. Then there's the arena itself—roughly fifty feet square, two stories tall, walkways around the edges, a few sniping posts scattered around the floor. Standing panels set at random angles to each other throughout, most of 'em with shoot-through openings, so keep your heads down. Best bet is to immediately step to one side as soon as you're in, stay flat against the wall, and inch your way around until you hit stairs to the walkway. Don't go up, though! That's a rookie mistake— actually makes you an easy target, and the walkways never go all the way around. Stay under them instead—makes you harder to hit, it's about the only real cover you'll find."

That's one of the longest speeches I've ever heard Tall make when he wasn't lecturing me on what I'd done wrong, and when I see the gleam in his eye I groan. "Oh, don't tell me, you were one of them, weren't you?" I accuse him. "One of those PhaserTag nuts."

"Omega-level regional champion," he agrees proudly, "three years running." Then he scowls. "And I would've had the nationals too, if not for Betty Chang from Boston!"

"You got your butt whupped by a little girl from Beantown?" I can't help laughing at that one, but Tall is definitely not amused.

"She was ten going on twenty-five but looked eight," he claims, "and I swear she'd had SEAL training before! Do you have any idea how small the strike zone is on someone who's barely four feet tall and probably forty pounds soaking wet? It's unfair!"

"Okay, okay, don't get all in a snit about it," I warn him. "We get it, you kick butt at this stuff, which we kinda figured you would. Can we go get Ned's family and leave the Twisted Land of Evil Arcade Games behind us now?"

"Absolutely." He glances over his shoulder at the three of us, all holding our weapons about as enthusiastically as a new parent who's just realized his pride and joy has that "not so fresh even for a cursed ancient bog" smell, and grins. "Just follow me."

This is a plan I'm surprisingly okay with.

Chapter Twenty-two
This is *not* tackle football!

We haven't even all cleared the doorway when the first mook tackles us.

By "us," of course I mean Tall, since he's out in front. Which is fine—he does this little hop thing like on a trampoline, the mook sails beneath him and crashes into the wall, and then Tall lands squarely on the guy's back. Given the way the new foot rug barely groans before going limp, I'm pretty sure he won't be bothering us again any time soon.

One down, umpteen million left to go.

I don't really remember PhaserTag much—I was too poor to play it much back when I was actually a kid, and though we did mess around in the nearest Arena a lot in high school and again in college we were usually drunk so it's all a laser-lit blur—but so far this one matches what Tall said. We're in a big room with a long table over against one side, clearly where you sign up. The other side of the room has cheap plastic chairs in neat rows so you can sit while you fill out your forms.

Or it would if those hadn't been shoved to the side to make room for all the goons packed in here.

It's like rush hour on the subway going through Little Italy.

Or that stupid veggie crisper drawer in the bottom of the fridge after your mom has been to the store, all crammed full of nice fresh fruits and veggies you'll do anything to avoid having to eat. There's not a lot of light in here, especially with the dark walls and carpeting, but I count at least twenty invader-modified goons standing there facing us, all in their dark suits and hats and shades. All carrying guns.

If this is the championship match I'm ready to concede. I'll even give up on getting my registration fee back.

Except that Ned's family is somewhere behind these guys, which means quitting ain't an option.

I look around for anything we can use to take these guys out fast. There's the table behind us, sure, but by the time we grab it they'll have put so many holes in us we'll look like a colander collection. I glance around again. Man, they're really packed in tight! If only I had a bowling ball I'm pretty sure I could get a couple good strikes easy, but wouldn't you know it, I left that in my other "storm the arcade" outfit back at the Matrix.

I do have my head, though. Which is way bigger than any bowling ball. Can't exactly detach it and throw it, but I can improvise. It's what I do best.

"Hey, look!" I shout, pointing back behind the goons. "Is that Old Blue-Eyes?"

They all turn, and I launch myself forward—then deliberately cross my ankles so I trip over my own two feet.

Hey, do anything often enough, you get to be an expert at it.

As I hit the floor I pull my arms in tight, mummy style. The air explodes out of my lungs with a loud "oomph!" but by then

I'm already rolling forward like the world's first feathered log—and these guys are the little rocks and twigs and shell-shocked squirrels right in my path.

I hear a few of 'em shout just as I slam into the first row, but gunfire from behind me tells me my buddies have my back. Like always.

Then there're pants and shiny shoes flailing everywhere around me. I get kicked a few times but I'm doing a lot more damage than I'm getting so I just keep rolling along. Finally I come up against the far wall and stop. For a minute I just lay there, breathing. I don't hear any more shooting, so I figure that's a good sign.

"Everybody okay?" I call out. I'd look around but right now that would be too much work.

"We're good!" Tall replies. "You?"

"I won't be breakdancing any time soon," I answer, "but I think I'm okay, yeah." I slowly lever myself up into a sitting position. There's Tall, Ned, and Mary all looking at me, and a mound of suited bodies and limbs between us. "Man, did I do all that?"

"Well, we helped a bit," Ned corrects. "But most of it, yeah." He grins at me. "That's using yer head, fer sure!"

"Good tactic, cutting 'em off at the knees," Tall agrees. He reaches me in two long strides, grasps my hand, and hauls me to my feet like I was made of Styrofoam. If I could make that horrible squeaking sound at him right now, I totally would. "Brief us next time, though, yeah?"

I nod. "Will do." He lets me go and then has to catch me by

the shoulder as I wobble a little. "I'm good." Then Mary's there, ducking under my other arm to help support me. Yeah, definitely good now. Hey, I just took out an entire room full of bad guys—I've earned some snuggle time!

"There'll be more in the Arena itself," Tall warns, glancing past the guys on the floor to the wide double doors in the far wall. "Maybe not this many, though. I'm sure they thought they'd stop us here."

"Nobody ever counts on a rolling duckman," I declare proudly. "We're the ninjas of the alien abductee world." I gesture toward the doors. "Let's go take out the rest of these guys, find Ned's family, and bring 'em home!" We don't quite cheer at that—too somber in here still—but everyone's nodding and we all look nicely hopeful as we march to the doors, fling them wide open, and storm into the Arena.

The first volley of shots almost takes Tall's head off.

"Find cover!" he shouts, diving to the floor off to one side. The rest of us follow. Mary and I wind up against a panel, and from here I can see Ned and Tall. They're both okay, though Tall takes off his trucker cap and stares at it mournfully. It looks like it was carved from Swiss cheese.

"You'll pay for that!" he declares, shoving the perforated headgear back on and hoisting his gun. He starts shooting wildly into the Arena, and I have to shout at him to stop.

"Tall! Careful, man! Ned's family, remember?"

"Oh." He stops shooting and gives Ned a guilty look. "Right. Sorry." Then he sets his jaw and climbs back to his feet, crouching to stay behind an L-shaped set of panels there. "Come on."

We stand too, and all ready our weapons. That barrage took care of our earlier euphoria. Now we're all business.

"Aim high," Tall instructs softly. "Snipers on the walkways first." He peeks around the panel and lifts his barrel. "Ready?" We all nod. "Now!"

This time there's shooting on both sides. Tall takes off around the panels, heading off to the side, and we all follow, firing our weapons up and toward the edges of the room. I think I hear a few groans but it's hard to tell with all the shots ringing in my ears. A minute later we're flattened against a wall, some sort of narrow overhang above us. The walkway. We're under it, just like Tall told us to be.

Only thing is, I don't see Tall.

Crap.

My first thought is, they cut him down while he was covering us. But I just don't see that happening—I'm sorry, but Tall's not the kind of guy who's gonna get mowed down by a bunch of tubers and legumes and whatnots in suits. It's like when I jaywalk in front of a car and tell it "sorry, you're not a Porsche or a Lotus or a Ferrari, you're not allowed to hit me."

Hey, guy's gotta have his standards.

Anyways, Tall's too good to get caught out like that here. My guess is, he's snuck off on his own to take out more of these mooks. Which means we've got to keep moving and draw their fire so he has a chance to get the drop on 'em. Which is why I tell Ned and Mary, "Okay, we stay under this as long as we can, got it? Shoot at anything that moves and isn't wearing a trucker hat. Let's go."

We hear shouting somewhere as we start our little trek, but I can't tell what they're saying or even exactly where it's coming from. This place plays tricks on the eyes, with its fog and black light and lasers, and those and the panels are messing with sounds as well, throwing them every which way and distorting their direction. I figure the best thing is just not to worry about it, so instead I concentrate on hugging the wall and watching for anyone coming.

When a goon's sunglass-wearing face pops up behind one of the panels not ten feet away, I plug him with a shot to the forehead and keep moving.

Another appears in the cut-out window of a different panel, and Mary's shot nails him in the throat. He drops with a gurgle and is replaced by a different mook, who earns himself a blast across the eyes and cheeks from Ned. He goes down, too.

Above us I hear pounding footsteps, then a thump, and then a louder thump. I'm pretty sure that was the noise a mook makes when he falls down. I knew Tall would take care of it!

We keep going, and come to a spot where there's a panel shielding us from the rest of the Arena floor. A panel with a cut-out in the upper half. Gesturing for Ned and Mary to follow me, I duck down so I'm below that opening and get right up behind the panel. They crowd in next to me. And then we wait.

There's some shouting, and some running, and then a dark shape blocks the light from beyond.

I point my gun up and angled outward slightly and shoot.

The shape disappears.

Several more try to creep up and peek in, and we shoot each

of them in turn. Then, when there's a pause in the action, we hurry across the empty space beyond to the next partition—and wait there until another group of goons rushes the first partition. We shoot them in the back and continue on.

Okay, I hate to admit it, but I'm starting to see the appeal here.

We round the corner of the room, still staying under the walkway, the occasional thud above reassuring us that Tall continues to take care of the threats on high. A few more mooks try rushing us, but the walkway gives us good cover above and a solid wall behind and some coverage in front so we're actually really defensible—all we have to do each time is duck down behind a partition and pick the goons off as they get close.

Then we run out of walkway.

There's stairs in front of us, leading up there. And beyond them is the back end of the room, which is completely exposed. Through the stairs, which are mesh platforms on bare metal legs, we can clearly see the nearby corner.

And the four people sitting huddled there, one big and three small.

"That's them!" Ned shouts, and practically dives over me in his hurry to reach them. I grab him by the arm and haul him back.

"I know, dude. And they look fine," I tell him. "A little freaked out, but these places always do that to me, too. But look where they are. There's no cover at all there. If you go to 'em right now, the goons'll cut you to pieces right in front of 'em."

Mary nods. "We are within reach," she promises Ned, "and

we know they are safe. Now we must be smart and careful and eliminate the rest of their captors so we may escort them out safely."

"Yea, what she said." I look around some more. There's a second walkway on the wall past the corner, with stairs leading up to it. "I'd have somebody waiting on those stairs," I tell them, pointing over there. "They'd have a clear view of the corner and of the walkway above us, and could probably see right over all the partitions, too." I frown. "But that's not gonna be enough. If we take those guards out, we're home free. They'd have to have another plan."

Look, planning's not exactly my strong suit. I try putting myself in the bad guys' heads. They're drones, altered to carry out the invaders' orders. They're cold and cruel and ruthless. They'll do anything to win.

Including play dirty.

And, thanks to growing up the way I did, that's something I know all about.

I reach past Ned, raise my gun, and—with a quick silent prayer that I'm right—I shoot the four figures in the corner. One, two, three, four.

"No!" Ned looks ready to pounce on me but visibly restrains himself. "What'd you do?"

"Saved our asses," I answer. "Look!"

We all turn to stare at the corner again. The four figures there are slumped over now, knocked out by my shots. And now that they are, we can just make out their dark clothes, their angular limbs, and the sunglasses askew on their pale faces.

They're mooks. All four of 'em.

"It was too easy," I explain in the face of Ned's shock. "They wouldn't leave your wife and kids here unsupervised. But they would make us think they were, so that we'd rush over and rescue them." I look over at the other walkway where it disappears up along the wall heading into the room's far corner. "I'd have them up there, all the way in the corner, with guards on either side. A real veggie sandwich."

Ned nods. "So how do we get to them, then?" he asks. "Won't they just shoot us if try for those stairs?"

"Absolutely." I study the stairs, then the walkway, and finally the walkway above us. Then I grin. "Yo, what all can your wacky piecemeal gun do, exactly? 'Cause I get the feeling the answer is gonna be a lot more than slicing, dicing, and Juliennes!"

Which is why, a few minutes later, I step out and start shooting while Ned ducks down low and darts across to the space beneath that other walkway. Mary's beside me, also blasting away, and the goons happily shoot right back at us. They keep it going a full minute or so after we've taken cover again.

"Let's give him a few minutes, then do it again," I suggest. Mary agrees. And, a few minutes later, we once again do our best Butch-and-Sundance impression, only minus the whole "charging out to die" part. I may not be as pretty as either Paul or Robert, but at least I'm smart enough to know the suicide charge isn't always the best option.

There's a loud tearing sound somewhere off to one side, then another, and then a series of thuds. "Now!" I tell Mary, and we step out and start shooting again, making sure all eyes are on us. We do that for another minute before hiding, and then we just wait.

A few more minutes go by before we hear footsteps approaching. "Don't shoot, it's us!" Ned whispers loudly. I raise my gun so the barrel's just visible through the cutout and wave it at him.

Then he's back beside us—and this time he's not alone.

"DuckBob, Mary, this is Nessa," Ned tells us proudly. His wife is taller than he is—which isn't hard—and slimmer—also not exactly grounds for Guinness—with a big head of curly green hair like a garden Afro. Apparently Ned not only found the perfect woman for him, she's even the same veggie type! Which I'm sure made a lot of people happy.

"Hey, good to meetcha," I tell her, offering my hand. Instead she lunges forward and wraps me in a big hug.

"Thank you so much." She's got a nice, soft voice, like my elementary school assistant librarian who was a mom herself and volunteered there to be close to her kids but who always had time for the other students, too. Even little boys who weren't all that great at reading and didn't like getting teased about it so stayed away from books whenever possible. She taught me to read properly, giving up her own lunch hour to work with me until I could keep up with the other kids. I still think about her every time I open a book—especially if there are pictures.

"Yeah, of course," I tell Nessa. "Hey, Ned's like family, which makes you like family, and that's good because I like family, and no way were we leaving any family, his or mine, here." Okay, time to stop talking now. I peer down at the trio of kids clustered around Ned like little leafy puppies, jumping up on him from all sides. "Cute kids. Everybody okay?"

"Great," Ned assures me. "Worked like a charm."

"Cool." It had occurred to me that the walkways were just panels attached to the frames. If you could cut through whatever nuts and bolts connected them, the panels would drop down into the space under the walkway—and into the arms of whoever was waiting there.

Why go up and over when you can do under and through instead?

"Okay, so how do we get out of here?" I mutter. We're still by one of the back corners, and I don't exactly love the idea of having to wade through the whole Arena again. If only there was another door, but of course the last thing the arcade owners want is a way for kids to sneak in and out unseen.

Then again, this isn't a real arcade. At least, it doesn't belong here in this spot on this world. It was created from whole cloth by the invaders to fill the space where trattoria/capitol building used to sit.

Which means I don't have to care what the owner would want—or about keeping this place undamaged for his return.

I raise my gun, level it—and swivel instead, so I'm aiming at the outer wall.

And then I let 'er rip.

The first blast tears through the panels covering the wall, those big padded cushions that dull sound and also keep you from hurting yourself if you slam into them. The second shot starts eating away at the materials beyond. Fortunately this is an arcade, not a bunker—its walls are masonboard and plywood and plaster and wood, not concrete and steel and stone. Ned immediately groks my plan and starts shooting with me, while Mary keeps her gun turned back toward the rest of the Arena and any goons trying to sneak up on us, and after only a few seconds of our combined efforts we start seeing daylight. Literally.

"It's working!" Ned shouts.

"I know!" I shout back. "Keep going!" We do, and the hole gets bigger and bigger. "Tall!" I shout over my shoulder. "We're cutting our way out! Get your butt over here or get left behind!"

A minute later there's a thump above us, and then the whole walkway creaks as a big shape swings down from above and lands beside us. "Smart," Tall admits, adding his firepower to our own. He's procured a second gun somewhere, presumably from one of the goons, and uses that to help Mary fend them off while his big gun tears massive chunks out of the wall, and now we've got a gap big enough for even my swollen mug to fit through. "Go!"

I nod to Ned and he grabs his wife and kids and hustles them out through the hole. Mary's next, then me, with Tall bringing up the rear and now firing both guns back into the Arena nonstop like he's a one-man artillery range. There aren't as many shots being fired back but there are still a few, and I have no idea if any of the ones we did hit are going to get back up again. I've gotta assume some of 'em will, and that there'll be more. That's kinda the point to goons and mooks, right? That there's a neverending supply of 'em, just like paperwork or dog poop or those crappy candies in the bottom of the Halloween basket that nobody ever wants to eat? For now, though, we've held them off enough for all of us to run through the parking lot and across the street, where we can finally lower our guns and catch our breath.

We did it.

"Thanks, guys," Ned tells us once we're more or less recovered from all that activity. I swear, if we did this three times a week I'd be in killer shape. "I mean it." He has an arm around Nessa and the other around his kids, and they all look pleased as punch. Or V-8, anyways.

"No sweat," I tell him. "Glad we could help." I glance over at the arcade—from this side you can't even see the hole. "The only question is, what're we gonna do now?"

I already know the proper answer isn't "wade back in there and go a few rounds on Tempest and Donkey Kong."

Which is a shame, because when Tall and I were first hunkered down in there I found a whole mess of quarters.

Chapter Twenty-three
Baa baa, blam blam

"There's gotta be somebody we can report this to," Tall grumbles, still keeping watch on the arcade like any minute all those mooks might come pouring out, spoiling for a rematch. Which they just might. Rematches and revenge are big in mob movies, at least.

Which makes me think of something else. "Hey, what about the black sheep?"

"What're you on about now?" Tall wants to know. But Ned's already nodding, his eyes so lit up I've gotta squint and look away. And it occurs to me, he's the first person I know who, if he glares at you, he really *glares* at you!

He's not glaring right now, though. "You're absolutely right!" he agrees instead. "The Black Sheep! Why didn't I think of that? That's exactly who we need!"

Now, normally whenever anyone reacts with that much enthusiasm to something I've suggested—not counting Mary because she's learned to trust my instincts, among other things—I get wary. Too often what's seemed like genuine agreement has turned out to be sarcasm, or leading me along in order to make me a punchline later. My siblings used to do that sort of thing to me all the time: "Oh, sure, Bobby, jumping off the roof with a rope tied around our waist so we swing down and around and land on the front porch sounds like a great idea—you go first." And so on. (And for the record, that would've worked, too, if not for the wind, the angle, and the fact that apparently TV antennas aren't actually strong enough to support a twelve-year-old in full motion.) But after studying Ned's face carefully—as best I can beneath the glow from his peepers—I think he actually means it.

Tall isn't buying it yet, though. "What exactly are we talking about here?" he asks both of us. "Who is this Black Sheep and how did you"—that last bit is aimed only at me—"know about him?"

I just shrug. "There's always a black sheep in mob movies," I tell him a little—you guessed it—sheepishly. "I figured maybe there'd be one here, too."

"And there is," Ned confirms again, his eyes still shining. I feel like I need sunglasses, though maybe putting sunglasses on him would be more cost-effective. "The Black Sheep is the Wiseguy Opposition leader. It's his job to keep the other Wiseguys in check, make sure nobody gets too much control, stuff like that. He's got his fingers into everything, so if the rest of the Wiseguys really are gone he should be able to step in and at least keep everything running for a bit."

"We should find this Black Sheep quickly," Mary offers, "before the invaders locate him and eliminate him."

"You got it." Ned hauls out his doodads again and summons us another cab. "I know right where he is—at least, it's where he usually is. He should still be there, provided it hasn't gone away already."

I see the way Nessa's looking at him, a little proud and a little angry and a little scared and a fair bit sad. "Hey, maybe you should stay here, get in some family time, keep the kiddies safe," I suggest. "Just tell us where we're going and we'll go talk to him." What? Family's important—they're the only ones you can trust for a really ironclad alibi.

Ned frowns, his eyes finally winking out, and I think he's gonna argue, but just then the littlest of his kids wraps a small green hand around Ned's and peers up at him with big green eyes so dark they're almost liquid black. "Please, Daddy?" the kid asks in that trembling just-on-the-verge-of-tears voice of trying-to-sway-parents little kids everywhere. "Stay here with us?"

I don't care if you tore your heart out with an old ice cream scoop and traded it from some Cadbury's eggs and a really nice fountain pen, that voice and those eyes would still get to you. Ned's no exception. "Okay," he agrees just as the cab appears. His kid squeals and wraps both arms around him like a starved octopus. "I'll program in the address for you, and tell it to bill my card so you won't have to worry about figuring out the currency exchange. Just be careful when you talk to him. He can be a little . . . prickly."

"You got it, man." I slap him on the shoulder, then tousle the little rugrat's hair. "Keep these guys safe, yeah? We'll be back soon as we can."

"I'll hang here too," Heidi offers. He was waiting for us

when we all got out, hovering anxiously by the lamppost. "Just in case." My first impulse is to ask what a cross between a Mood Ring, a terrarium, and a soap bubble can do if there's trouble, but I know better. I've actually seen Heidi handle some pretty tough customers. And it's always good to have somebody watching your back, regardless, so I just nod, as do Tall and Ned, and it's settled.

Tall, Mary, and I hop into the cab and, after getting its instructions from Ned, it bolts upward and then takes off like a bullet. We all get tossed around a bit, and I feel like that lone carrot your mom sent as part of your lunch but you didn't want to eat so you left all alone in your lunch bag to rattle around in there until you got home and your mom gave you that disappointed little sigh that meant you'd failed her somehow.

At least, that's how I'm guessing it would go. And I guess this time it's the veggies' turn to toss *us* around.

Good news is, the ride doesn't last very long—maybe ten minutes later we're touching down again, this time in front of an old-school butcher shop. There's a tailor's and a dry cleaner's alongside, so this is obviously a little downtown area, and just as obviously working class. I've seen places a lot like this in the Bronx, in Brooklyn, in Queens, and out on Long Island—you're walking along and you turn a corner and suddenly you're back in the fifties somehow, all the same storefronts and buildings, only the cars and phones and people's clothes have changed. I'm also relieved to see that none of these places look all creepified. I guess the invaders haven't found this area yet, or maybe they just didn't think it was important.

We head into the butcher shop and look around. It's exactly what you'd expect, one long display case running all the way down, with the butcher and his assistant on one side and any customers on the other. Ropes of sausage hang overhead, and in the case are chickens and various cuts of beef, pork, turkey, and so on. Guess the Wiseguys didn't bother bringing kosher with them. They definitely remembered the pepperoni and the prosciutto, though, so I'm not complaining. In my house we were loudly kosher, which means that when Ma was cooking something and one of us would say "hey, Ma, what's that?" she'd reply "It's kosher beef, of course—what else?" Loudly. Even when it clearly wasn't kosher *or* beef. I guess she figured God was more likely to be listening than actually taking a peek.

"What can I get ya?" A raspy voice calls out, the butcher obviously tipped to our arrival by the little bell over his door. He comes into view a second later, almost hidden behind the case, and it takes me a second to realize what seems familiar about him. Then I get it.

"Black Sheep, I presume?"

He eyeballs me through the case—he's too short to see over it, even perched on a tall stool. "Yeah. I know you?"

Now that I'm seeing him clearly, I laugh. "No, but I know you—Dante Spataro!"

Spataro's eyes narrow. "What of it?"

I'm actually pretty amazed. "How're you still alive?" I blurt out, earning me a groan from Tall beside me. "I mean, you came here in the fifties, right? That was sixty years ago for us, but it's been what, a couple hundred years here?" Yet there's no question

I'm right. I remember the images Ned showed me. This is Dante Spataro, in the flesh. Admittedly, it looks like he took one of those vacuum sealers to himself, sucking out any additional air or fat and leaving his skin so shrinkwrapped to his bones you have to worry that he's gonna cut himself open on his joints every time he moves. What few strands of hair he still has are white and plastered across his forehead, and it's clear he's curled in on himself the way so many old people do, like he traded his bones for a couple of Crazy Straws. But it's definitely Spataro.

He shrugs, not even bothering to deny it. "No idea," he says instead. "I just stopped looking—or feeling—any older. So if you came through to kill me, I don't think that's gonna work out too well for ya."

"We're not here to hurt you, or to harass you about your past back on Earth," I assure him. "We just need to talk to you. An alien race is invading your world as we speak! They're replacing people and places with dark, twisted versions of themselves! They turned your capitol trattoria into a video arcade! And if they have enough time they'll make it impossible to get rid of them here, then they'll start moving through the rest of the universe, devouring everything in their path!"

"What?" Spataro bangs a gnarled fist on top of the display case. "They can't do that! We stole this planet fair and square! They can't steal it back!"

"Great," I agree. "So how exactly do we stop them?"

"We?" He gives me the stink-eye again. Old men are really good at that, I've noticed. It must be all the years of practice. "I don't know you, fella, and while I appreciate the heads-up I don't see how it's any of your business."

"It isn't," I admit, "but one of my pals lives here, so it's definitely his business. And I stick up for my friends, so that makes it my business, too." Which is true, I've always been the kind of guy who'll get into trouble to help a friend. Of course, a lot of my friends have pointed out over the years that I've gotten them into just as much trouble, so I suppose it evens out, really.

Nonetheless, the ancient mobster looks impressed. "Okay, you got loyalty, kid," he tells me. "And guts. And one helluva big head. I like you. Fine, here's what we do—you know where these upstarts are?"

"Boy, do we," I answer. "They're holed up in the arcade right where the trattoria was before."

"Okay, good." He cracks his knuckles—the rest of him is all old-guy scrawny, I realize, but his hands are huge, like somebody stuck a gorilla's mitts on him one night when he wasn't looking. "We'll gather everybody who's left, march on that place, and toss 'em out on their ears. They wouldn't dare come back after that!"

Personally I'm not so sure the invaders are going to let a little wounded pride destroy their plans to remake our universe, and that's assuming this petrified *patron* can even gather enough bully boys to take out the altered goons, but for once I manage to keep my mouth shut. We wanted this world's last real authority figure to step in and that's exactly what he's doing—it won't help anything if I start confusing the issue this early in the game. Besides, this is definitely one of those cases where I'd love to be proven wrong.

"Good idea," Tall offers, earning the geezerly Godfather's attention for the first time. Spataro doesn't frown or squint at Tall, of course—his heroic frame earns a clear nod of approval.

"You looking for a job, sonny?" Spataro asks him. "I could use a guy like you."

"Thanks, but no," Tall answers. "I've got a job. But I think I can get us a few more able bodies to help put these guys down." He pulls out his cell phone and presses a single button. Uh oh. I tend to worry whenever someone makes a big statement like that and then uses speed-dial. It smacks of pre-planning, and that sort of thing always makes me nervous.

I get a lot more nervous when I hear Tall say, "Hello, Agent Smith."

Tall listens for a minute, then says, "I understand, and you'll have my full report soon. Don't worry, that's all fine now. But I'm calling about another matter. I'm sure you remember the invaders we fought off before? Well, they're making a second attempt. We could use some help repelling them." Another pause on his end. "That would be excellent, sir, thank you. Ask our other friends for transportation—they know where we are." He hangs up and nods to me. "They'll be here."

The MiBs aren't always my favorite guys—just like I know I'm not theirs, and if not for Tall I'm sure I'd be a punishment duty, like "ooh, you shouldn't've let that Rangorian go on that rampage through Times Square with that digitized light-scythe, that's gonna be hell to clean up, you'll probably get stuck with DuckBob Detail now"—but I'm not ashamed to admit I'm relieved when he says that. We may not see eye to eye on everything but the MiBs are committed to protecting our reality and a squad or two of them would be pretty handy in what sounds like is gonna be the fight to end all fights.

Speaking of which, I haul out my own phone. Tall isn't the only one with reinforcements a single button-push away.

Chapter Twenty-four
It's not a family reunion
without pickle relish and bloodshed

"**I'm really not** sure this is a good idea," Ned tells me as we traipse across the street—well, more like dash between honking, speeding cars, but still—and into the arcade parking lot. "Tall calling the MiBs is one thing, but this could get dangerous."

"You don't think they've seen their fair share of danger?" I ask. "Come on, man, this is me we're talking about, and I'm not even the tough one in the bunch. I could show you decorated combat vets who've seen less action and less danger than they have." I pause, which is a bad thing to do when straddling the median like a delusional zombie attempting the pommel horse and making its way up onto the thing before realizing it just lost both feet. "Or, wait, did you mean it might be dangerous for the MiBs and the Black Sheep and anybody else around? That could be true—they tend to think 'collateral damage' means you put forth the idea of hurting someone or something and then they put up something as payment for you not to do it." I almost pause again but a car horn warns me not to. "Actually, that's what I thought it was too, for a long time. Which probably explains why I didn't get that job as assistant bank manager when I promised to just punch the clients right back."

Ned sighs. "There's just no talking you out of this, is there? Or talking to you at all, sometimes."

"Nope." We stop in front of the wormhole, though of course I'm trusting Ned and his toys to tell me where that is. I wish there was a way to tag it so we could see it—does Home Depot sell some kind of paint that's "perfect for use on astronomical anomalies"? And mold-resistant?

There isn't anything to see, no light show or shimmery glow or any other kind of visual distortion. There's just a spot somewhere right in front of us that's the wormhole—and then, a second later, there's a spot and somebody I'm related to is standing in it.

"Hey, Frank," I tell him, giving him a quick hug. Hey, he may not be my favorite relative but he's still blood. And he did come through first.

"Yo, Bobby," he replies, hugging me back. Then he turns and leans over, and I swear the top of his head disappears. "All clear!" I hear him holler, though it sounds like when you put your mouth right up to a fan and talk through it. Not too close, though, because let me tell you, even with a cheapie little plastic fan that can sting. On the plus side, great way to get the whole "swollen, bee-stung lips" look dirt cheap!

A second later there's a smaller, blonder person next to Frank. This time my hug's a lot tighter. "Hey, kiddo," I tell her. "Surprised you didn't push him aside and jump through first."

"What, and get eaten by rabid space beasts or fall into a flaming lava pool or get cut down by laser fire? I watched all those movies with you, remember?" Lizzy asks. She gives me her usual "ain't I clever" grin. "That's why I shoved Frank through first."

Ah. Yeah, that actually makes a lot of sense. Nor can I blame her. Hell, I'm glad at least one of us has enough smarts to think about self-preservation.

Right behind Lizzy are Tricia, Caitlyn, Eddie, Jimmy, Grant, Andy, and Bonnie. And after them are three more of my siblings, Matt, Joe, and Marty. This is starting to look like a proper family reunion, only without all the food. At least I'm pretty sure we can still expect the senseless violence, so that's something.

"Wow, I can't believe you all made it," I tell them after exchanging hugs, fist bumps, high-fives, and various other greetings. "Thanks, guys."

"Hey, Ma told us to get our butts over here and make sure you made it home safe for the holidays," Matt tells me. "So that's what we're here to do." He looks around for the first time. "Where is here, anyways? We were in Brooklyn, but Brooklyn hasn't looked like this since La Guardia was mayor." Matt's a history buff, at least when it comes to New York—ask him anything about its mayors, its streets, its subways, its parks, and he knows it. Ask him why he's still working the same dead-end job for the same crappy salary when he could do so much better and he hasn't got a clue.

Yeah, okay, this is the part I wasn't looking forward to. "Okay, so here's the thing," I start to tell them. "Y'see, that job I got last year? I may not've told you the exact truth about it. Really, it's—"

Lizzy interrupts me. "You look different than when you came to dinner." She's talking to Ned. "Your skin's all green, and your face is flat, and are those broccoli growing out of your head? You're an alien, aren't you?"

Ned laughs. "Well, technically you're the aliens right now, seeing as how you're on my world and not the other way round."

She glances around, and I can pretty much see all the little details clicking into place for her. "So you're an alien and we're on another world," she says after a minute. "And your new job has to do with all that, right? And with the whole head thing." She ignores the gasps from the others. "And now something's wrong and you need help, probably to do with those guys I heard you all scared off Grandma's lawn earlier today." She hits me with another of those patented grins. "How'm I doing so far?"

Did I mention that not only is she my favorite niece but she can probably outthink all the rest of us put together?

"Yeah, pretty good," I tell her. "See, there's this thing called the Matrix, it kinda protects the whole universe from people outside trying to get in. Bad people. And I'm the Guardian of the Matrix. Me. That's my job—I keep the Matrix running so it can keep all the bad guys out." I cough. "Only this time they snuck in, all subtle-like, and started rearranging the furniture behind our backs. Now they're a lot stronger and they're holed up right over there and we need to grab 'em and stomp 'em and not let up, both to protect this place, Ned's world, and to keep them from getting any more footholds in our reality. Clear?"

Frank raises his hand. "I just got one question," he says.

"Really? Just one? Are you sure?" I sigh. "Go ahead."

Frank points again, this time over my shoulder. "Ah, so, those would be the bad guys you're talking about, right?"

Turning, I see what looks like a rolling wave of smoke, only with legs and arms and sunglasses. And guns. That's a detail I'd like to somehow miss, or at least not have there to even notice, but no such luck.

"Yeah, that's them," I answer. "And it looks like they're our welcoming committee." Because, right now? They're all heading straight for us. "So, now'd be a good time to, y'know, put up your dukes or lock and load or whatever. We're about to have company."

"Company?" Grant grins and hoists a wrench that's nearly the size of my head—and believe me, that's saying something. "I love company. Think they brought pie?"

"I like pie," Andy agrees. His wrench is every bit as big as his dad's. Must be the genes. The first of the mooks is almost on us, and Andy steps forward, raises that monster wrench, and does his best Babe Ruth impression—with the surprised mook as the ball. "Give me pie!" my nephew bellows as he swings through. For such a normally quiet guy, Andy's got one hell of a pair of lungs. I'm not sure which surprises the goons more—the shouting, what he's shouting, or the fact that he just sent one of their number sailing over their heads like he was a paper airplane with a strong tailwind.

The respite only lasts a few seconds, though. Then some of the goons snap out of it and charge us again. I feel like Cary Hiroyuki-Tagawa should be standing off to the side somewhere shouting "Fight!" and "I declare—mortal combat!"

At least I've got the theme music stuck in my head now. Better than nothing.

One of the goons—celery, tall and gangly with finger-in-the-socket hair—takes a swing at me with a baseball bat, or at least what a baseball bat would look like if it decided to get gussied up for a night on the town. It's basically a giant glow-stick, and I'm pretty sure it's humming just a little. I'm tempted to make a Kevin Matchstick reference but I'm pretty sure this guy wouldn't get it, so I settle for stomping on his feet with one of my own, then kneeing him in the face when he doubles over from the pain. And down he goes. I grab the Electric Bataloo out of his hand—hey, he's not using it!—and turn to face the next guy in line—

—when a sheet of lightning arcs across the parking lot, cutting me and my clan off from the sea of mooks. Really, it looks like somebody just ran a giant sheet of plastic wrap between the two sides, only the wrap's electric. Wicked.

"Come on!" I glance around and there's Ned off to the side, waving us over. He's holding a long, thin, sparkly metal oval like a crushed version of Liberace's hula hoop, and I realize that's where the electric wrap originates. Of course, leave it to Ned to cook up some crazy science gadget to save us. Not that we couldn't have held our own, mind you, but there're more mooks pouring out of the arcade and I've only got so many siblings.

"Let's go!" I shout, and lead the way over to him. "Hey, thanks for the assist, man." I clap him on the back.

"Figured it was better to gather all our forces and then face them all at once," Ned says with a shrug. "Besides, I like some of your family."

I grin as Lizzy reaches me, Grant and Bonnie right behind her. "Yeah, me too." Then I raise my voice to the rest of them. "Time to regroup, mi familia!" Some of 'em seem determined to stay and fight some more, so I have to pull out all the stops: "Hey, look, free food!" That does the trick, and Ned and I lead them across the street to where Tall's waiting.

And, behind him, just past where Heidi's hovering, are a whole bunch of guys who look like they're either doing a Blues Brothers remake or are here to sell us life insurance. Including one who's glaring at me again like we've never been apart—and like I just stole her last Milk-Bone.

"Hello, Agent Jones," I tell her as we reach them. "Miss me?"

"I never miss," she answers, completely deadpan, and I honestly don't know if she's kidding or not. Tall laughs, though, which puts a crack in her stony façade. Yes, Virginia, you really can show emotion, even have fun occasionally, and still be a bad-ass. Who knew?

"Okay, so you got yours," I tell Tall, "and I got mine." I turn to Ned. "Now where's yours?"

"Right here," a crotchety old voice replies, making me spin around further—I'm starting to get dizzy—and there I spot old Spataro, the Black Sheep, and his men. Who look an awful lot like the goons we've been fighting off, really, except that they don't have the whole weird distortion effect going on. They're just your regular, average, everyday sentient veggie people trapped in a 1960s Mob movie.

Yes, this is my life. Most days I can't decide if I should laugh, cry, make popcorn, or tell Pixar they'd better try to keep up.

"We want to help, too," somebody else calls out, and I'm running out of places to look but then I spot another group of people behind Agent Jones and the rest of the MiBs. A group that's dressed like normal folk—well, from the '50s and '60s, anyway—and with skin in varying shades of white, orange, green, red, and even a few purplish-black. And they're all carrying shotguns, hunting rifles, bats, hockey sticks, golf clubs, butcher knives, and so on. It's like an angry-mob tossed salad.

"I made a few calls," Ned says when I glance his way. "Lot of people I know aren't too happy with the way things are going right now, and don't feel like letting other folks do their dirty work."

"Hey, the more the merrier," I assure him. "And I don't blame them. I'd fight for my world, too." Of course, my version of fighting would probably involve challenging them to cards or maybe an online game or even ping pong, but it still counts. At least to me.

I look over at Tall, who's already got that "shut up, I'm thinking here" faraway expression on his face. Good, Mr. Action is on the case.

"Okay," I ask him after a minute, as much to remind him we're still here as to get an actual answer—yes, I'm needy, just ask any of my elementary school teachers or any of the regular bus drivers on my old work commute—"what's the plan?"

Tall's face splits into an evil grin, which gives me the shivers. It's bad enough when he smiles a little, but this? This is the cat about to eat not only the canary but also the mouse and the cheese from the mousetrap and possibly a few nearby books and maybe one or two random passersby. The fact that his smile widens when his eyes latch onto me doesn't make me feel any better but I do have a sudden, desperate urge to twitch my whiskers.

"How would you feel," he asks me, still grinning like that, "about putting your talents to some use again?"

Somehow I don't think he's referring to my ability to shape adult content from mashed potatoes, or the fact that I can do all of "My Country Tis Of Thee" in a single good, long burp. And, while it's nice to know I do have some other usable skills floating around, I don't mind admitting I'd rather they didn't all seem to come down to me dangling on a wire like a piece of meat.

At the very least I should be offered some mint jelly to help take the edge off things.

Chapter Twenty-five
Chum is more than another way to say pal

"I don't see how you expect they're gonna fall for this twice in as many hours," I grumble as I stomp my way back across the parking lot. "I mean, really, how dumb do you think they are?"

Tall's voice crackles in my ear. "They're mooks," he reminds me. "So, pretty dumb."

"Fine. But when this doesn't work and they just gun me down from the safety of their arcade fortress, I hope you feel bad!" I stop talking to him then because I've reached the middle of the parking lot, which is where I stop and take a deep breath.

Showtime.

"Yo, come on out!" I shout toward the arcade. "Come on, I know you're cowering in there like little dogs or snails or earthworms or something else that cowers, maybe high school freshmen! Stop being such chickenshits and step on out here! I dare you!" Nothing. "I double-dog dare ya! I triple-dipple Vanilla Roadmonkey dare ya!"

Still nothing.

"Wow," I say loudly. "That's . . . well, pathetic, actually. I'm one guy, for crying out loud! Sure, I've got a duck head, and yes,

I've been kicking your collective asses for the last several days or weeks or however long it's been since I arrived on this salad bar of a planet, but even so, I'm one guy! And every single one of you is afraid to face me, even as a whole big group?" I shake my head. "Man, I've met kindergartners with more balls than you guys."

That gets a response. Finally. I watch as the arcade door opens and a single mook steps out, sunglasses firmly in place, gun in hand.

"We are not afraid of you, strange little duck man," he calls to me. "But we know you are not alone. You have all your little friends, the ones in the suits and the ones who want pie and the ones with the rakes and shovels and the ones with clubs and tire irons. You are waiting for us to come out there, where you and your friends can surround us." He smirks. "We will not be doing that." Wow, the Wise Guys not only imported things like egg creams and pastrami and knishes—mm, egg creams and pastrami and knishes!—and their whole Mafioso culture, they even brought over the Russian mob. Which was years after their time, but there's no arguing that this guy—who I think is a Romanesco because he's a pale yellow-green and his hair is done up in spikes but they're like fractals at the same time—is Russian or at least Cuban. It's like talking to the *Veggie Tales* version of Max Headroom if he was playing Al Capone. Yeah, wrap your head around that one!

Anyway, this guy's clearly waiting for a response, and I hate to disappoint my audience. "Huh. You know what?" I scratch at my bill. "That's a great plan. Damn. Say, could you wait right there while I go away and get things set up and then we'll try this again?" I start to back away as fast I can without looking desperate or tripping over my own feet.

His smirk gets wider. "You did not think of this? You are not the best planner, no? You truly came here all on your own?" His gun drifts upward, now pointing straight at my head. Which, sadly, is a hard target to miss.

"What, you think that's dumb?" I ask him. "To sneak out while they're all still planning and come over here to call you guys out?" I stop. "Oh. Yeah, okay, maybe it was. Crap."

If this mook's grin grows any more it's going to eat his ears. Which, ew—I don't care if you are a vegetable, cannibalism is still gross. Though now I can't help but wonder, do Ned's people ever eat vegetables? Do they not need to, maybe because their own bodies already produce all the Vitamin A and B and C and so on they could ever want? Do veggie people only eat meat and cheese and maybe grains? Weird.

Definitely one to ask Ned later—assuming there is a later. Maybe, if we get out of this, I'll try sitting down in front of him with a big tossed salad, just to see if he turns pale and says, "No! Cousin Joey!"

"This is very fine," the mook is telling me, now in full-on gloat mode. "I will shoot you, and suddenly I am big hero. Everybody will know my name."

"Sure—if they believe you," I mutter. But he hears me. It's tough to do whispers and mutters properly without lips—I tend to either be inaudible or really loud. Which, in all honesty, was true even before the duck head.

"Why would they not?" he replies, taking a step closer to me. "Especially once I show them your head."

"Oh, you can prove I'm dead," I tell him. "That's the easy part. But proving you killed me? What're you gonna do, call *CSI: Other Worlds* and have 'em swab my body? Nah, without eyewitnesses nobody's ever gonna believe you. Which means you won't get any credit for it. None. Zero. Zip. Nada. Zilch—"

He cuts me off, which is just rude. "I have the witnesses!" he shouts. He hauls upon the arcade door and yells inside. A few seconds later several more goons step outside to join us. "There," he tells me with a sneer. "Witnesses."

They just keep coming, too.

"Uh . . . okay. Sure, that'll work," I admit. "So now all your buddies are gonna see you gun me down like a stray cat, huh? Standing way over there and shooting me with that big gun. Well, that's . . . technically acceptable, I guess." I put as much disdain into my voice as I can. Then I sit back and let him and all his new buddies pour out into the square. It's not like I can stop them.

I've lost Fractal Face again. "What is the technically acceptable?" he asks. Oh goody, I love it when I get to give language lessons. That hasn't happened since I got kicked out of synagogue the one time I went back to visit and the rabbi was sick and they asked me to cover for him with the Sunday school students. Hey, it may not have been Hebrew exactly but the words I taught them were probably a lot more useful! Especially if any of 'em decided to become a New York cabbie.

"What I mean," I explain slowly, "is that, yes, you could

shoot me from over there and it would count. It'd look a little like you were still a chickenshit, too scared to face me up close and personal, but hey, it gets the job done, right?"

That gets his back up. "Am not scared of you!" he insists, taking two big steps toward me. "See?" Then, when I don't incinerate him or whatever, he takes two more. We're maybe twenty feet apart now. "There, see? Is close enough."

Naturally his whole posse moves with him. It's almost laughable—so I go ahead and laugh.

"Dude, what the hell?" I ask. "Are we playing catch here or are you planning to shoot me? Because if you wanna toss a ball around, this is a good distance. If you're gonna shoot me, maybe you should be close enough to see the whites of my eyes?" Actually, I don't have whites to my eyes, not anymore, but the expression still holds. Though it'd be better if I had a red coat. Or red feathers. Or a big funny hat.

"Oh, we are with the shooting," Mandelbrot Mafiaboy assures me. "Yes, most certainly that." He walks closer, though I can't help noticing his fingers are white-knuckle-tight on his gun. "You see?" He stops maybe five feet from me and lowers his sunglasses so he can peer over them. "Whites of eyes."

"Yep, those are white, all right." I take a step closer. "How'd you get 'em like that, anyway? Even back when I had whites they were more Tabasco red, really. Do you guys use Visine? Isn't it made with vegetable oil or something? Wouldn't that be like using stem cells for you guys?"

"I do not know what this all is," he admits, backing up a pace to maintain the distance between us. His gun, which he'd lowered a little while walking, lifts up again. "But this part I know. I know well. Now, Mister Duck Head, you die."

"It's DuckBob," I correct him. "Not 'head.' Not 'Mister DuckBob,' either. Just DuckBob." I step toward him again, and he tries backing up but all his buddies are right behind him and there's nowhere for him to go. "Oh, there's just one thing, though." I gesture for him to come closer.

And he does. That "I need to tell you something" gesture is really hard to resist. "Yes?"

I give him my best shit-eating grin. "Surprise."

Which is when the whole mess of everybody else—my family, Ned's friends, the Black Sheep's boys, the MiBs—spring out around them, weapons leveled.

Yeah, turns out Tall was right. They really are that dumb.

Naturally, after that initial shock, the first thing Pixelated Produce Man does is shoot me.

In the head.

He looks even more unsettled when the energy blast or whatever it is just bounces off.

Thank you, Ned! He warned me that the forcefield he was rigging up would only hold for maybe thirty seconds, which is why I waited until "Surprise" to activate it. And now, before the mook can try again, I reach out and snatch his gun out of his hands. "Give me that!" I tell him. "Before you hurt somebody! Like yourself. Or one of your friends." I turn the gun on him. "Now, are you guys gonna surrender or do we have to get rough?"

Huh, I had no idea radicchio could get as dark and purplish

as his face does now. Maybe he's got a little eggplant on his mother's side? Or it could just be rage and embarrassment because he shouts something completely inarticulate—it sounds like "Glarrgh!"—and leaps on top of me.

Or would have, if I hadn't shot him full in the chest. His leap turns into more of a flop, and when I sidestep he just slams down onto the parking lot and lays there, groaning.

But I think that's a definite "no" to the surrender.

And apparently his pals have all spontaneously designated him their spokesveggie and role model because when he falls they all gasp and then, almost as one, bellow incoherently and charge.

Looks like the battle's on.

It's funny—you know how, in movies, battle scenes always move in slow motion, each person distinct and clear, every action clearly delineated? And how, in books, fight scenes are all spelled out, with each person's moves fully described?

Yeah, in real life it's not like that at all.

I've been in my fair share of fights—plenty when I was growing up, a bunch in college, a few after I was out of school, and a few more since my "big change." The craziest one was definitely the fight against the invaders the first time, at the Matrix, with Tall and Ned and Mary and I holding off an entire swarm of 'em, and then Tall and Ned and Mary trying to keep the crafty little buggers back while I restarted the Matrix and plugged the hole they were pouring through.

This fight is worse.

With that one, at least it was just the four of us against a whole bunch of 'em. Not great odds, but it was really easy to tell who was on which side.

Here? It's like somebody piled a whole mess of colored strips of paper into a blender, put the lid on, and then hit Purée. All around me it's a sea of chaotic motion, arms and legs flailing, heads and torsos twitching, weapons swinging and firing. There's all kinds of noise, shouts and curses and gunshots and laser bursts and thuds and groans and so on, so much so that you can't pick out any one noise or even any one person, it all blends together into one big, deafening sound blanket. And the same is true of the sights—there's so many people filling the parking lot, and all of them thrashing about, that your eyes don't know where to focus. It's like one of those op art paintings except the lines and swirls are constantly shifting so you can't even turn them into a picture. Every so often I see a face swim out of the crowd, someone I know or recognize or can at least clearly identify by affiliation, but then it's gone again, swallowed back up by the living, battling maelstrom.

I can't tell who's winning. Hell, I can't even tell who's still standing! Whenever a shape that's clearly "modified mook" becomes visible I bash at it with my fists or my feet or my bill or shoot at it with my confiscated gun but I don't really know if that's helping any. At least nobody's attacking me directly right now—I'm apparently the eye of the storm, all the action's swirling about me but nobody's stepping clear of the fight long enough to take a good shot at me. Which I don't mind, except that I feel like I'm letting my friends and family down by not taking part more, or at least drawing enemy fire.

"Over here!" I shout as one mook becomes partially visible in the chaos. "Yo, come and get me!"

He grimaces, glances around, sees me, and breaks free of the rest to stomp toward me, gun up. "You!" he shouts.

That's all he has time to say before somebody nails him in the head with something that looked a whole lot like a pink baseball. He goes down like a sack of potatoes, and I glance around for the deadly pitcher—and stop, staring, when I see who it is.

"Lila?"

She glares at me, but she's grinning too, which is a difficult combo to pull off but she manages it. And she's tossing another baseball from hand to hand, clearly itching to use it. It's pink, just like the last one. I remember when she got those. She wanted to play baseball, but the only kids' baseball in our area was for boys, they said. Ma wasn't having any of that—she's never been one to let others tell us what we could and couldn't do, barring national and occasionally natural laws, at least—and insisted that the coach let her play. He said "fine, but I'm not gonna take it easy on her just 'cause she's a girl."

"Good," Ma had replied. "I wouldn't want you to."

So the first practice, Lila shows up in the team shirt and team hat the coach gave Ma for her. And she's got a bat, which is a hand-me-down from Eddie. But his old glove was toast, so Ma bought her a brand-new one, and a package of nice new baseballs to go with it.

In hot pink.

Lila's choice.

She gets to the field and her new teammates start howling

with laughter. "Aw, look at the pretty princess!" one of 'em, Stevie Lancaster, calls out. "Hey, where's your tiara?"

Lila looks over at Stevie and smiles. "Wanna catch?" she asks.

"Sure," he tells her, smirking at his buddies. He holds up his glove. "Do ya need me to come closer?" He's maybe forty feet away, almost half the distance from one base to the next.

"Nope," Lila answers. Then she winds up and throws.

The good news is, they were able to rewire Stevie's jaw and get it mostly straight. He's had some drool problems ever since, but nothing major, and as long as he doesn't get too excited he speaks just fine.

Nobody ever made fun of those pink baseballs again.

Lila was ten at the time.

And I know it happened like that because I was there with her. Ma had told me to go along and make sure nobody messed with my little sister. Even back then, I knew it wasn't Lila we should be worried about.

Now here she is, with those baseballs, and she just clocked a guy with one. A guy who was about to jump me.

I'd wonder if her aim was off—she missed me by a good six inches or more—but I know it isn't.

I look at her, wanting to ask but afraid to, and she shrugs. "Ma said there was trouble," she explains, targeting another mook and taking him out with the second ball. She's got a messenger bag slung across her, and draws a third ball out of it, searching for a new target while she talks. "And that you needed everybody." Another shrug. "I'm part of everybody."

"Yeah. Yeah, you are." How is it that there's a crazy-ass

battle raging all around me, people are getting shot and hit and punched and all that, and yet I suddenly feel like I want to cry, with my chest all tight and my eyes watery? I just can't believe that, despite everything, when I needed help Lila came running. I start to say something to her, I'm not exactly sure what, but then two more goons emerge from the melee and rush me and I'm too busy defending myself to talk.

When I look around again, Lila's gone. But she's still here somewhere, I know. And maybe, after this is all over, we can finally talk. That's something I'd pretty much given up on ever happening, but I guess if reality's being altered around here then anything is possible.

Now maybe I'll get really lucky and it'll start raining pastrami sandwiches. And knishes.

Mmmm.

Chapter Twenty-six
Thomas Aquinas says stop!

I'm getting tired, my arms feel heavy, my head's aching, my stomach is rumbling so loud I think I swallowed the San Andreas Fault, and my feet are killing me. On top of that, the gun I took off Rowdy Radicchio ran out of charge or energy pellets or nanoscopic light-bunnies or whatever—I wound up having to literally hurl it at somebody, and it klonked him good, giving me enough time to pull the pistol I'd taken off that mook back at the Matrix and start shooting with that, but I'm still surprised. I guess I never really thought that spaceguns could run out.

But anyway, the good news is, we're winning.

I know this is true because, though it's still like I'm standing in the middle of a giant flesh hurricane, there are fewer and fewer limbs flailing about. And more and more of them are people I know, while more and more of the debris piled up at their feet looks like altered mook.

So, yay.

"Keep it up, gang!" I holler, fulfilling my role as team mascot. "We've got 'em on the ropes!" Or would, if we had any rope.

Of course, the second the words leave my mouth my stomach

clenches and my throat dries up—and it isn't because of something I ate. It's because I just realize what I did. I brought the universe's attention to our current good fortune.

Crap.

Sure enough, that's when things start coming unglued.

Literally.

The first thing I notice is that the ground under my feet feels funny. Soft, like the asphalt just melted all at once. But not exactly melty, either. It's more . . . grainy. Like suddenly I'm standing on loose sand and the tide's coming in, sucking away the surface a little at a time. I glance down, and sure enough the parking lot is starting to dissolve beneath me.

This can't be good.

"What's happening to the ground?" I hear somebody—I think it's Frank—shout. "I've got no traction!"

"It's the invaders!" Tall hollers back, loud enough for everybody to hear. I'm pretty sure they heard him back on Coney Island, actually, and that's without the wormhole channeling his voice through. "They're altering reality around us!"

Well, isn't that just swell?

"Their guys're loosing their footing too!" I point out loud as I can. "Just keep hammering 'em!"

Except it turns out that's easier said than done when your feet are suddenly slipping and sliding every which way. I've got it better than most—my feet are like built-in snowshoes so I've got a lot more surface tension going for me—but even so when a mook leaps out behind me and I spin around at the sound of his snarl I almost topple over.

He doesn't seem to have as much trouble with the shifting surface as I do, though. And when I glance down—after shooting him in the chest and again in the head just to be sure—I see why.

He doesn't have feet anymore.

Not exactly. Instead, where his feet should be are these things that look an awful lot like ATV treads, only smaller and cabbage-colored and ridged with thick calluses. It's like somebody fleshscaped his feet into tank treads.

Three guesses as to who did that one.

"They've adapted the mooks to handle the sand!" I shout out. "Be careful!"

"I see it!" Grant answers. "Jam something into their feet, it'll lock 'em up!" I hear what sounds like a cross between a groan and a grinding noise and figure he did exactly that. I always knew having a mechanic around would come in handy someday, besides when I lock myself out of my car or need to know how to disable the obnoxious neighbor's car alarm that goes off every time someone drives past and continues for a good ten minutes every time, no matter what time of day. How hard is it to set the alarm to shut off after a minute? Any car thief worth his salt's long gone by then anyway, so really the only reason to let your alarm go on so long is to piss off all your neighbors, which may just result in your car being disassembled and then put back together somewhere else.

Like inside a subway car.

Anyway, the next few minutes are filled with grunts and the sound of people falling over as everybody gets to work fouling up the mooks' new appendages. A couple of our guys have gone down—fortunately Ned had rigged up these things for everybody that looked like holographic brooches but were actually wave emitters or something like that, he said they'd block out portions of the weapons' rays and basically convert lethal fire to stun rays instead—and a few of theirs have shaken it off and gotten back in the game, but we've still got the advantage in numbers and position. We're still holding our own.

Until I feel my feet start to lift off the ground.

"We're losing the gravity!" Somebody—one of the MiBs, I think—warns. "Hold onto something if you can, keep your body spread out, and don't make any sudden upward motions!"

Ooh, good advice—and a second too late, as another mook appears and shoots at me and I jerk back away from his attack.

Which sends me flipping end over end, backward, like I'm doing a cross between a moonwalk and a backward somersault. If only I could've done that when I tried out for the yell team all those years ago! Of course, if I'd known from the start that they were just male cheerleaders I wouldn't have bothered—I thought they were simply kids the school had given permission to yell when they wanted and maybe used as the equivalent of town criers.

A hand lashes out and grabs my ankle, stopping my flight like a brick wall, and then reels me back in. It's Tall, of course. I don't know how he's staying so solidly on the ground, but knowing him he's learned how to alter his center of gravity so much he sent it down below street level and is basically anchored to the planet's core.

"No flailing about," he warns me. Then he seems to remember who he's talking to. "No flailing all in one direction," he corrects. "If you flail every which way at once, all that energy might just cancel itself out."

Right, yeah, okay. But I've got bigger problems to think about than how to control my hands. "What do we do?" I ask him.

The frown he gives me is not encouraging. "No idea," he admits. "If they're going to keep altering the local conditions on us, and adapting their own boys to match, we could be in trouble."

"How much trouble?" I start to ask, but get cut off as a dark figure suddenly looms up over us. It's one of the mooks, only he looks like a radioactive flying squirrel bit him. His dark suit basically billows out between his arm and leg on each side, creating something like wings, and he's tilting his hands and feet to control which way he goes. I remember little remote control fliers like this, they were crazy maneuverable, and it looks like he is too as he pivots about, glares down at us, grins, and raises his pistol.

Tall shoots the mook down before he can fire, nothing but his own weapon moving the whole time. If I'd tried that I'd have thrown my entire body into it and would've sent myself sailing backward into last week.

But Tall's only one guy. And the rest of the MiBs aren't going to be total full-body-control Zen masters like he is, much less the Black Sheep and the locals and my kin.

I think we're screwed.

"We need to fall back," I tell him, "before they wipe us out."

"Sure," Tall agrees, eyes swiveling to another target and gun realigning to follow. It's like watching the Tin Woodsman back when he was still rusted stiff, if he'd been a Tin Shootist instead. "But how're we gonna do that when trying to move will bounce us all over the place?"

I look around. "We need some way to anchor ourselves," I point out. "If there were still cars in this lot we could use them. If we could get to the mailboxes and lamp posts across the street, those'd work." I eye a few of those. "Hmmm."

Studying the fight still going on around us—albeit slowly, with the earlier frenetic pace now decidedly off-kilter—I spot the people I'm looking for. "Lila! Grant!"

Both of them hear me and basically air-swim toward me. If Grant's surprised to see Lila there, he doesn't show it, though he does nod hello.

"Grant, you got any rope on you? Or cord or bungee or something?"

He pulls a wad of something out of one pocket of his jump-suit. "This do?" It's a length of woven silk rope, about as wide around as my little finger but easily strong enough to haul crates.

"Perfect." I pass it to Lila. "Lila, I need you to tie this around something and then hook it onto one of the lamp posts over there." I gesture—carefully—across the street. "Can you do it?"

She gives me a look. Then she holds out a hand, but not to me. "Wrench," she demands.

Grant grins and slaps one into her hand, though not too hard. It's not his great big battle wrench but a more normal-sized one, maybe a foot long and an inch thick. She quickly ties the rope around it, makes sure it's secure, and then squares off and studies her target.

Then she hauls back and throws.

Ever seen a good knife-thrower? When they release the blade, it whips end over end toward its target, a lot like I was floating earlier from the mook but much smoother. That's what the wrench does. Grant thought to position himself behind Lila, so our petite little sister doesn't go sailing away herself, and all three of us plus Tall watch as the wrench zooms across the street, curves around the lamp post, and then circles it several more times, looping the rope more with each pass, until it finally loses momentum and falls against the post with a dull clang. Lila kept the other end of the rope wrapped around her fist, and now she hands it to me with a triumphant smile.

"Thanks," I tell her, and I'm talking about more than just the rope. I'm pretty sure she knows that, too.

I hand the rope off to Tall. "Here," I tell him. "Let's start getting our people out of here."

He nods and braces himself. "Everyone grab the rope and follow it back across the street," he orders, his voice carrying. "Now!"

One of Ned's neighbors is the first to respond, latching onto the silken lifeline and hauling himself hand over hand out of the fray, across the parking lot, and toward the relative safety of the street and the sidewalk beyond. Tricia is next, with Lizzy right behind her. More and more of them get the idea, using the rope to keep from drifting away and hauling ass out of the combat zone. Heidi, of course, doesn't need the rope—he's the only one of us who wasn't affected by any of the changes, since he floats anyway. I stay with Tall, my back to his, shooting anybody who tries taking him out. Beside me Ned and Mary have regrouped and are firing at those mooks targeting our fleeing army, keeping the ropeline clear. Eventually everyone is out of here except the four of us. Only, that means we're pretty much surrounded.

"Well, at least everyone else is safe," I point out, eyeing the mooks massing around us.

"You three go," Tall instructs. "I'll cover you."

"Yeah, not happening, big guy," I reply. "I'm not leaving you here."

"No sense all of us going down," he points out, but I ignore him and shoot a mook who was getting a little too close. I brought my gun up too fast, though, and the motion causes me to float a little, so I hook one arm through Tall's to steady myself. Mary hooks an arm through mine, and Ned links with her and then with Tall so the four of us are now standing like our own little square, all connected, each facing a different side.

Unfortunately, there's mooks everywhere we turn.

"Anybody got any bright ideas?" I ask. "Because now'd be a great time to hear 'em."

"We are out of time, I fear," Mary says sadly. "If only we had more we might be able to plan a counterstrategy, but alas, time marches inexorably on, regardless of our desires." I don't think I've ever heard her wax poetic like that before. At least, not in public, and not about something like that. It's usually more along the line of limericks.

Then my brain processes what she actually said—yeah, I get

distracted watching her, or listening to her, or thinking about her, or . . . what was I doing again?—and I almost laugh out loud.

"That's it!" I tell her, leaning around to kiss her. "Babe, you're a genius!"

She smiles. "Thank you. What is 'it'?"

"The answer," I assure her. "Not just to dealing with these goons, but to taking care of the whole situation!" I glance around at my three closest friends. "Listen, just let me do the talking, okay?"

That gets varying degrees of concern from them, but they all nod.

After all, at this point, what've they got to lose?

Chapter Twenty-seven
Working the exchange rate

"Yo, invader dudes!" Okay, maybe not the most respectful form of address but it's the best I can come up with. It's not like I know their names—or if they even have names where they're from—and tacking on things like "your worshipfulnesses" and "your most awe-inspiring luminaries" just smacks of sucking up. Besides, I'm a big fan of calling a spade a spade and a hoe a hoe and this is why I got in so much trouble as a kid tagging along when my older relatives went to bars, isn't it?

Nothing impressive happens when I shout this, other than a bunch of modified mooks all turning toward me, but I hold up my hands as I—very carefully—disengage from Mary and Tal and walk—even more carefully—a few paces away from them, back toward the arcade. Over my shoulder I gesture for Tall and the others to get the hell out of Dodge and I hope they listen but I can't worry about that right now as I return my attention to the horde massing all around me, hungry for blood. Like weird vegetable vampires, though you'd think they'd be busy stalking bottles of salad dressing and fruit juice instead.

"Chill, dudes," I tell the goons. "I'm here to parley." I feel like one of 'em needs a parasol and a wooden eye, but I know

they won't get the reference. This is why interstellar communi-
cation generally falls apart, if you ask me. No common frame
of reference, specifically no way to tell each other jokes because
so much of humor is based on the fact that you and your buddy
saw the same movie last week and can spout random quote from
it at appropriate—or wildly inappropriate—moments. Mark my
words, if we were to send a slew of comedy videos along with
our astronauts and Earth emissaries? We'd have peace with
other races in no time. Either that or a reputation as being really
lethal with a banana peel.

Right now, though, these mooks are still eyeing me like
they're trying to decide which body part to carve off first, so I
repeat myself. Slowly. "Par-ley. Capisce? Talk? I'm here to talk."

"We got nothing to say to you," one of the mooks, a great
big cabbage of a guy, tells me with a snarl. "Unless we're talkin'
with our fists."

"Simmer down, 'Roid Roughage," I warn him. "I'm not here
for you. I'm talking to your bosses."

That gets a smirk out of him. I swear, I'm never gonna look
at salad the same again, I'm always gonna think it's mocking me
from now on. Especially the endives, those smug little bastards.
"They don't wanna talk to you," Sal Slaw insists.

"That's not up to you, now, is it?" I point out, and waddle a
little closer. "Hey, invaders!" I shout, raising my voice to be heard
over the goons' grumbling. "You hear me? It's me, DuckBob.
You know, the guy who stomped your butts the last time?"

And there it is, just at the edge of my hearing, or maybe the
edge of my brain's ability to pick it out of all the background

noise. A rustling sound, like somebody's gotten into the Saran wrap again. Only this rustling, if you listen to it long enough and sort of unfocus your ears the same way you cross and then uncross your eyes, letting the sounds themselves just drift in and take on their own shapes without any help from you, this rustling forms words.

"Yes, we remember you," the rustling says, sounding as if somebody were talking by way of a pile of dead leaves. Through a bunch of thick curtains. "What do you want?"

I scratch at my bill. "Believe it or not, I'm here to help."

"To help?" The rustling grows later—either they're agitated or amused, or possibly both. Or it could just be windy in whatever reality they're in, like trying to talk to someone who's in a car with the top down on a brisk winter's day. "Why would you want to help us? You oppose our efforts at every turn."

"Yeah, and look how far that's gotten me." I gesture all around us. "You've got control of this city, of this whole goofy little planet. You're beating the pants off us." I shake my head. "I'm not exactly big on the whole 'throw your life away for a worthy cause' thing. I mean, it sounds good and all, and looks great in the newspaper obit, but there's that one little problem of YOU'RE NOT AROUND TO READ IT BECAUSE YOU'RE DEAD!" I shrug. "I'd rather stay alive, and so would a whole big mess of other people. So I figured I'd come over here and talk to you about it. Discuss terms and all that."

"Terms?" The rustling sounds confused—yeah, I know it seems weird that I can empathize at all with a special effect and a bunch of cheap drapes, much less ascribe them real emotions, but that's just the way I roll. "We have no need for terms," the rustling explains after a moment. "We will take this world, altering it until it suits our needs. Then we will come through in great numbers and begin changing each world we encounter, until all the solar system is ours. From there we will extend out into the greater cosmos. It seems the most efficient way to convert all such flimsy lifeforms is to alter one first and then that one will spread its new knowledge to the rest. There is less trauma this way." Ever see an invisible, tentacled space monster try to pat itself on the back for being so "humane"? Me either, but I'm pretty sure that's exactly what it wants to do. Weird.

"Uh, yeah, okay." I rock back and forth on my heels, fiddling with some loose change in my pocket. "So, here's the thing. You do realize it's gonna take you, like, hundreds of years to modify everything until it suits you, right? Maybe longer?"

No answer. I'll take that as a "What you talkin' about, Willis?" frown on its non-face.

"Look, I get it—you change the air, you change the gravity, you change the light, you change the people, so on and so forth, until everything's the way you want it. Maybe even the way you need it to survive, I have no idea. But the thing is, even you can't change everything all at once. Like you said, this world first— but how long's it taken you already? And you've still got a long ways to go."

"What is it you suggest?" the rustling asks, trying to keep cool and calm. But I sense the pink ripple of its concern washing over me. I feel slightly unclean after—and a bit fuchsia.

As long as it's not mauve, though, I'm okay.

"Well, I figure you're in a hurry, right?" I ask. "I mean, I suppose you could've just been strolling around back in your home reality one day and suddenly somebody said 'Gee, I'm bored, let's go invade the next reality over' but I'm not buying it. I think something's up with your own reality and that's why you're so desperate to get over here into ours."

Still no reply, but either I'm getting better at reading the rustling—and the lack of it—or I'm projecting, because it sure feels like that uncomfortable silence you get when somebody says "Robert, are you the one who thought creating a mudpit in the living room was a good plan?" and you both already know the answer is "well, yeah" but you just can't bring yourself to admit it out loud. I still think Ma would've been okay with it if I'd cut her in for a share of the ticket price, though.

"Okay, so you're in a rush to get over here," I continue, pacing back and forth. They've let the gravity and the ground revert, I notice, which is certainly making this easier for me. I'm more or less in front of their wormhole now, or maybe a little to the side of it—and between it and the one to Coney Island. This is not by chance, either. For once, I know exactly what I'm doing.

More or less.

"And you'd probably be a lot farther along," I say, "if people like me didn't keep getting in your way, right?"

"Yes," the rustling agrees, finally on a topic it feels is safe to discuss. "But we will soon eliminate you and your friends, and then we will be free to continue unopposed." At that, the goons all perk up a little, and a few of them grin at me in a really not-nice way.

"Yeah, uh huh, sorry, it's not that easy," I reply. "You could bump me off, sure. And my friends. But there's a whole lot more people over there, you know? And some of them're already talking to their friends and family, calling for more reinforcements. You'd have to wipe out everybody on this planet, and then hope the word hasn't already spread to other worlds."

It seems to consider this. I'm actually just assuming there's only one invader speaking right now, but I really have no idea. For all I know there're a dozen of them all clustered around the equivalent of the Speaker's conch, wrestling for it and shouting "my turn, my turn!"

Mrs. Scandariotto in junior high English would be so proud I remembered that.

"You have a proposal?" the rustling asks finally.

"Yeah, well—sort of." I scratch my bill again. "Look, the guys who were running this place all came through that wormhole over there, see?" I gesture toward where I think it is. "From my world, maybe fifty years ago. They took over here a few centuries back and started rearranging things the way they liked, but they're still from Earth. So if you just let them, and everybody else, go back there, we'll clear out of here and leave this planet to you. You can reshape it to your hearts' content, nobody to say ye nay. Then, when you're done—well, maybe you'll decide this one little corner of our cosmos is enough for you. Maybe we can negotiate, set up borders, embassies, a cultural exchange. How's that sound?"

Another pause, but this one feels different. It feels . . . sinister. And gloaty. Don't ask me how silence can feel like gloating, it just does. You'd understand this if you had as many older siblings as I do. Way too many times, growing up, one or more of 'em would manipulate me into doing something, or get me blamed for something, and they didn't have to say a word, they just sat there and somehow I knew.

Huh, and here I am treating these invaders who act like my big brothers and big sisters as if I'm the den mother and have to settle the whole "he's on my side of the couch!" debate. Bizarre.

I wonder if this is what it's like to have kids. Invisible, shapechanging, bent-on-conquest kids.

Mary and I are gonna have to be a whole lot more careful.

Finally the rustling comes back. "We think . . . no," it says, and yeah, it definitely sounds smug now. "But thank you, both for your offer and for your unwitting assistance."

"What? Whaddyamean? What assistance?" I glare at where I think the sound's coming from. "I told you we'd leave peacefully! What more do you want?"

"Conquest," it answers. "Total domination. Expansion without restriction." The rustling gets softer and higher and quicker now, and there's no mistaking that patter. It's laughing. "And you have just handed it to us."

"No I didn't," I shout, spinning around in the vain hope of seeing something. "What're you going on about?"

"The other wormhole," it whispers. "Those who came through from your world—fifty of your years ago on your world, hundreds of years here."

I stop mid-shout, and I'm sure if I was an actual puppet and somebody'd just cut my strings I couldn't slump any faster. "Oh. Crap."

"Indeed." You know how you can't actually laugh and talk at the same time, like people always write "'That's ridiculous,' he laughed" and it *is* ridiculous because if you really tried that it'd come out as "tha-a-a-ha-ha's-s-s-s-ha!"?

Well, apparently if you're an invader from another reality and you talk by rustling and whispering and barely making any real sound, you actually can do that.

"All we have to do," it continues, and there's a clear note of glee in its words now, like the curtains just got gilded or dipped in chocolate, "is alter the time dilation. A day there becomes a hundred years here. A thousand. A million! We will have all the time we need to alter this reality, and for our brethren it will seem as if no time at all has passed."

"You really don't wanna do that," I tell it. "Besides, we'll just find a way to reset it and you'll be right back where you started."

"We will lock in the change," it rustles angrily, which sounds a lot like it just swapped the Saran wrap for tinfoil. "No one will be able to alter it on us."

"Oh." I watch as a faint shimmer appears near the wormhole and then expands around it, allowing me to actually see it for the first time. The mooks are staring too, all their insults and threats forgotten as we all gape at the lightshow. It isn't even like there are colors exploding around the wormhole, really. It's more that the space and time seem to be bending about it, twisting and knotting and forming a lace doily or one of those cutout rows of paper dolls. Looking at it is actually making my eyes hurt, and my brain, so I glance away, only to see Ned and Tall and Mary watching from across the street. They all look a little worried, like they can't quite tell yet if things are going really well or really badly.

I can't help it. I catch Mary's eye—and then I wink.

I barely have time to see her face relax into a small smile before I turn back toward the wormhole, just as the invader rustles out "It is done!"

"Yeah?" I say. "You really did it, then? You reset the time dilation between this end and that?"

"Yes," it replies, the answer long and drawn out the way a very self-satisfied cat might.

"And you locked it in so nobody can change it?"

"Indeed."

"Not even you, if we were to somehow force you to?"

It does that laughing-while-talking thing again. "Not even me."

"Oh. Right." And finally I let myself break into a big-ass grin. "Well, gee, son. I'd say you're totally screwed, then. In fact, you just got played!"

Chapter Twenty-eight
Heaven and earth, Ho-ratio

Ever heard a faint, creepy, almost-all-in-your-head rustling sound that's barely more intelligible than the wind in the tall grass sound completely and utterly befuddled?

Let me tell you, it's a treat.

Especially when that same barely-there voice has been tormenting you and everyone you know—and, let's face it, when it's been featuring pretty heavily in your dreams and nightmares for several months, too.

So, yeah, I'll admit it—I'm enjoying this part. It's like the moment when the good guy rips open his shirt to show the bullies that he's really a superhero and is about to clean their clocks. Taa-daa, it's DuckBob to the rescue!

I totally need a cape.

"What?" the rustling manages. "What do you mean, 'played'?"

"I mean you got fooled, boy," I tell it gleefully, rubbing my hands together, I'm so excited—I haven't been this wired since I "accidentally" touched my tongue to the mini-particle accelerator Ned "loaned" me so I could heat up my coffee and hot cocoa more quickly. What? It totally goes from lukewarm to boiling in like half a second! But the thing itself never gets hot, something about exciting molecules, so I was curious what'd happen if I tried it on liquid that was already in my mouth. Besides, exciting something has got to be a good thing, right?

Turns out, when that something is the molecules in your head?

Not so much.

This time, though, my enthusiasm is totally legit, and not caused by strange vibrations or imminent seizures. "You got took," I continue. "Bamboozled. Taken for a ride. Led down the country lane. Schooled. Tricked. Conned. Hustled." It's not really making words anymore, just little shuddering sounds. I think that's its equivalent of shrugging and sighing and going "huh?"

I sigh myself. I can't help it. It's no fun getting the jump on somebody if they don't even know how to jump. "Look," I say, "there's this old question about God, right? God's almighty, he can do anything, make anything. He's all-powerful, he can lift anything. So can he make something he can't lift?" That one got me out of Sunday school early. Two years early. Ma was none too thrilled. Neither were my siblings, but that's just because they didn't think to ask it first.

Anyway, the invader apparently does get parables. "Yes, I have altered the wormhole so that even I cannot alter it further," it agrees. "But why would this make you feel you had tricked me? It was what I wanted."

"Naw, it's only what you think you wanted," I tell it. "Listen, there's, what, three of you here right now?"

That gets a little gasp out of it, which sounds almost exactly like air leaking from a balloon. "How did you know that?"

Ha, lucky guess, I think, but of course I don't say it. Hey, even I'm not that dumb! "There couldn't be many of you," I tell it instead. "Otherwise you'd have done a whole lot more damage to this world a whole heck of a lot faster. But there's more than one of you, definitely. So I figured two to four was about right, and three was smack dab in the middle." Which really is how I figured it out, actually. So a lucky but carefully thought-out guess. "Anyway, there're three of you here. And all the rest of your people are on the other side of that wormhole. And will be for thousands—even millions—of years."

"What?" Ooh, I know that tone of voice, even through the rustling! It's the same tone I use whenever I do something really stupid and then somebody—usually Tall, or, going back, Ma—points out exactly what I've done. Often in excruciating detail. "But for them—"

"Yeah yeah, for them it'll be a few minutes, maybe an hour," I agree. "But for you? It'll be practically forever. How long do you guys live, anyway? I'm guessing not *that* long. So you're stuck here all by your lonesome, just three of you trying to reshape an entire world and a whole universe after that, and they're trapped in the passageway, like flies in amber, moving so slow they might as well be frozen solid."

"You." Wow, you can pack a lot of menace into a weird rustling sound if you really work at it. "You did this."

"Actually, no. You did." I hook my hands in my pockets, all casual-like. "Oh, maybe I suggested it, encouraged it a little, but you're the ones who ran with it. And there's no way to undo it, either. You said so yourself."

That gets a momentary pause. I can't see the invaders, of course—I have no idea if they're naturally invisible or just invisible when they're in our reality or if they're deliberately hiding themselves all the time they're here, maybe they have really awful hair and funny-shaped ears and they're real sensitive about their looks—but I can't help wondering if right now the three of them aren't busy kicking themselves. Or kicking each other. Maybe they're in a little masochistic circle, each one kicking the next and around and around again.

Alien invaders are wacky business.

Finally the rustling comes back from wherever it went, or just from its sulk. "What happens now?" it asks. I've never heard a more defeated almost-noise in my life—the closest is that sound a kitten makes when it contemplates attacking your foot and, in a brief flash of good sense, realizes how much bigger than it you are and how you could just scoop it up and drop it in a desk drawer or something if it even tries such nonsense, so it actually gives up the idea as a really bad one and just stretches and yawns and goes back to looking all cute and innocent.

Never trust a kitten. Before I got altered my toes had the scars to prove it.

"Well, you've got a choice," I tell it. Because I've actually thought about this for a change. "You could go on fighting us, of course, throwing your tricked-out goons at us and reshaping this world a little at a time. But you're not getting any backup, not for at least a millennia or two, and with only three of you, well, eventually we're gonna get lucky. And then you'll be done for. Of course, it'll be an ice age before the rest of your family even gets here, much less figures out what happened to you."

I shrug. "Or you can take what's behind door number two. It's a better deal than you're gonna get anywhere else, I guarantee it. And, in all honesty, it's better than what most of my friends—and family—would give you if they were in on this conversation right now." I glance across the street, where everybody's watching, and give them all a big thumbs-up. Ha, that doesn't seem to have helped Tall's mood any!

The rustling sounds puzzled again. "Why would you offer us something your friends would not?" it asks. "We have attacked you repeatedly."

"Yeah, I know. But"—I shrug again—"what can I say? I guess I'm just not that vindictive of a guy. Unless you take my last Twinkie. Or mess up my comic book collection. Or take one of my classic collector's-item action figures out of its box. Because then, oh man, I will hunt you down!"

I can tell I'm getting a little sidetracked here, so I bring it back around and lock it down. "Look, I get it. You're here all alone, you're trying to bring the rest of your family across, that doesn't make you bad guys. But warping this world and the people on it without anybody's permission? That does." I look around—not for the first time I wish the invaders would just pick a visible form and stick to it. It'd make exchanging death-glares so much easier! "So," I ask the area I think the rustling is coming from, "what's it gonna be? Door number one, fighting a hopeless battle against overwhelming odds, or door number two, the best deal you're gonna get?"

A bit of silence again. If they hadn't been so bent on universal conquest and all, these invaders could've made great comedic actors, or great car salesmen. It's all about the timing.

Then it whispers its answer.

"Explain this to me again," Tall asks a little while later. "You let them go?" Behind him, Agent Jones is making apoplectic sounds. Either that or she's choking on the apple fritter I saw her wolfing down—and believe me, that term is wholly appropriate for the manner and speed with which she devoured that poor pastry. I was tempted to try sneaking a tiny little red cloak onto the thing, but couldn't avoid the image of a nine-fingered DuckBob that arose from the idea. Hey, maybe I'd get a ring out of the deal, though!

For now I just ignore Jones's apparent outrage and focus on Tall, who doesn't seem as much angry as confused. And maybe annoyed, but that's more or less his permanent emotional state anyway.

"Yeah, I let them go," I admit. "After they changed everything back to the way it's supposed to be." I glance over at the trattoria, and at the Big Boss, who's once again sitting at his table, drinking espresso and slurping down pasta and listening to somebody complain about some problem or other. I don't really grok how these invaders do what they do. I mean, they alter reality, I get that. But when they replaced the trattoria with the arcade, did they literally mold the one into the other? Or did they make the first one cease to exist and then somehow conjure the second into existence to fill the gap? What happened to the Big Boss and the rest of the people who were dining here or working here or just waiting to be seen here right before it happened? None of them seem to remember anything from when they disappeared to when they reappeared, and it wasn't even like when you've forgotten the middle verse of a song and you sing the first part and then skip to the last part but know there was more in there originally. They don't even realize there's anything missing. For them, they were here one second, and the next second—they were still here. No time had passed. Which I guess at least avoids the post-traumatic stress of things like "And then I was this video arcade game, you know, from the seventies, and this big guy and this duck-headed guy were standing on my head, and it still really hurts!"

Heh, those invaders could put the entire fraternity of ambulance chasers out of business! Hard to sue when you don't even remember what it is you're suing about!

"It was very good of you to ensure that Ned's world was returned to normal," Mary offers. Her lovely brow's a bit furrowed, though. "But are you not concerned as to the invaders' whereabouts, and whatever future plans they may hatch?"

"Not at all, my love," I tell her, giving her a quick squeeze and a peck on the check. "See, I didn't just let them go. I sent them home. And that's where they are right now." I wave at the corner of the courtyard where the wormhole still sits.

"You sent them back through that?" Ned asks. "But didn't you say they—"

"Cranked the here-to-there ratio all the way to the top," I

confirm. "Yep. Which means once those three make their way out the other side they won't be able to come back for thousands of years either." I grin. "Of course, they've gotta get home first. They twisted that wormhole so outta whack, they might've skewed the trip from here to there too. They could be stuck in there for centuries or more." I shrug. "But at least they won't be stuck here all alone."

"Not too shabby," Ned agrees. He offers me his hand, and we clasp, all manly-men even though we're both shaped more like Papa Pears. "Thanks for saving my world, man."

"Eh, no worries," I tell him. "Not like I could leave you and yours without a place to hang your respective hats, am I right?"

Of course, other than Ned's trademark baseball cap I don't even know if his people wear hats. Most of the mooks have been bareheaded, not a fedora or trilby or even a pork pie in sight. I suppose that last one makes sense, though in a way it would sort of work to see a human carrot or radish wearing a pork pie—like a regular person wearing a straw skimmer. Irony aside, though, I'm having a hard time picturing what hats for overgrown veggies would look like, beyond some sort of stylish equivalent to that elastic-lined Saran wrap you sometimes see keeping the broccoli and cauliflower nice and clean and ready to go. Which, it suddenly occurs to me, looks almost exactly like what the lunch ladies always wore over *their* hair back in school.

Curious.

But whatever Ned's people wear on their heads, at least now they've once again got places to put them.

Ned's busy nodding. "Definitely." There's an odd look on

his face, though, one I don't remember seeing there before. He looks almost . . . guilty? "And about that," he adds. "I think I'm not gonna be around the Matrix quite as often for a while."

"Yeah? Why not?" I ask. "Don't dig the new drapes? Come on, I thought they were cool—how often do you find home furnishings that're made of water held together by its own electrostatic bonds? It's like having a waterfall right there in the room, only you can part it to peek outside whenever you want."

"It's not that," Ned assures me. "It's just. . . ." His eyes swivel—yes, they can do that—to one side, where Nessa and the kids are sitting, waiting, and looking up at him with what I can only call adoration. "I think I'm gonna spend a little more time at home for now." The kids squeal and basically throw themselves at him like little monkeys, wrapping their skinny kid arms all around him. If they're trying to topple him they should've grabbed on lower, around the knees.

"Good for you, man," I tell him, and I mean it. "I think that's great. Why the change of heart, though?"

He frowns over his kids' heads, but only for a second because it's kinda hard to look even remotely serious or annoyed when you've got three enthusiastic salad-people bouncing around you like manic puppies. "I just . . . with everything that's happened here lately," he says, hugging his kids, "I realized how much I've been missing. I never used to think I needed this stuff, you know? I didn't wanna let myself get tied down. But now I'm thinking, maybe there's something to be said for being tied down a little. Like maybe it helps ground you, gives you something to fight for." He smiles at the top of his kids' heads. "And I think I got that something right here."

"I think you do, too," I tell him, stepping back out of the way as Nessa gets to her feet and joins the kids in hugging the hell out of Ned. "You've got a great family, amigo, and you should absolutely take some time to enjoy that."

He nods. "I got you to thank for that," he says. "Both for helping keep 'em safe and for showing me what real family can be like—and how much it's worth. Thanks, pal."

"Any time." Would you believe ducks can cry? Me either, but apparently I've got the best of both worlds—I can get tear-eyed AND I've got nictitating membranes. And I'm definitely a little dewy watching Ned's Hallmark moment. And knowing I'm partially responsible for it.

I'll admit, I'm pretty pleased with myself right about now.

Despite which, I still go weak in the knees and dry in the throat when a new trio of figures shimmers into existence just behind Tall and Mary.

A very familiar, very short, very gray-skinned, big-headed trio.

One of whom is still wearing the same little-kid footie pajamas as when I first met him back in that MiB safehouse.

Gulp.

Chapter Twenty-nine
Who knew HR made house calls?

"DuckBob Spinowitz."

"Holy crap, you can talk!" I clap a hand over my bill, which of course is about as effective as trying to shore up a dam using masking tape. "I mean, sorry, it's just been a while since one of you has actually, you know, said anything. Out loud. To me." I'd also forgotten about their voices, which are a weird cross between sub-bass and whiny child. It's like Satan's Whinging Little Offspring, both annoying and strangely unsettling. "But, uh, yeah. Hi."

"You have defeated the invaders," the Gray in front—the one in the pajamas—continues. "Again. Clearly, our faith in you was well-placed."

"Oh, yeah?" I straighten up. "I mean, yeah! Thanks!"

The Grays aren't looking at me anymore, though. They're glancing around at our ragtag little army, or what's left of it. The locals have all gone back to their homes, and the Black Sheep disappeared with his crew though not before sharing one of those "yes, you are my adversary and I totally respect you and will happily golf with you when we both retire, assuming we live that long" looks with the Big Boss. A lot of the MiBs left, too, though Agent Smith and Agent Jones are still here.

And then there's my kin.

"You have revealed the nature of your work to your family," the Gray points out. "We understand that this may have been necessary at the time in order to obtain their assistance, but to allow them to retain such knowledge now that the crisis has passed is unwise. Their awareness of the Matrix, and of your connection to it, could put not only you but them and all of us at risk."

Crap. I see what it means. Anybody trying to get at the Matrix—the invaders, the MiBs, other races, people who collect strange shiny things, anybody—could somehow hear about it from my family, who aren't exactly renowned for their skill at keeping secrets. Hell, Frank and Jimmy would be blogging about it right now if they knew how to use a computer. And if either of them or Eddie figures out a way to make money off the Matrix, I'm pretty much doomed.

"So, what're you suggesting?" I ask the Grays. "You're not gonna say we haveta kill 'em, are you? Because they're my family."

"Death will not be necessary," the lead Gray assures me. "We will simply alter their memories. They will remember the general conflict but not that it took place on another world, or that your job involves anything other than oversight and maintenance of some business somewhere."

"Call center," I mumble. "They think I work at a call center." I glance over at them—everybody's in that half-euphoric, half-catatonic stage you hit after a fight, when you're happy to be alive and to have won but so utterly wiped it's too much effort to even sit up straight, and blinking and breathing only happen because your body isn't letting you anywhere near the controls.

And I sigh.

Most of my life, my family's thought I was the world's biggest loser. Oh, they still loved me and all—that's the thing about family, they can love you and still be horribly, terribly, massively disappointed. Which only makes it worse. So really, ever since I left college they've thought I was wasting my potential—I'd get lectured all the time by this older brother or that uncle or that great-aunt about how smart I was and how clever and how, if I'd just apply myself, I could really make something of my life. And then the next time I'd see anyone I'd get those pitying looks like "oh, well, we never really expected you to take our advice and turn your life around."

Things didn't get any better after the whole abduction and duckhead business. Then the pity wasn't just about how I'd been wasting my life, it was about this horrible tragedy that had befallen me, and how sad and awful and how now there really wasn't any way I could dig myself out of this deep, dark hole I was in.

And of course, when I became the Guardian of the Matrix all my family knew was that I'd been hired on by a call center out of the country and had to move there right away. Which at least meant I was employed.

But today? Today has been different. Sure, they were all shocked when I brought them here—shocked to be on another planet, shocked to be dealing with aliens, shocked to be helping protect the universe. And shocked when I told them what I really do for a living. As in, I'm the freaking Guardian of the freaking Matrix. I protect the whole bloody cosmos. Me, DuckBob.

For the first time in my adult life, my family treated me with respect. They were actually impressed.

And now the Grays want to take all that away.

"I get it," I tell them. "I do. They can't know about the Matrix. It's too dangerous." I look over at my siblings and cousins and nieces again. "But do ya think there's any way you could leave at least a little bit of how impressed they were? Maybe they think I *run* the call center?"

Mary puts a hand on my arm and smiles warmly at me. "I believe I may have a solution," she says softly. And when my gal, whose IQ is higher than most zip codes, says she's figured something out? Suddenly that whole knot in my stomach and the matching one in my throat disappear.

"We will erase their knowledge of other worlds," Mary offers, alternating her gaze between me and the Grays. "And of other races. We will also erase their knowledge of the Matrix, and of your role as its Guardian. But we will leave them their sense of how important this battle was, and of how pivotal you were." She hits me with another of those smiles—between her and Lizzy it's like I'm basking in a human heat lamp, all warmth and light and not even the slightest risk of a burn. "And we will leave them the awareness of how important your job is, and how you are the only one who can perform it properly."

Even though she's talking to me she's really addressing the Grays, and I stare at them too while we wait for their reply. Finally it comes, in the form of a single short nod.

"Very well," the lead Gray says. "We will do as you suggest. As long as they can no longer link you to the Matrix, they may retain their sense of your importance in the scheme of things."

I let out the breath I was holding. "Thanks," I tell them. "I really appreciate it." Hey, I may act all tough and carefree and silly a lot of the time, but my family's still important to me. And not having 'em look down on me means a lot.

Plus this way, Frank will stop trying to set me up with jobs. It's like your aunt who's always trying to fix you up: "I know just the girl for you, she's a lovely little thing, so sweet, and someone clearly bribed that judge against her" or "oh, she's very smart, has her own business, I understand she even owns real estate—I wouldn't ask too many details, though, she has this thing about thinking everyone's wearing a wire." The thought is nice, but the actual execution? Not so much.

Two of the Grays turn and start toward my kin, but the one in the PJs stays. "You continue to impress us, DuckBob Spinowitz," it tells me, "with your dedication, your creative problem-solving, and your loyalty. We remain well-pleased with our choice of you as Guardian."

"Thanks," I reply, and sort of fold my arms over my chest to keep from lunging forward and giving him a huge, back-breaking hug, which is what I really want to do. I get to keep my job! All that worry for nothing! Still, there are probably a few details we should get out of the way. "So, about the whole mobile thing. . . ." I start.

As is often the case, the Grays seem to have anticipated me. Or maybe they're reading my thoughts. Or my blog posts. Anyway, this one says, "you will continue to reside at the Matrix, as this will allow you to be on hand in case the Matrix requires repair or assistance." What's it gonna do, call out asking me to bring it a glass of water or wanting me to read it a story? Still, what Señor Sleepover is saying makes sense. Better for me to be close by, just in case. "However, we recognize that you will wish to take advantage of your newfound mobility more, and we encourage such activity, which will keep you more alert and more physically fit." Crap, they've been talking to Tall! But then the Gray reaches into its pocket—who knew footie PJs came with pockets? I really need to see about getting a pair!—and pulls out something small and dark and shaped like a flattened oval, which it offers to me.

"This device grants you prearranged access to our teleportation network," it explains, and I see that the thing is basically a little key fob like the kind you use on a car, with three buttons. "The first button will automatically transport you and anyone touching you back to the Matrix." There's even a little circle on that button, kind of like a rough sketch of the Matrix itself. "The second will take you to a particular corner in the building you know as Grand Central Station, in Manhattan." Ooh, smart—Grand Central's open twenty-four/seven, so I'll always be able to get in and out, and there's always people around so it won't look weird for me to show up there, but the place is so big you can definitely find spots where nobody's gonna notice you suddenly blinking into existence. "The third button is only for emergencies—press that and we will know that you are in danger and will send help."

It smiles at me, which is always disconcerting because when

a Gray smiles it looks like it's just unzipped its entire head only instead of zipper teeth it has sharp, needle-like teeth, and several rows of them, so it suddenly goes from being sort of vaguely cute to being a pint-sized shark on two legs, and you start feeling like you might just be a plate of sushi. Brrr.

"This is a mark of our appreciation for your work," it tells me, which offsets the smiling and the teeth a little—but only a little. "And a sign of our trust. We hope you will continue to serve as the Guardian for a long time to come."

"Uh, sure, thanks," I tell him. I'm a little stunned, to be honest. I mean, this is way better than a gold watch, and those are only for retirement and it's not like I've ever been at a job long enough to retire and who wears watches these days anyway? This is also way better than those little plaques some places give you for being there five, ten, twenty years, or the flowers, or whatever else. I mean, my own teleportation key! How cool is that? Now I can go see Ma and Lizzy and Bonnie and Grant whenever I want, I can go get real, proper New York pizza and cannoli and pastrami on rye, I can take Mary to a Broadway show, and then afterward I can go back home. My home. The Matrix.

This is awesome!

Tall and Ned and Mary crowd around to congratulate me and to admire the key, which is when I catch a glimpse of Agent Smith lurking in the background. Glowering at me.

"Uh, Tall?" I mutter.

He sees where I'm looking, glances that way himself, and nods. "Don't worry, I'll take care of it," he promises. "You'll still only have to deal with me." Which is all I need to hear, because

Tall keeps his promises. Sometimes to my detriment, like his promise to whip me into shape, but still.

"Cool. Thanks, man." He nods. "So," I tell the three of them. My posse, triumphant once more. "I've still got the coolest job in the universe, and the best pad, and the best girl"—that earns me an elbow from Mary, though she's blushing when she does it—"and now I've got a way to get to New York and back in a flash. Plus we've put Ned's world back to normal, including, hopefully, the ever-legendary Gus's All-You-Can-Eat Melva Buffet. So I've just got one question for y'all."

I look at the three of them and smile. "What're we doing for lunch? Because I've gotta tell you, I am starving!"

About the Author

Aaron Rosenberg has not been altered by aliens, as far as he's aware. He is, however, very silly, and he and DuckBob share similar taste in shirts. When Aaron isn't busy taste-testing fried chicken and barbeque or watching movies or sleeping, he's writing. So far he's written roleplaying games (including the award-winning *Gamemastering Secrets*, work for *Warhammer*, *Dungeons & Dragons*, *Deadlands*, *Vampire: The Masquerade*, and many others), children's books (including the middle-grade series Pete and Penny's Pizza Puzzles, the #1 bestselling *42: Jackie Robinson Story*, and books for *iCarly*, *Ben10*, *Chaotic*, and *Transformers Animated*), educational books (including books about cryptology, the Bermuda Triangle, and various biographies), and of course novels (like his two WarCraft novels, his Daemon Gates Warhammer trilogy, *Stargate: Atlantis: Hunt & Run*, and the Eureka novels *Substitution Method* and *Road Less Traveled*). He is also the author of the *Dread Remora* space-opera series and one of the creators of the O.C.L.T. paranormal thriller series and of the *ReDeus* anthology series. If he did meet Grays, he'd probably ask them to increase his typing speed. Aaron lives in New York City with his family, and makes sure to always have a MetroCard and a finger puppet handy. You can read more about his life and his books at gryphonrose.com or follow him on Twitter @gryphonrose.

Missed out on DuckBob's first adventure?
No problem!
Here's the opening chapter of

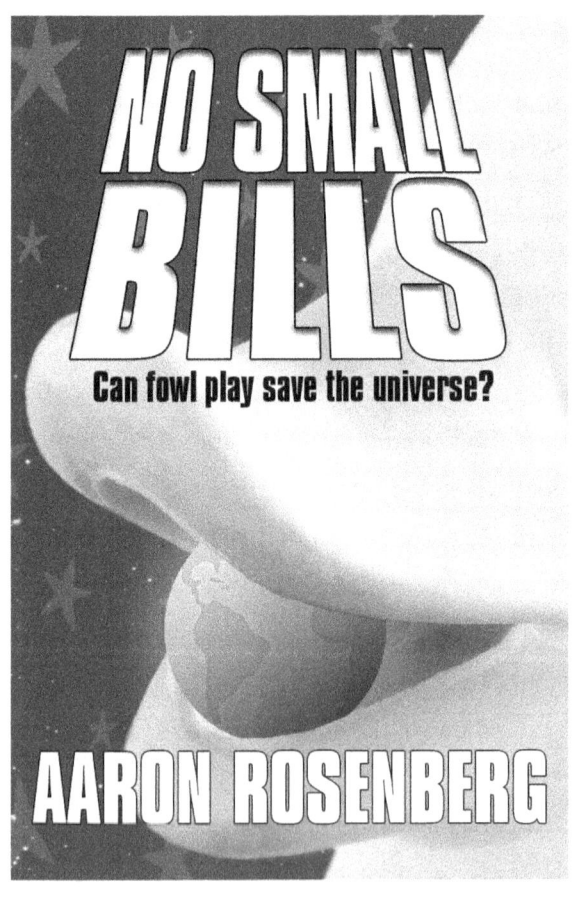

Chapter One
DuckBob, meet the Universe.
Universe, meet DuckBob.

Ever have one of those days where nothing ever seems to go quite right? Where you miss the train by seconds each time, fumble your change at the snack machine, click away from the porn site too slow to fool your supervisor, kick yourself in the head when you're trying to tie your shoe, take a swig of your beer only to realize it's a canister of baking soda instead?

That's pretty much every day for me.

The name's DuckBob. DuckBob Spinowitz. No, that's not a nickname or a pet name or any of that other funny stuff. It's my name. I had it legally changed. Figured it was easier to join 'em than try to stop 'em, and when you beat 'em to the punch, it stops being funny. A little. Sometimes. Why "DuckBob"? Well, okay, here's the thing—

—I've got the head of a duck.

I know, right now you're thinking, "oh, he's got a flat nose" or "he's got a weak chin and a high forehead" or "he must have feathery blond hair." No. That's not it at all.

I.

Have.

The head of.

A duck.

Really. My head? It's that of a mallard—a Wood Duck, to be precise. Complete with black-tipped red-and-white bill, white below the bill and down the front of the neck, a touch of yellow rising up from the bill and leading to a white streaks above red eyes, and emerald green feathers covering the rest, with a few white streaks mixed in.

A duck.

Only, y'know, man-sized.

I've also got webbed feet. And feathers instead of hair. All over. Soft downy feathers, looks just like fine hair until you feel it. Speckled brown down the chest and on the feet, tan across the arms and hands, emerald green on the back (yes, all the way down!), and white on the belly, groin, and legs.

It's pretty slick-looking, actually. If I were a crazed xenobiologist with leanings toward ornithology, I'd say I was an impressive specimen. I even won a few awards at bird shows, before I was disqualified—seems the entry and the owner can't be the same person. Purists.

Plus there was that whole "disrobing in public" thing. But hey, is it my fault they wouldn't take my word for it about the feathers, y'know, Down Below?

On the plus side, I can walk in the rain and not get wet. And swimming? Fuggedaboutit.

No, I wasn't born this way. And no, I don't want to talk about it. Just another example of the colossal bad luck that routinely plagues my life. Because that's what it was—bad luck. I mean, was it my fault I was hiking through a restricted area in the Catskills in the dead of night, waving a lighter in one hand and a neon-orange fishing pole in the other? While naked?

Long story. There was a girl involved. At least I certainly hope so, because otherwise I've got no excuse.

Beyond that—let's just say that, all those stories about alien abductions and crazy experiments? They don't know the half of it. Those little gray buggers are downright cruel.

So you're probably thinking, "Okay, this guy's half man, half duck. That's weird. I'll bet he's a superhero, with a face like that—DuckBob the Aquatic Avenger. Or a mad scientist. Or a professional deep-sea diver. Or at least a sunglasses model."

Nope. Sorry. I'm just your ordinary average guy, and when I'm dressed I look completely normal, 'cept for the whole duck-head thing. I'm no superhero. I work at—aw hell, does it even matter what the name is, really? It's an office job, okay? I'm a pencil pusher, and not even a glorified one. I shuffle papers and push buttons in a little cubicle all day. Then I leave.

Whee.

Some life, huh? Well, it beats the alternatives. At least that's what I like to tell myself. Hey, whatever it takes to get through the day. For me that usually includes watching a few minutes from old Donald Duck cartoons at some point. It's about the only way I can convince myself things could be worse. Look like this, not be able to talk straight, and be forced to walk around with my butt and my business hanging out all the time? Yeah, that would pretty much be the last straw.

Anyway, I'm used to being the butt of some cosmic joke. That being said, I was still surprised when I walked into work one Tuesday and two guys suddenly showed up alongside me and grabbed me by the arms. Big guys, too—they lifted me right off my feet, and I'm not small myself. Plus the bill weighs a lot— I've got amazing neck muscles.

"Hey, what's the big idea?" I demanded as they turned and carried me back out the door. "I've gotta punch in!"

"Mr. Spinowitz?" One of them asked. He had a face like a microwaved potato—squishy and overflowing—and a voice like a hoarse bulldog. He was wearing a suit, a dark one, and I was pretty sure I heard fabric tear each time he shifted.

"Yeah. Who the hell are you guys?"

"We need to speak with you about an urgent matter of national security," the other guy said. He was taller than his buddy, athletic where Mr. Potato Head was just squat. (I'm big-boned and slightly rotund, by the way. It's the slacker lifestyle that does it.) Matching suit, though. I thought that was sweet. Like jewelry but washable.

"National security? I was just curious what sort of brownie recipes it had," I said quickly. "I didn't try any of the other stuff, and even if I did Missus Gries down the hall had it coming! I'm sure the twitching will stop soon!"

The shorter guy raised an eyebrow but shook his head. "That's not why we're here."

"What, then?" I thought for a second, then gasped. "Oh, come on! I know the porn was from Yugoslavia but I only traded an old Steve McQueen movie for it! It's not like I was selling state secrets! It's not even a clean copy!"

By this time we'd reached the curb, and a big black sedan idling there. Mr. Potato Head opened the passenger door and slid in, then Mr. Tall shoved me in after him. I've never understood the whole "dark sedan with government plates" thing, actually. Why that kind of car? Why not those crazy monster SUVs, so the agents can drive over anyone who gets in their way? And nobody'd escape custody—it's not like you can get out of one of those without a ladder and some pitons. Or go for sports cars, classy and great in a car chase. Or the old kidnapper classic, the white Econoline van— cheap, ubiquitous, and now with faster sliding doors! Or maybe something to counteract their whole "we're not really on your side after all" image. I bet government agencies wouldn't seem half as scary if they all drove brightly colored compact cars or minivans with "My Kid's an Honors Student" bumper stickers.

Instead, there I was in the back of a dark sedan. The windows were tinted—I could have made faces at my co-workers and they'd never have known. Not that I can do many faces anymore— duckbills are not very versatile. I'm great at Charades, though. As long as it involves water fowl.

"Where're we going?" I asked as the car pulled away—there must have been a third guy driving but I couldn't see him. "Who are you? What do you want from me? Say, what's that?" That last one I asked while pointing at the Empire State Building, just to get a reaction. I did. They looked at me like I was a moron. I know that look all too well.

With a head like mine, it's hard getting people to take you seriously.

"Our superiors want to speak with you," the taller guy answered.

"They never heard of the phone?"

He glared at me. "It's a matter of national security."

"Yeah, you said that already. Couldn't they have used a nationally secure phone?"

That got snorts from both of them, and I think from the driver as well. "No such thing," Mr. Potato Head said. "You have any idea how easy it is to tap into a cell phone conversation?"

"No. Could you show me? I'd love to know what my boss says about me." Though actually I think I have a pretty good idea. "Quack, quack" is surprisingly easy to lip read.

They didn't answer, and we spent the rest of the ride in silence. I hate silence. It gives me time to think.

Finally we pulled into a building down near the south piers. A warehouse, it looked like, on a narrow street full of warehouses. I didn't see a sign or a street number or anything. Which I guess was the point.

"Out," Mr. Tall demanded once we'd stopped and the garage door clanked shut again. He got out first and Mr. Potato Head shoved me from behind to make me move, then clambered out after me. Maybe his door was broken. I looked around as I got out but it just looked like a warehouse. There was a guy standing there watching us, though. Average height, skinny as a razor blade, with features to match and glossy black hair that looked painted on. Same suit as my escorts but his looked better on him.

"Mr. Spinowitz? I'm Mr. Smith," he said, offering his hand. "Thank you for joining us."

"I didn't really have a choice," I pointed out, but I shook hands with him anyway. Hell, I was in a nondescript warehouse somewhere in Manhattan with at least four guys, all of them probably armed. Being rude didn't sound like a good idea.

"I apologize for our insistence," Smith explained. "But this is an urgent matter and we couldn't risk you refusing our invitation."

"Okay, so I'm here." I glanced around again. Nothing to see but rusty walls and stairs and railings, concrete floor, the car we'd pulled up in, and us. "What's this all about?"

Smith started to say something, stopped, and started again. "We have a situation, and we think you may be uniquely qualified to handle it for us," he said finally.

"Qualified? Me? You haven't read my performance reviews. What makes me so qualified?"

Smith pointed at my head. "That."

"Oh."

"Yes. You see, we've been approached by extraterrestrials. We have no idea what they want, and none of our attempts to communicate have worked. But you've encountered them before—we hoped that might have granted you some rapport with them."

I stared at him, at the guys behind me, and then back at him again. "Let me get this straight—you've got some aliens you want to talk to, and you want me to do the talking because I got abducted and given a duck head so you figure I can relate to them better? Are you mental?" Okay, I might have forgot about the whole not-pissing-off-the-men-with-guns thing.

"You may be correct," Smith admitted. He actually didn't look pissed-off at all, which was unusual for anyone I talk to. "But we have little to lose at this point, and it seemed an avenue worth exploring. Would you be willing to make the attempt? For the good of your country?" Man, this guy was good! Those callers from the Fraternal Order of Police had nothing on him!

I took time to think about it, though. I didn't want to just jump into anything. "Yeah, okay, sure."

"Excellent!" He actually rubbed his hands together. I thought they only did that in cheesy movies. "Come along, it's right this way." I followed him to the back of the warehouse, which had several doors. The floor above continued back past this point so I was looking at the doors to several rooms rather than a whole set of back doors. Which makes sense because why would anyone need more than one back door, especially all in a row? Why not just have one great big giant door? Smith gestured toward the door to the left. "After you."

"Oh, the alien's in there?" He nodded. "And you want me to talk to it?" Another nod. "Alone?" Nod number three—one more and I walked. "But you just said 'after you'—doesn't that mean you're going in with me?"

Smith smiled then, which looked like something you'd see on a buzzard that suddenly found itself at a breakfast buffet. "I lied." He indicated the door again, and rested one hand on his side. Right below the bulge I suspected was his gun—either that or he had a hideous growth under his left arm. Either way I figured I'd better do what he wanted.

"Okay, okay, I'm going." I turned the knob and pulled the

door halfway open. At least it looked dark on the other side, no blinding lights and sets of examining tables and rows of glistening tools. Not that I think about such things. Much. Ever.

"Right." I took a deep breath. "Here goes." And I stepped inside.

And promptly screamed as the door slammed shut behind me. Then the lights came on, showing me four plain metal chairs and a small folding table—and the little figure sitting in one of the chairs facing the table.

Short, skinny, gray skin, huge head, huge eyes, no hair. An alien. Just like the ones who . . . anyway, an alien.

Though I wondered where he'd gotten the Halloween-themed footy pajamas. Those didn't seem like standard issue. At least the black-bat pattern went with his skin tone and his eyes.

I was trying hard not to panic. I figured I could always do that later, in a pinch. I'm good at spontaneous panic. Also, shooting spitballs. I've got wicked velocity.

Right now, though, I figured the best thing was just to get this over with. Face my fear. All that.

"Uh, hi." I like to think my voice didn't shake much at all. I walked over to the table and leaned over it so we were roughly face-to-face. "I'm Bob. DuckBob. Um, have we met?"